STONEWALL'S

HEAD

Also by Richard Beeson:

Seduction of a Wanton Dreamer

STONEWALL'S HEAD

A MYSTERY-THRILLER

by

Richard Beeson

iUniverse, Inc.
New York   Bloomington

Stonewall's Head
A Mystery-Thriller

Visit the author's website at www.richardbeeson.com

iUniverse books may be ordered through booksellers or by contacting:

iUniverse
1663 Liberty Drive
Bloomington, IN 47403
www.iuniverse.com
1-800-Authors (1-800-288-4677)

ISBN: 978-1-4502-3509-9 (sc)
ISBN: 978-1-4502-3510-5 (dj)
ISBN: 978-1-4502-3511-2 (ebk)

Library of Congress Control Number: 2010908278

Printed in the United States of America

iUniverse rev. date: 6/9/2010

For ELLI

CHAPTER ONE

TUESDAY, APRIL 26, 6:00 AM (EDT)

The gym resounded with the grunts of contestants, the squeal of rubber soles on hardwood floors, clanging of blades, cries of *touché!* and *point!* as members of the Fairfax Fencers Club squared off against each other. At 6 a.m. they could squeeze in a full hour's workout before the high school students arrived.

Achilles Smith was busy with a foil match. A burly man with an aquiline nose and solid chin, he was still limber enough in his middle age to indulge his passion for fencing. He felt more comfortable with a saber, but forced himself to practice the foil occasionally to keep in touch with its different weight and balance. He had just scored his first point when he felt an unexpected touch on his shoulder. Holding up a hand to stop the match, he turned to see who would be brazen enough to interrupt an active duel. Through the screen of his fencing mask he saw one of the young apprentice-scorers holding an object in his hand—and the object was ringing.

"I'm sorry, sir," the apprentice said. "But your cell phone keeps ringing—thought it might be important…"

"Excuse me a minute," Achilles said to his partner. He removed the mask, wiped the sweat away from his thick hair, and put the phone to his ear. "Achilles Smith."

"This is Perly," a familiar voice replied: P. Ransom Lyman, Achilles' long-time friend and colleague, a fellow field agent in the Pentagon's Ring Zero. "Sorry to bust in on your match, ole buddy," Perly drawled, "but this is real big, can't wait. What do you know about Sodom?"

"Sodom? As in the Bible? Isn't that the town where people did kinky stuff?" The Old Testament was not one of Achilles' strong suits.

1

"No, no, I don't mean Sodom like in the Bible," Perly said. "I mean Sodom spelled S-O-D-M, Sodm. You ever come across it in your code books? Know anything about it?"

Achilles, in addition to being a field agent, was one of the last old-time code-breakers alive, a man who used intuition and history instead of computers, and his expertise was still much in demand for certain types of cases.

"Nothing," he said. "Never heard of it. Why?"

"Start packin', pal of mine. We're takin' ourselves a little trip to New Mexico. Taos, to be exact."

"Perly, slow down. Why are we going to Taos?"

"Malcolm's orders. That's all I can say now."

Achilles cupped his hand over the phone and distanced himself from the other members of the fencing club. "You have to give me a clue, at least. What's in Taos?"

"A head. They found a head."

"Right. And?"

"The head has no body."

"Right. But whose head?"

"It had a domino stuffed in its mouth, and it's been branded, four letters, smack over the eyebrows—S-O-D-M, pock, pock, pock, pock."

"Branded? As in cattle?"

"Branded, tattooed, stamped, whatever! I haven't seen the thing myself."

"So why aren't the local police handling it? Why have they called RZ in?"

Ring Zero was a new agency, more secret and powerful than the CIA or the British MI6. Following the terrorist attacks in September 2001, the U.S. intelligence agencies had been restructured several times. The most secret division—the one whose existence had been on a "need-to-know" basis, even for other CIA and FBI operatives—had been removed from CIA control, moved to the Pentagon, and renamed RZ, for Ring Zero. If Perly had been ordered to call Achilles and tell him they had to go to Taos ASAP, it had to be for something big.

"They called us in," Perly said, "because they thought they could use us."

"Perly, come on. This is Achilles. Since when do you play coy with me? Give me the memo."

"Okay. Think about this for a minute. Think about someone who used to have a high profile—probably made a lot of enemies, especially in the Muslim world—went off to spend his golden years at his ranch, a ranch near Taos, you gettin' me yet?"

"You don't mean Ke…"

"Yeah, I do. Stonewall."

"Somebody took out Stonewall?"

"Let's say—took most of him and left the head."

"Iraqis? They called in their fatwas?"

"Could be. But there's too many things don't add up. Might be somethin' else. There's no video of the sendoff ceremony, no bad guys wearin' masks. You got enough of the memo now?"

"I have to get home to pack."

"Malcolm is requisitioning a Learjet. A car will pick you up at 11 o'clock. We're takin' off from Bull Run at noon."

———

Later, in the back seat of the car, Achilles took in the colorful blur of spring blossoms decorating the Virginia countryside, and pondered the situation. A severed head belonging to an influential member of the inner circles of government, discovered on or near his property—Perly hadn't been specific about that. A domino stuffed in the mouth and the letters SODM branded on the forehead.

SODM. Could it be a different way of spelling Saddam? Or was it some other word? Strange one, if it was. Not that strange words were new to him. His own name, for instance. His mother, determined to have a son who stood out from the crowd, couldn't bear to give him a normal first name. No John Smiths for her, especially no John Smith Juniors, since she had already married a John Smith. She wanted a son whose name exuded the aura of strength and invincibility. So Achilles he became. If she could have dressed him for school in Greek armor she probably would have done that too.

And Perly: hardly a normal name. Perly resolutely refused to tell anyone what the initial *P* stood for, so he had become P. R. Lyman, or Perly for short. Achilles had met him in CIA boot camp when they were both fresh out of college and filled with anti-Soviet fervor. Perly, a graduate of the University of Virginia, had done a stint with the Cavaliers as a tight end before an injury forced him out of the lineup. He loved to poke fun at Achilles' Columbia connection—a school that hadn't won a football trophy since the 1930s—and his love of an "effete" sport like fencing. Never mind that Achilles had grown up out West and was a better horseman than his buddy. For Perly the issue was football vs. fencing, end of discussion. Thus, proving once again the old saw that opposites attract, they became the best of friends.

Back to SODM. It might be a keyword to a code or it could simply be a code word in itself, a use of the late Saddam Hussein's first name that had developed a quasi-mystical meaning to Islamic terrorists. At first glance this had the hallmarks of a revenge killing, an act committed to exact just due for the U.S.-led war in Iraq and the execution of the Iraqi president. But Islamist groups didn't usually brand code words on the foreheads of their victims. And they would have shouted the deed from the electronic rooftops, videotaping the execution and broadcasting it on the Internet, sending a copy to al-Jazeera.

An even bigger question was how anyone could get close enough to such a heavily guarded personage to kill him. Where had Stonewall's security fallen down? Who could have breached his defenses, killed him, beheaded him, and disposed of his body, all of it undetected?

How, indeed, had anyone managed to murder former Secretary of Defense Chandler Kean?

CHAPTER TWO

Achilles' driver knew exactly where to go. After threading his way through the streets of Manassas to the back end of the municipal airport, he pulled up in front of a small cinderblock building that was little more than a utility room attached to a hangar. Next to the doorway an old sign with fading red letters on a weathered white background identified this as the headquarters of the Bull Run Flying School. Achilles had flown out of this same facility many times.

Perly, impatient as ever, paced in front of the doorway. He was a big man with a narrow, oval face decorated by bushy eyebrows and a thin moustache, and his springy gait bespoke his days as a tight end for the Cavaliers. He might have been crossing from one side of the backfield to the other, waiting for the snap of the ball. Even the process of breathing seemed to try his patience: he wanted to get to the bottom of things almost before they'd actually happened, and he couldn't bear waiting for answers. As compensation, however, he had great flashes of insight, a way of putting in context things that Achilles would have missed by being too methodical. The two had often talked of opening a private detective bureau together; they worked so well in tandem it would have been a logical next step. Yet neither one of them felt ready to give up playing secret agent.

"C'mon, let's hustle," Perly said, opening the door to the car before it had even come to a stop. "The plane's warmed up and I'm sproutin' wings."

They raced out the tarmac to a waiting Learjet with civilian markings. To anyone watching through the chain-link fence nearby the partners would look like a couple of corporate oafs going to a conference. Once airborne, they unbuckled their seat belts and sat on opposite banquettes with a conference table between them. Except for a steward puttering in the galley they had the cabin to themselves. Perly extracted a small notebook and some papers from his computer case, spread the papers on the table, and filled Achilles in, punching out the main points with his finger while he spoke.

"Whoever killed Stonewall did it Friday night. Wife not home, at a fundraiser for the Santa Fe Opera. She got back maybe 11 p.m., maybe midnight—details fuzzy in her mind. At first she didn't see anything out of order, but then she couldn't find the big man himself. Thought he might be watchin' some late news on the TV—went to the entertainment center. Not there. Tried the bedroom, the kitchen—not there either. Tried the stable next. He had a thing about wrestlin' with the horses at bedtime."

"Wrestling?"

"That's how she put it. He used to do some bulldoggin' in rodeos when he was a young pistol—liked to keep in practice by pullin' the horses down in their stalls, still strong enough to do it. Guess the horses knew it was a game. They had to play with him if they wanted their beddy-bye nibbles."

The image of the staid secretary wrestling with a horse in its stall both amused and distracted Achilles. He was brought back into the present by Perly's sharp rap on the table.

"Achilles! You with me? Good. The SecDef wasn't in the stable, either, and the Mrs. was about to go back to the house when she noticed that one of the horses had gone AWOL. Damn, can't read my own writing—oh yeah, she thought Stonewall might have gone on a night ride alone, she was afraid he might get hurt, he hardly did that anymore—you catch the drift?"

"Right. She was too frantic to think straight."

The steward emerged from the galley with coffee and bagels, and put the snack down next to Perly's papers.

"So, long story short," Perly continued, "she finally called in the Secret Service—Stonewall was a special-order protectee, but he kept 'em at arm's length, didn't want guards interferin' with his life. The SS called the county sheriff. At that point everyone still thought he might've gone for a night ride without tellin' anyone—he'd given the household staff the night off, so they didn't know anything either. No one suspected murder.

"The sheriff's office poked around with dogs, horses and helicopters, but when they couldn't find anything by midday Saturday the SS called in the National Guard. Still no luck the rest of Saturday or Sunday. On Monday an Indian from the Taos pueblo came into the sheriff's office, said he'd been hunting rabbits just inside the ranch property, and stumbled across a severed head near an old mine shaft. The head was Stonewall's, and the sheriff detained the Indian as a material witness."

"Native American."

"I can't stand those PC labels. Indians is what I call 'em. They have a website called Indianz.com, and they call each other NDN man and NDN woman, for chrissake. That's good enough for me."

"Okay, okay, I didn't mean to set you off."

"So the SS called the White House, the White House called the director of national intelligence, and the DNI called Malcolm. Took 'em all day to go through channels. Malcolm called me early this mornin', gave me our marching orders."

"Has the press gotten hold of this yet? I'm surprised I didn't hear anything on the news."

"Major squelch in effect. Anyone who talks gets banished, including locals. But that can't last long."

"You said they found the head. What about the body?"

"Haven't found it yet, at least not by takeoff time. Some storyboards, but no body. Storyboard one, it was dumped down the mine shaft, one of those old vertical jobs, too dangerous to go down. Storyboard two, the coyotes et it."

"Bizarre. No notes, no clues at home, no videos on the doorstep of our embassy in Riyadh?"

"Nothin'. What we got is the domino in the mouth and the brand on the forehead."

"Dominoes," Achilles thought out loud. "A popular game in Spanish countries. I don't know about Muslims or the Indians, though."

"What about Indians? What makes you think they figure in this?"

"At least one of them was hunting on the ranch. How did he get inside without setting off alarms? Why was he detained as a material witness instead of arrested for trespassing?"

"Good points." Perly scribbled in his notebook.

"Maybe the Indians don't take to their powerful neighbor," Achilles mused. "Maybe it's that simple."

"Interesting storyboard. I'll include it in the report." Perly feverishly scribbled more notes.

"Anything else?"

"That's it for now. We'll find out more when we land."

While Perly worked on his notes Achilles stretched out on the banquette and dozed off for the rest of the flight. Over the roar of the engines, through the stupor of his sleep, he could hear Perly tapping his fingers on the table, leafing impatiently through his notes and muttering to himself.

CHAPTER THREE

After what seemed like a dream-visit to a jet engine testing facility, Achilles felt a bump as the plane landed, and heard the high-pitched whine of the engines reversing thrust. Then he felt Perly shaking him.

"Achilles, snap to, ole buddy. We're here."

Achilles sat up and looked out the window, expecting tarmac, some buildings, or signs of an airport; but all he could see was sagebrush, stubby pine trees, and mountains nearby.

"What the hell?" he said. "Where's the airport?"

"Stonewall's ranch is sixty thousand acres. When you're master of somethin' that big you got room for your own airstrip."

Waiting for them when they disembarked from the jet was a young Secret Service agent complete with shades, a radio device in his ear, and a shoulder holster under his dark brown suit jacket.

"Mr. Lyman?" the agent said. "Mr. Smith? May I see your IDs, please?"

"Taking no chances, eh?" Achilles joked as he and Perly handed over their cards.

The SS man was in no mood to joke. "I think under the circumstances you can understand." He scrutinized the cards, put them through a portable scanner to verify their authenticity, then handed them back. "Welcome. Please come with me."

They followed him to a black Ford Expedition turned chalky with collected dust, piled their luggage in the cargo area, and scrambled into the back seat.

"Young fella," Perly said to the driver as the SUV lurched into gear, "you Browncoats learn anythin' since last night?"

"I can't say."

"You can't say 'cause you don't know, you can't say 'cause you're not authorized, or you can't say 'cause you don't feel like it?"

"Yes," the driver answered.

Perly grunted. "Thank God I didn't join the Secret Service," he muttered. "They make us look like kids on an MTV talk show. Can't even have a beer with one of 'em without givin' the password."

Achilles watched the driver's expression in the mirror. He thought, but couldn't be sure, that the fellow cracked a tiny little smile—an upward curl at the corners of his mouth—that in any other person would have gone un-noticed, but in this case was an almost blatant expression of emotion. Then the curl vanished and the man focused his attention on the bumpy ruts of the dirt road.

In the distance Achilles could see a large ranch compound nestled in a notch at the foot of a mountain range. The buildings were surrounded by a grove of tall pine trees, a variety different from the stubby piñons he had noticed when their plane was landing.

"The airstrip's pretty far out," Achilles observed.

"The big man came here for R&R," Perly said. "Would you want a jetport in your living room?"

"Had one, when I was on assignment to the U.N. mission in New York. Three jetports, in fact."

"So if you built a ranch in the desert, your version of hog heaven, would you move the jetports in with you?"

"Sure. To me the planes are like flocks of honking geese. Airports are lakes along the migratory flyway."

Perly snorted and fell silent.

Another Browncoat decked out in a shoulder holster and shades greeted them when they pulled up in the spacious courtyard of the ranch house, a sprawling stucco building that formed three sides of a square, almost repli-cating an entire Mexican town. A couple of dogs—one black, one yellow—lounged in the shade of the portico. After looking around and sniffing the air they decided there was nothing worth getting up to investigate, so they went back to their naps.

"Mr. Lyman? Mr. Smith?" intoned Browncoat N° 2. "Follow me, please."

He led them through a side door and down a long hallway past a series of small conference rooms, where the great man in his heyday had probably hosted simultaneous strategy sessions. Kean, or Stonewall, as he was called by those who worked in other government agencies, had been renowned for his ability to hold the press at bay—which was how he had earned his nickname—and his skill at multitasking, which had been given its own nickname: Cirque du Soleil.

During Kean's term as secretary of defense he had overseen many foreign military actions stemming from the terrorist attacks on the U.S. in September 2001—Afghanistan and Iraq being the most prominent. Could he have enemies, one might ask, people who would want to even the score with him? The answer was an unequivocal yes: enough to fill a couple of good-sized countries.

And now for the first time Achilles was privy to the home base of this most powerful of men. Pentagon West had been its rather loose name. It actually had a more prosaic code name the staff used in official communications, but in conversation it was simply "Pentagon West," as in "Stonewall is doing the Cirque du Soleil at Pentagon West this weekend," which meant several high-ranking officials from the Joint Chiefs or NATO or the U.N. had been hauled off to the ranch for "special conferences"—conference being yet another code word, replacing more accurate terms such as "arm-twisting" or "browbeating."

When they reached the end of the hallway the Browncoat escorted them into a hotel-sized kitchen, which had been sufficiently equipped to prepare meals for all those who attended the famous Cirque du Soleil. Several men in white lab coats were waiting for them.

"So you're Asa," Perly said warmly to the man at the front of the group. "This is my partner, Achilles Smith."

The two RZ men shook hands with Asa, who had the gray-tinged appearance of a doctor on a poster trying to entice new patients to join his HMO.

"This is Nestor," Asa said, steering their handshakes toward a younger man by his side who looked faintly mid-Eastern. "Nestor al-Kindi."

Hmm, Achilles noted. *Al-Kindi. Why is that name familiar?* Then he remembered that someone named al-Kindi, an Arab from Baghdad, had invented a code-breaking system called frequency analysis centuries earlier. Might there be a connection spanning the generations, one that would facilitate the Iraqi thirst for revenge?

"Nestor is the best pathologist we have on the forensics staff," Asa continued. "I brought him with me. Here, you'd better put these on." He motioned to a man on the fringe of the group, who handed surgical gowns, masks, gloves, and caps to the two newcomers.

"It's not pretty," Asa said as Achilles and Perly put on their gear. "The tissues are badly deteriorated. Brace yourselves."

At a signal from him a man opened the large door to the freezer, and they all stepped through. Along the left side of the freezer, beef and hog carcasses hung on hooks, each stamped with a date on one flank. On the right side stood shelves stocked with cardboard boxes marked "chicken wings," "whole chicken," "French cut green beans," "tortillas," "navy beans," "jalapeño peppers," and so on. In the middle was a gurney, on which lay a body covered with a shroud; and on a table nearby was a box like the others, but with the words "chicken thighs" crossed out. Below the crossout someone had used a magic marker to scrawl the words "victim's head."

"So you got the body," Perly said, wrinkling his nose as he lifted the shroud. "You told Malcolm you only had the head."

"They found the body this morning, after you were already in the air," Asa said. "We didn't bother calling you. Nothing you could do until you got here anyway."

"Where'd they find it?"

"At the bottom of the mine shaft. Our SS friends flew in a cage from a mine rescue outfit."

"You're sure nothin' was left behind?"

"We sent a man down after we had extracted the body. The shaft was totally dry, so he would have found anything that might have been down there."

"I'll want to take a poke in that hole myself, check things out," Perly said. "Okay, let's see the head."

Asa went to the box and opened the flaps, then reached in and gingerly positioned his hands under the large object inside. If Achilles hadn't known better he would have thought he was watching a museum curator remove a rare vase from its shipping carton.

"Here it is," Asa said, placing the head on the table next to the box. The room was filling with fog from the exhalations of so many visitors, which obscured the victim's features; but when Achilles moved closer he could see without a doubt this was the face that had antagonized the world press and defied Islamic militants for years. In life it had been a benign, even friendly face, concealing its owner's ruthless determination to have his way as he marched on his path through world history. The hair, carefully slicked back for the showing, was thin and gray; the forehead broad, with the grotesque letters SODM blazoned across it; the mouth, open wide, the teeth in full view—not open with a smile, the way Achilles had been accustomed to seeing it, but rather open in a grimace, a scream frozen in place at the moment Chandler Kean's mind came to grips with the fate in store for him.

11

The headlights of the Escort poked ahead into the darkness, transforming stones into boulders, picking out a fence post here, a horse there, a lone tree or bush somewhere else. The night shadows emphasized the agents' isolation and gave Achilles a sense of eerie foreboding, a feeling that people of the modern era did not belong in this place. He could almost see the spirits of the Indians' departed ancestors beckoning from their lost world. Not that the lost world had been peaceful. He knew that often as not, many tribes were at war with each other well before the conquistadors came on the scene. He thought back to the skull domino, and the possibility it might have come from Yucatán. Mesoamerican natives were known for some unsavory body mutilation rituals. Could the practice have been revived, and traveled north?

They reached the parking lot outside the pueblo, which was pitch black except for dim lights visible in the doorways and windows of some nearby bungalows. The Escort's headlights and noise had brought out a group of curious residents, who slowly approached the car with kerosene lanterns in hand. Now that he saw the place Achilles wondered how Sam Rains could have thought it would be possible to hold a clandestine meeting here. This wasn't exactly an old ruin. Perly had goofed, big time, on this one.

"What do you want?" said an elderly man who seemed to be the spokesman, when the group reached them. "Why are you disturbing our peace?" The anger on his face was intensified by the shadow play of darkness and flickering light, which turned him into a modified version of Bela Lugosi in *Dracula*.

"Sam Rains," Perly said, flashing his ID. "He asked us to meet him here."

"Sam Rains is not of this pueblo." The spokesman's voice had a beautiful lilt to it. "He has no right to ask you to come here at night."

"Sorry, didn't think to ask if he'd cleared it with y'all. He said he had somethin' important to tell us."

"Sam Rains will not be able to meet with you. He has left."

"What do you mean, left?" Achilles said. "Why would he set up a meeting with us, then leave?"

"The mountain was displeased. The mountain asked him to leave. And now you should leave also."

They heard a woman keening inside one of the bungalows. Perly and Achilles both caught on immediately.

"His wife," they said to each other.

"May we speak to his wife?" Perly said.

"No. She needs to be alone."

"Just for a minute—"

"I think that you might be a little more sensitive to the effects of your intrusion. Sam's wife needs to be alone with her grief. She is in no condition to talk to strangers."

"Grief? What do you mean by grief? Are you tellin' me Sam Rains is dead?"

"She needs to be alone with her grief," was all the spokesman would say. With a wave of his hand, he dismissed them and returned to the pueblo with his group.

————

"I can't believe I was so stupid," Perly said on the way back to the motel. "Gettin' sucked into a trap like that. As if he could schedule a secret meeting with us in the middle of an active pueblo."

"Don't be too hard on yourself. I'm not sure it was a trap."

"What else could it be?"

"Maybe he was trying to call for help."

"Or," Perly said as they pulled into the parking lot, "it was just a ruse to get us to leave the motel. Which makes me even more stupid."

"What makes you think that?"

Perly nodded toward their units. The doors were wide open.

————

The carnage was even worse than Achilles feared. His laptop had been destroyed, the parts scattered around the room like pieces of a smashed robot in a Japanese kids' cartoon. Fortunately, he had brought the digital camera and his scratch pad with him. But everything else was in total disarray. Perly's room had fared no better: laptop destroyed, clothes thrown all over the place, and even his toothpaste had been squeezed out of the tube into the toilet.

Whatever the intruders had been looking for, they couldn't have found; the laptops had been completely password protected. Now Achilles and Perly would have to go through the discomfort and irritation of explaining things to Procurement and get new ones sent Fedex.

"Pretty amateur job," Perly said. "As if I would put important goodies in my toothpaste tube. Maybe they thought they were gonna steal some plastique."

"Maybe amateur, maybe just for effect."

Perly's motel phone rang. "Lyman," he said into the receiver; then, after a pause, "I thought you were dead." While he listened, he rubbed the stubble on his chin noisily, a sign he was nervous.

"Guess who," Perly said when he hung up.

"Sam Rains."

"He apologized for not showin' up. Said he had to make himself scarce suddenly. He still wants to talk to us."

"Did he say what about?"

"Not exactly. Just repeated that he had some information we needed. Then he hung up, same as before."

"And we still don't know how he knows about us."

"I think it's safe to assume he didn't learn it from the local sheriff."

"Which leaves the SS, or someone on staff at the ranch."

"SS never leaks, I'll say that much for them. Ranch staff wouldn't have enough to pinpoint us."

"So that leaves…," Achilles began, then stopped. The two men looked at each other with dawning apprehension.

"…One of our own," Perly finished. "Makes sense. Who else would be able to get close enough to Stonewall?" Perly started collecting his belongings and methodically repacking his luggage. "Achilles, I do believe that we're lookin' at an inside job. A rogue operator in our own backfield."

CHAPTER FIVE

Wednesday, April 27, 6:15 am (MDT)

P erly roused Achilles at dawn and nudged him to the car so they could find a place for breakfast.

"Sleep well?" he said as he pulled into the heavy traffic on the Paseo, dodging a hurtling pickup truck like a practiced ranch hand.

"No. Had to call Kirtland to order our new laptops. And then I kept dreaming of a death's-head domino talking to Stonewall's head in the box of chicken thighs, asking him what he knows about horse wrestling."

"Me, I spent the night dreaming about what it would be like to brush my teeth with plastique. I kept waking up just before it blew."

"If we keep this up we'll both end our days babbling in a VA hospital."

They found an open coffee shop, grabbed a quick breakfast, and headed for the ranch. When they pulled up in the courtyard, the SS man who had picked them up at the airstrip was sitting next to the dogs, idly whittling a piece of wood. He folded his pocketknife and sauntered over to them when they got out of their car.

"Sleep well?" His voice had a sarcastic tone that made Perly's identical comment earlier seem more akin to a mother cooing over her baby.

"You bet, sweetheart," Perly replied, returning the sarcasm. He and Achilles had agreed beforehand to say nothing of the previous evening's events. "Where are your pals?"

"Mostly out looking for evidence. Riley took a squad to Kirtland. They're flying Kean's body back to Bethesda for more testing."

"Where's the widow?"

"Still inside, sedated. She hasn't been coherent since it happened."

"We're gonna ride out to the mine."

21

The SS man shrugged. Now that the action had moved elsewhere, he had lost interest in the whole affair. "We already picked over everything. But suit yourself. The stable is up that service road a couple hundred yards." He pointed toward a narrow road that went around the north side of the portico and led up into the hills. "The groom's there. You have to bang hard on the tack room door. He's asleep most of the time."

Achilles and Perly followed the track until they reached the stable, a two-story wooden structure with a small flat-roofed tack room attached to the front. Sure enough, the groom was asleep, and it took some loud pounding to rouse him. When he finally flung open the tack room door, a blast of stale air laden with the odors of neat's-foot oil, saddle soap, and whiskey billowed out from behind him and enveloped the two RZ men.

"Whaddaya want?" the groom demanded, obviously irritated at having his slumber interrupted. His cropped hair was gray mingled with sand—the sand could have been his natural hair color, or real dirt that had taken up residence permanently—and he had the obligatory three-day stubble that went with such a character, as if he had been studying to play Bogart's role in *The Treasure of the Sierra Madre*.

Achilles and Perly flashed their IDs. "We need a couple of horses," Achilles said.

"We're goin' out to the mine," Perly added.

The groom now took them in more thoroughly, with their stiff new jeans and shiny boots.

"More fools," he said as he shuffled from the tack room into the darkness of the stable. The floor was loose dirt, unlike the concrete floors of stables back East, and deep ruts had formed in the aisle between stalls. Birds flapped around in the rafters, and a few brazen magpies pecked at horse droppings near the open door at the far end, which led to the exercise paddock. Horses whinnied and knocked their feet against the gates of their stalls, anticipating being let out into the paddock for a free run.

"Sorry, beauties, no play today," the man said, walking back and forth along the aisle, trying to decide which horses to select. "You two ever ride before?" he called back to Achilles and Perly. "Or are you like the other eastern dudes?"

"Grew up on a horse," Achilles said.

"Ridden some, but mostly English," Perly said.

"One dude, one bragger," the groom muttered to himself. He continued pacing until he decided on two horses stalled across from each other. "Come on, Pasco," he said to a handsome bay, entering the animal's stall and fastening a lead to its halter. He brought Pasco out and tied him to the grooming hitch in front of the stable, then went back for the other horse. Achilles and Perly went over to the horse to inspect it. Pasco eyed them with a wild look, snorted, and stomped his foreleg in the earth, sending up a cloud of dust. In a few seconds he had filled the air with floating dirt.

The groom emerged with a sorrel mare, who followed him placidly.

"This one's called Cerrillo. She's nice and gentle, should be just right for the dude. She was the favorite of the Missus, when they took long rides."

"What's Cerrillo mean?" Perly asked. "I see it all over the maps here."

"Little ridge of hills, like the bumps on her backbone. But don't worry, you won't feel 'em with the saddle."

"You have an English saddle?" Perly said.

"Nah. Mr. Kean always rode western. He used to do some bulldogging in his early days. Got a great kick when the high and mighties came here and clung to the saddle horns for dear life. One way he kept 'em in line."

The groom set to work cleaning the horses' hooves and brushing their coats.

Perly gave Achilles a knowing glance and went to work pumping the man for information. His name was Ray, Ray Muller, and he had been Chandler Kean's groom for close to twenty-five years, ever since Mr. Kean, flush with cash from some financial dealings, had bought the ranch. This had been well before he entered government.

Ray was sound asleep the night Stonewall disappeared—no surprise—and hadn't awakened until he heard Mrs. Kean pounding on his door with a horseshoe. She was so hysterical he couldn't understand much of her babbling, other than the fact that she couldn't find her husband. Over the next few days he had been kept busy providing horses to the first investigators on the scene, so there was nothing he could add in the way of information. Despite his gruff exterior he seemed to be confounded and upset by Stonewall's death, and didn't really want to talk about it.

Horses. The night Stonewall disappeared. A memory came to Achilles, a comment Perly had made on the Learjet.

"What happened to the missing horse?" he asked Ray.

"What missing horse?"

"We heard that Mrs. Kean came out to the stable searching for her husband, and noticed one of the horses was missing."

Ray, who had gone from grooming to saddling, paused for a moment and gazed at the low hills nearby.

"Funny you should bring that up," he said as he started to tighten the cinch on Pasco. "No one else did."

"How'd they think Stonewall—sorry, Mr. Kean—got out to the mine, then?" Achilles said.

"Dunno. You'll have to ask them."

"So tell us about the horse," Perly said. "What's the deal with the missin' horse?"

Ray looked at them both intently. "You gotta promise me you won't tell the others."

"How can we not tell the others? They're investigatin' this murder, same as we are."

"Can't put it in words, exactly, but you two seem all right. The SS, they're too much like the cops in Santa Fe who run you off the street if you smile at a rich tourist. As if the dudes and the tourists are the only ones with the right to be in the precious adobe paradise."

Hmm, Achilles noted. *Lot of bitterness there.*

"Okay," Perly said. "We promise. We won't tell 'em."

Ray waited for Pasco to let his breath out, then pulled the cinch home. The horse grunted in discomfort. Ray moved on to Cerrillo and lifted a saddle onto her back, whistling as he worked.

"Ray," Perly said. "The missin' horse."

Ray was now tightening the cinch on Cerrillo.

"She was a cute little thing," he said after a long pause. "Piebald, with a bob tail. I called her Maggie, cause she looked like a horse version of a magpie."

"Where is she now?" Achilles asked.

Ray, the tough cowpoke, spat on the ground to cover up the emotion in his voice.

"Lyin' up a side canyon a piece, past the mine. The vultures are doin' their work on her."

"For chrissake, man," Perly said. "Why didn't you tell anyone? This could be important."

"You gotta understand. Mr. Kean wanted me to get rid of her. I bought her so I could ride ahead of his groups and clear the trail of rattlers. The snakes spook the other horses, and I didn't want his high and mighties gettin' thrown into the cactus. But he thought she didn't look good enough. Too native, he said. Didn't even want her in his stable."

"But why would that stop you from telling the investigators?" Achilles said.

"Come on, use them eastern brains. They'd think I killed Mr. Kean, because I was mad at him about the horse."

"Why this one horse?" Achilles persisted. "Why did you have to use this one horse?"

"Like I said, to clear the trail of rattlesnakes."

"Why wouldn't some other horse do?"

Ray sighed, kicked the ground with the toe of his boot, and then went into the stable. He returned leading a third horse, which he began to groom.

"You see, it don't happen that you can use any horse in the stable to clear rattlers off the trail. Most horses freak out, begin bucking and rearing. This horse was specially trained, didn't just hear the rattler, she picked up on the smell. She could sniff one out under a bush twenty feet away, and instead of bucking she'd race over to the bush and attack with her front feet. If she didn't get the snake on the first strike, it took the hint and went away. I wanted one of these horses all my life, but they're next to impossible to get."

"That still doesn't tell us why you didn't tell someone about this horse being missing."

"Mister," Ray said in exasperation, throwing a blanket and saddle on the new horse—without any words being exchanged, Perly and Achilles understood that Ray meant to lead them on the trail—"my piebald bein' missing didn't have a thing to do with Mr. Kean's death."

"But the sheriff thought Kean had gone for a night ride. Maybe he rode her up into the hills to meet somebody."

"No, he didn't."

"How can you be so sure of that?"

"Because she wasn't broke to saddle. Mr. Kean may have been a bull-dogger once, but he wouldn't be caught dead riding bareback on an Indian pony."

Indian pony. Suddenly Achilles realized what Ray was trying to tell them. "You mean Indians train these rattlesnake hounds?"

"That's right. I spent years looking, finally found an Indian who'd sell one to me, and now, only a month after I get her, she's dead."

He finished putting the bridle and bit on his new horse, went to the tack room, put on a gun belt, came back to the horse, and mounted. "C'mon. I'll show you where she is."

"Wait a minute," Perly said. He led Cerrillo to a cinderblock mounting step that had been provided for Stonewall's guests, and clambered up on the saddle hand over hand. Achilles swung onto his horse fairly easily, considering how out of practice he was. They followed Ray out of the stable yard, taking a

"No. She knew you had bought it recently." The groom let himself relax a little. "Ray, I hate to say this," Perly continued, pouncing on the moment, "but I don't think you've been entirely straight with us, pal."

"What the hell do you mean?" Now the muscles in Ray's neck tightened like bridge cables. He stood up tall and glared at Perly. "I told you everything I know."

"Except Persimmon."

Caught in his lie, Ray could do nothing but sit down again.

"Persimmon was the other horse, wasn't he, Ray?"

Ray remained silent.

"I guess my question is, did you ride Persimmon out to the mine and carry Mr. Kean's body on Maggie?"

Ray averted his eyes and dug his boots in the dirt, then finally looked at Perly.

"I didn't tell you about Persimmon because I knew you'd follow that exact line. All I can tell you is, I was asleep. Mrs. Kean woke me up with her pounding. When I searched the stable Maggie was gone, but Persimmon was still here. I swear he was. I helped Mrs. Kean back to the ranch house so she could make her phone calls, got the house staff to watch after her. When I came back to the stable, Persimmon was gone too. Near as I can figure it, whoever killed Mr. Kean had been out back, loading him up on Maggie, when Mrs. Kean busted in. And soon as I was out of the way, they took Persimmon too, so they could ride lead."

"But Ray," Achilles broke in, "Mrs. Kean said the missing horse was Persimmon."

"Come on, she was hysterical. The only thing I'd trust her to remember is the fact she couldn't find her husband."

"Where's the horse now?"

"Don't know. He never came back."

"Where'd he go?"

"How would I know?"

"Ray," Achilles said, determined not to give up, "did Persimmon have the special horse shoes you mentioned?"

"Yup."

"Why didn't he have your local shoes?"

"Farrier comes once a month. Hadn't been here yet to change them."

"What color was he?"

"Reddish-brown body and legs, same color mane and tail, a white blaze between his eyes. Classic dark chestnut. I guess you could say—he looked like a persimmon."

"And where did Persimmon come from?"

"Ranch in Texas, near Bunavista, I think that's what Mr. Kean said. He told me the shoes are their mark. They breed Quarter Horses for rich people all over the world."

"What's the name of the ranch?"

"The Double Six."

CHAPTER EIGHT

On the way back to Taos, Perly swung off the main highway and headed up the rutted road leading to the pueblo.

"What gives?" Achilles said. "Why are we going to the pueblo?"

"Two reasons. One, it's lunchtime, I'm hungry, and the Indians run a restaurant nearby—motel clerk told me about it. And two, I want another crack at seein' Sam Rains's wife."

"What makes you think they'll let us?"

"We can pretend we're tourists, buy tickets. Whatever we have to do to get in there, see if we can locate her. Maybe once we're in they'll be friendlier."

The Indian restaurant, called the Tiwa Kitchen, was about half a mile from the entrance to the pueblo. A typical Southwestern adobe structure, it was bracketed by a parking lot in front and a pasture in back, where a couple of horses grazed peacefully. Inside, it had the retro look of a '50s diner, with linoleum floors and table tops, and a potpourri of chairs and benches in different styles. The odor of cooking oil hung heavily in the air.

A middle-aged Indian woman greeted them. She was dressed in blue jeans, running shoes, and a simple green smock with lots of pockets for silverware, pens, and check pads. No attempt at being "native" for the tourists. Achilles appreciated that. She escorted them to a table in the rear with a view of the pasture, and gave them menus. The other customers—mostly off-season tourists—looked with idle curiosity at the two dusty dudes.

The menu combined Mexican/Spanish dishes with what Achilles assumed were authentic Indian ones, but he was no more an aficionado of Taos Indian food than he was of New Mexican. He ordered a cornmeal-coated fresh brook trout with roasted vegetables; and Perly chose green chili with blue corn bread—really an Indian version of tortillas, the waitress explained—and they both ordered some iced Indian tea, which came right away, and was made of some herb Achilles had never tasted before.

While they waited for their food, they reviewed the situation.

"I have a couple of questions," Achilles said.

"Shoot."

"One, why did you tell Ray we'd keep him out of this, when you know that'll be impossible? And two, why did you cut the interview short with Mrs. Kean? I sensed you had more questions, but you ended it suddenly. You know we won't get another chance."

Perly thought for a minute, then took a sip of his tea. He shuddered briefly and smacked his lips in distaste. "This stuff is really weird. I think it would be better if we smoked it."

"Probably their joke on us. Might be a mixture of roadside dirt and weeds."

Perly laughed. "Or boiled-down manure from the horses out back. I should buy a container and ship it to Hadley. She was always big on these herbal infusions."

"I don't think that's wise. She'd accuse you of trying to poison her, and you'd get pulled off the case while they investigate you."

Perly laughed again. He seemed in high spirits, overall. "What about yours?"

"My what?"

"Your ex-wife. Phyllis. Ever hear from her?"

"Only when she needs extra money."

"I thought she remarried."

"She did. A Marine colonel assigned to the White House. He swaggers around like he's Ollie North. They're both living the high life in my house, while I hunker down in that roach-infested apartment in Arlington."

"So, why does she ask you for money?"

"Habit, I guess."

"And you give it to her?"

Embarrassed, Achilles didn't want to answer; but he and Perly had known each other so long that lying to Perly would be as bad as lying to himself.

"Yeah, I give her some—sometimes."

"Why, for chrissake? Hadley would be lucky to get manure in the mail."

"Habit in, habit out."

Perly was now warming to the subject. "Achilles, really, you ought…"

"Perly." Achilles said his partner's name slowly, deliberately—saying *enough* without using the actual word. "I asked you a couple of questions about the investigation. We're here on an investigation, remember?" Every once in a while Achilles had to snap his friend to. It was part of the process. Achilles had long ago realized that when Perly started to ask personal questions it meant he was probably struggling with an issue he couldn't put into words yet.

Just then their orders came.

"After we eat," Perly said. "I'm starvin'."

The food was actually quite good, and Achilles, happy to get some nourishment in his stomach, held his questions in abeyance until they had been served coffee.

Finally Perly was ready to talk. "I told Ray we'd keep him out of it," he said, patting his stomach with satisfaction, "because I mean to do just that. It's obvious he doesn't trust the SS. He could be valuable to us. Don't want them mauling him and ruinin' things."

"I thought the DNI had ordered all the services to cooperate with each other."

"Achilles, get real. Since the reorganization, the turf battles have only gotten worse. The DNI can issue all the orders he wants—the services only obey them when they feel like it, especially since the new administration came in and let up on the pressure. The SS kept the FBI and the CIA out of this altogether, 'cause Stonewall was a special-order protectee. I guess we got called in because he was the boss of our boss, so to speak. But the others resent us whenever we jump in the sandbox. They just can't accept the idea that the Pentagon's secret intelligence arm is on a domestic case, and they're workin' every day to pull the plug on us."

"That still doesn't explain how you think you can keep the others out."

Perly sipped some coffee and looked out the window at the horses in the back pasture before answering. "I got a hunch, but that's all it is. This is above my pay grade, so I can't know for sure."

"What's the hunch?"

"Goes back to what I said after our rooms were trashed."

"You thought there might be a rogue operator in our own backfield."

"Exactly. Maybe somethin' personal is goin' on, somebody at the CIA settlin' scores for Stonewall's raid on his turf."

"Perly, this goes way beyond bureaucratic revenge. I can't believe anyone at the CIA would go so far as dissolution of the ex-secretary of defense."

"Achilles, don't be naïve. Lot of stuff went down durin' Iraq Two. Bad feelings between agencies, especially the ones who lost out to Stonewall. Anythin's possible. Not only do I think we oughta keep the SS out of the loop, I think it's our constitutional duty, if you get my drift."

"No, I don't. I think we could use any help we can get."

Perly thought some more, drained his cup of coffee, and motioned to the waitress that he'd like a refill.

"I guess I have to be more blunt," he said after she'd refilled their cups and left. "We're not sharin' with the other agencies because Malcolm ordered us not to."

"Why the hell didn't you tell me this before?"

"He told me not to say anythin' unless I was forced to. So now you've forced me."

It was Achilles' turn to sip his coffee and think. His head was spinning. "Jesus. I wonder what we've gotten ourselves into. This could blow up in our faces."

"Right you are, ole buddy. We better be sure to strap on our padding. We could get our own selves in trouble if we make a wrong move."

"Great, man. Very comforting thoughts. You just made my lunch taste like the whole meal was roadside weeds."

"Really? My chili was excellent."

"Very funny."

"You see, it's quite simple, when you think about it. Malcolm is takin' advantage of our new status. Before, when we were CIA, we didn't exist, but everyone knew about us. Now we're RZ, and we really don't exist. The other services can't squawk, 'cause they'd be compromising national security.

"So, on to your next question," he said with finality. He had shut off the previous discussion, end of story, no matter that Achilles was a friend as well as a colleague. "Why did I cut Mrs. Kean's interview short? 'Cause I could hear the orderlies talkin' in the hallway outside the library—I could feel bad energy comin' through the door. We weren't gonna get anything more out of her anyway, and besides, I wanted to check out Ray's story ASAP, before he decided to hit the road, which I have a feelin' he might."

"Do you think Ray is involved in this?"

"Maybe. Most likely not a big player, but he might be on the junior varsity. Or he could just be a standard-issue drunk. Between his alcohol and Mrs. Kean's sedatives, there's no guarantee we can go by anything either one of 'em said. Most likely, not."

CHAPTER NINE

They paid the bill and drove the rest of the way to the pueblo. The unpaved parking lot by the entrance was filled with Indian kids returning from school, being greeted by their excited dogs. Several tourists' cars were parked in the lot, but no buses, since it was off season.

In its daytime setting the pueblo had an entirely different appearance, more like a Diego Rivera fresco than a real place. A gigantic mountain, invisible at night, towered over them. Its crest sparkled with the harsh, brilliant white of snow, offset by black rocks peeking out from underneath. Farther down, green pine trees blended seamlessly into the brownish vegetation of the valley, the blue-green frothiness of the river that ran through the middle of the pueblo, and the mud-earth tones of the pueblo itself. All this was set against a turquoise sky speckled with puffy white clouds.

The building nearest the ticket booth had apparently been a Spanish mission. They were standing to its rear, but even from this compromised vantage point Achilles could make out three distinct crosses rising above the front of the building. The sense of spirit—heaven, earth, a people, timelessness—was palpable. Uncharacteristically, Achilles felt an impulse to drop to his knees and pray. Instead, he hauled himself up to his full G-man height and proceeded out of the lot with Perly. Before they had gone a hundred feet they were stopped by a young Indian in his twenties.

"Excuse me," the man said. He was smiling, polite, without any hint of menace or unfriendliness.

"Yeah," Perly said.

"Would you come with me, please?"

"Why? We were just about to visit..."

"We've been expecting you." The man turned on his heel and walked toward the narrow road that threaded between the many bungalows bordering the main pueblo. Curious children poked their heads out doorways, only to be pulled back inside by the adults. After a hundred yards or so the guide led them into the dark cool interior of a low bungalow, where a fire burned in a kiva fireplace in the corner. The logs were stacked vertically, leaning against each other in the shape of a blazing teepee. Sitting cross-legged on a blanket in front of the fire was the old man who had confronted them the previous night.

"Welcome," he said. "Please sit." He pointed to a bench near the doorway. Achilles and Perly sat and waited for the old man to open the conversation. The guide sat on another bench next to the fireplace and busied himself whittling a piece of wood.

"You have come seeking Sam's wife," the old man said.

"Yes," Perly said. "And your name, are we allowed to know that?"

"Francisco. Francisco Orozco. And this is my grandson Charlie," he said, gesturing toward the guide. Charlie nodded in their direction, acknowledging their presence, then resumed his whittling.

Perly and Achilles introduced themselves to complete the opening ceremony.

"Now," said Francisco, "I am curious to know why you have such an interest in Sam Rains and his wife."

"Can't really say," Perly said. "Government business."

"We know about Mr. Kean's murder. The sheriff has already been here. And in no time it will be in the papers. Worse, all over television. This pueblo, the entire state of New Mexico, will be swarming with TV vans and their satellite dishes, reporters asking everyone in sight if they've seen any Arabs hiding in the pueblo. We'll have no peace."

"I'm afraid that's true. We—the two of us—have no control over that, sorry to say."

"Well, your desire to find Sam Rains and his wife concerns us. We don't want to be involved in this business. It has absolutely nothing to do with us. The privacy of the pueblo will be invaded, through no fault of our own."

"Sorry to say we have no control over that either. But I have to disagree with you about not havin' any involvement. Whether you like it or not, Sam was married to a woman who lives in this pueblo. That's number one. Two, Sam found Mr. Kean's head and was detained by the sheriff."

"And released immediately. The sheriff has no jurisdiction over us. Neither do you."

"All we want is to ask him what else he knows, what he might've noticed. The site is a mess now, but he was the first one there, might've seen things that've been wiped out since then. We're not threatenin' him, or accusin' him.

And if we can't find him, we'd appreciate bein' able to speak to his wife, see if he told her anything."

"We told you last night, Sam has left."

"Yeah, that's right, so you did. But when we got back to our motel our rooms had been ransacked. Someone knew Sam had lured us out here, and took the opportunity to invade our privacy, as you would put it. Someone in this pueblo knows something, and we need to find out what."

Good job, Achilles thought. Perly hadn't said anything about Sam's second phone call.

"We have our own police force," Francisco said. "If you want to explore leads in the pueblo you'll have to work through them."

"This is a *federal* matter," Perly said, dropping his voice into its most official-sounding bottom octave. "I believe our jurisdiction supersedes that of your pueblo police force."

"You need to review the relevant regulations with your superiors," Francisco said, going legal himself. "You might be surprised at how limited your powers really are in this situation."

Perly had to backtrack. "Francisco, I'm not tryin' to have a confrontation here. I'm askin' for your help. I don't think for a minute any of your people are actually involved in this murder, but I do think someone may have information that could be useful to us. And I think Sam, and maybe his wife, are most likely to be of help. Since he isn't here, couldn't we at least talk to her? We'll do it in your presence, if that'll make you happy."

"I'm afraid that in this situation, nothing will make me happy. I'm also afraid I can't grant your request."

"Why?"

"Because she slipped away sometime during the night. We don't know where she went. We sent men out in all directions, but they couldn't find her. Sam must have come back for her."

"You tried to give us the impression he was dead," Achilles said, speaking up for the first time.

"No I didn't. I merely said his wife needed to be left alone with her grief. He disappeared after the sheriff released him."

"So now he's gone, and she's gone," Perly said. "And you have no idea where they are?"

"That's correct. I wish we could help you, but as you can see, gentlemen, we really can't."

"We only got your word for this," Perly said. "How do we know they're not holed up in the sanctuary of the mission, for instance?"

Francisco shook his head sadly. "The old mentality of the Bureau of Indian Affairs, still strong after all these decades. Indians are always lying, isn't that the mantra?"

"That's not what I meant at all. I meant…"

"You meant what you said, which was, if I may speak between your lines, how can you trust our word, how can you be sure we're not hiding them somewhere? The answer is, you can't. Just as we can't trust your word that this place won't be overrun with other investigators once we let you break into our jurisdiction."

"I never gave you such a promise."

"No, but it's the kind of promise you federals make all the time. And when things don't happen the way you have promised, you shrug and say you couldn't help it. I can tell you this: if Sam and his wife are hiding somewhere on the reservation, or in the sanctuary of the mission, we don't know it. If we find out they are, we'll be the first to call the tribal police and have them get in touch with you. Maybe the mountain will smile on you yet."

"How do you know where to reach us?"

"If Sam knew, we also know."

"Can you at least tell us his wife's name?"

"If we find anything out, the tribal police will call you."

With that, the interview was over. Francisco and Charlie watched from the doorway as Perly and Achilles, shaking their heads in consternation, returned to their car.

"What crap—worse than their tea," Perly said, once they were in the car and driving down the road to Taos. "Talk about stonewalling—Kean had nothin' on this guy. Maybe we need to pay the sheriff a visit. I want to find out more about Sam, like how he got all that information about us."

"Maybe you're right about the rogue operator. This is spooky." Achilles felt a shiver go up and down his spine. No matter how many situations he had been in, each one had its unpleasant surprises, its moments of uncollated fear. "But for now I need to think about something I can have a little control over, like the cipher. You can deal with the spooky stuff, like the vanishing Indians. In fact, before we go back out with Ray, we should stop by the motel to see if our laptops have come in from Kirtland."

"Wish to hell RZ would let us use Blackberries. We could have taken pictures already and wouldn't have to make an extra trip."

"Well, there's no way around it. We have to get back to the pony, and while we're at it I want to look for Persimmon's hoof prints too."

"Why?"

Richard Beeson

"I only have Ray's word that the shoes have domino pips. I want to see them for myself and get pictures. There are all sorts of connections to dominoes here—the domino in Stonewall's mouth, the name of the ranch that sold Persimmon to him. And the Spanish names of the Indians at the pueblo—dominoes came up from Mexico, brought in by the Spanish, if my memory serves me. I have some research to do on the Internet."

They pulled into the lot of the motel and went into the office to see if the computers had arrived.

"Anythin' come for us?" Perly asked the day clerk, a grizzled old westerner who reeked of cigarette smoke.

"Yep," said the clerk. "A piece for each of you, actually." He fumbled around behind the counter and produced two boxes that obviously had to be their laptops.

"And somethin' else. This is for you," the clerk said to Perly, handing him an envelope.

"Huh," Perly said, sliding his finger under the flap to open it. "Wonder what this is."

Achilles was too busy caressing the box containing his laptop to notice Perly rubbing the stubble on his chin.

"When was this delivered?" Perly asked the clerk.

"Few minutes ago. Some guy in a brown jacket, driving a big SUV."

Perly passed the note to Achilles. "Read this."

From now on have your cell phone turned on, the note read. *Come to the ranch immediately.*

"I swear it was turned on," Perly said as they raced back to the car. "We must've been in a dead spot."

CHAPTER TEN

The ranch was swarming with SS men and SUVs. Achilles and Perly had to show their IDs at three different checkpoints before they were allowed near the ranch house. Finally they reached the courtyard and got out of their car. A huge man with close-cropped hair and a beefy face came up to them, breathing fire. It took a moment for Achilles to recognize him as the *hauptmann* in the freezer.

"Just what the hell have you two been up to?" he said.

"Investigating," Achilles said. "You know who we are. Do you think we're here on vacation?"

"Never should've let you sewer rats near this. I can't even leave the ranch for a few hours to take a body to the air base. Do you have any idea what's been going on since you were here?"

"Excuse me," Perly said, in his best steely tone. "Introductions would be nice. Who are you, and why are you talkin' to us this way?"

Straining to recover his composure, the man introduced himself. "I'm Harmon. Riley Harmon. I'm in charge of this investigation."

"Not our part of it, you aren't. You're not in our chain of command."

"Never mind the turf business. We got a problem here, and we want to know what you two had to do with it."

"What *is* the problem, exactly?" Achilles said.

"I think it's better if we show you." Riley made a sign to the others, and two of his men came over to them, pushing motorized dirt bikes that had already been fired up. "You know how to ride these?"

"We prefer horses," Achilles said.

"Don't got time. Besides, there aren't enough for all of us, and the groom has—just never mind, hop on these and follow us."

"Wait a minute!" Perly said. "These damn things will tear up the trail and obliterate any evidence that might be left."

"Too late to worry about that. Damage has already been done. Come on." Riley and his men mounted their dirt bikes and headed for the trail. They looked completely out of place, like oversized kids defying their elders by riding the trails without helmets. There was nothing Achilles and Perly could do but follow them and eat their dust—a meal that had obviously been planned.

Instead of taking an hour and a half to get to the mine it took only fifteen minutes, although Achilles nearly didn't make it at all, because he almost went off the trail over a steep embankment. He hadn't been willing to tell Riley he had never ridden one of these things. In fact he hated them, with their whining mad-hornet racket.

The area surrounding the mine had exploded with activity since the morning. The mine rescue crane chugged and groaned as it hauled an object from the depths of the shaft. A dozen men picked over the ground near the shaft itself. *How did they all get out here in the last few hours?* Achilles wondered. He had to admit that when the SS men decided to mobilize they were pretty swift about it.

The object being raised was the rescue cage; when it emerged from the shaft the crane operator placed it gently on the ground, and a man stepped out, calling for help. A couple of his buddies came to his aid, disconnecting the cage and looping another cable over the hook.

"Okay, winch it up," said one of the men to the crane operator. The winch started whirring, the cable tautened, and the crane struggled to lift what was obviously a heavy weight.

"What the hell," Achilles said to Perly. "Guess there's been a lot of action since we left."

"Or before we got here. Damn. I thought the mine was done. There could've been somethin' down there this morning, and we didn't even look."

They walked over to the mine to observe.

"Jesus," Perly said when the heavy object appeared at the mouth of the shaft. It was the body of Ray's pony, Maggie. "How did that get here?"

"That's what we want to know," Riley said. "The groom can't tell us. He's gone missing. Found his pickup on the fire road out by the back gate, not far from here."

"But he was sittin' outside the tack room whittling, not three hours ago."

"That was three hours ago. This is now." Riley walked over to the pony's body as it hit the ground with a *thunk*. "So what I want to know is what else happened when you were out with the groom this morning? What happened between then and when we came out to do one last check on the mine? What did you find out that you didn't tell my men, and should've?"

"I don't get this," Perly said. "Everything's come unscrewed." He didn't attempt to answer Riley's charges.

Riley glowered at Achilles with fierce hostility. "You?" he demanded. "You got any ideas?"

"Have you been to the canyon?" Achilles said.

"Canyon? What canyon?"

Achilles hadn't really wanted to say anything about the pony, or the canyon. The coded note was still weighing down his shirt pocket, safe in its little plastic bag for now, and he hadn't had a chance to study it yet. If he said anything about the canyon he ran the risk that the SS would find out about the note and try to take it away from him. But this situation was spinning out of control, and he couldn't, in good conscience, leave Riley and his crew in the dark about what he and Perly had seen earlier.

"Ray brought us out here this morning, but first he took us higher up the trail. His Indian pony was lying up there in a side canyon. Someone had killed it and left its body to rot. I don't understand how it could have been brought down here and dumped in the mine shaft."

"Take us there. Now."

This time Achilles rode point and got to stir up dust for the others to eat. In a few minutes they had reached the mouth of the canyon, and pulled to a stop. Perly and Achilles leaned their dirt bikes against a rock and waited for the others to catch up, then led them on foot toward the rock outcropping.

"Ray told us he hadn't mentioned the pony to your guys because he was afraid he would come under suspicion," Achilles said to Riley as they walked. "Seems the pony had been used to cart Stonewall's body to the mine, then whoever murdered him brought the pony up here and killed it, too."

"Okay, fine. They brought the pony here. And then by some miracle, right after you saw it here, it wound up in the mine shaft? And I'm supposed to believe you didn't have anything to do with it?" Riley's gorge, bubbling just below the surface like hot lava, erupted again. "You spooks had better not be diddlin' with me," he bellowed.

Perly cut him short with a wave of the hand. "Respect us as professionals, at least, for chrissake. Do you think we'd play reckless games? There must be some explanation."

They reached the spot where the pony had lain. The ground had been swept clean of evidence, as if someone had taken a broom to the sand. Yet it was apparent even to an untrained eye that there had been a heavy body dragged across the ground, and that efforts had been made to cover up the fact. The group followed the drag marks out of the canyon toward a small plateau a few hundred feet away.

"Look, over there." Perly pointed to a spot nearby. "Flattened sage-brush."

They rushed over to the site, a large circle of broken plants and disrupted ground about thirty feet in diameter. The plant stalks had been mangled, in some cases uprooted, and beyond the circumference of the circle the men could see plain evidence of peripheral rotor wash: dirt embedded in foliage, small rocks overturned, general signs of lesser disruption.

Now it was Perly's turn to rage at Riley. "Airlifted out! You bastards knew about this pony the whole time, y'all came up here with one of your birds and airlifted her out, then dumped her in the mine, and you have the gall to accuse us!"

It was Riley's turn to be nonplussed. "I swear, we didn't."

"Come on, man! How could anyone have flown a bird in here that's big enough to carry a horse, without y'all knowing? The sound alone should have tipped your men off."

"Our own stuff is all over the place. Maybe we just thought it was one of ours…"

"And nobody looked? Nobody bothered to make an ID of a bird landin' up the hill, where it didn't belong?"

"Don't worry your pretty spook head about our logistics," Riley said, finding his voice again. "We'll figure this out, and we'll get back to you—if we feel like it." He turned on his heel and headed for the dirt bikes. "C'mon, we gotta get back."

"Perly," Achilles said quietly, poking at Perly's ribs. "Wait a minute."

The SS men raced to their bikes and took off down the trail, but Achilles and Perly hung back.

"C'mon!" Riley ordered, waving for them to follow as his head receded below the horizon.

"What is it?" Perly said to Achilles.

"Look. There's some hard ground over here."

He led Perly to a spot of hard earth on the edge of the helicopter blast zone. Although more solid than typical desert sand, it wasn't so hard that it wouldn't register any impacts whatsoever.

"Check these out." Achilles leaned over a set of clearly defined hoof prints, which had left a perfect pattern of dots in the soil. Six dots on each side of the shoe: the double six.

"Persimmon's prints. They must have been keeping him nearby, maybe in a trailer, or in another canyon, and they airlifted him out along with Maggie's body, then dumped Maggie in the mine."

"But the prints are headed away from the helicopter," Perly said. "Riley said they found Ray's pickup by a back gate not far from here. Maybe the live horse went out that way."

They were interrupted by one of Riley's men, who had come back for them.

"Hey! Riley said to shake it! He wants to talk to you guys!" He parked and stood with his arms folded, obviously intending not to leave until the RZ men came with him.

The ride down from the foothills was not fun. Achilles had trouble focusing on the trail; he kept thinking about the missing groom, Ray Muller, and about Sam Rains and his wife. Somehow, he knew, they were involved in Stonewall's death or its immediate aftermath. And it was quite apparent their disappearance had been related to this involvement. Possibly they had been killed or taken hostage because they knew too much. So far, so good. But the airlift of the dead pony, what had that been about? Obviously the killers had wanted somebody to find the pony; otherwise, why bother with the brand and the note? But would the airlift have taken place even if Achilles and Perly hadn't seen the pony and removed the message from its ear? Had someone been watching them the whole time?

When they pulled up in the courtyard they saw Riley on the portico, pacing like a caged mountain lion. His men tried to act nonchalant, but betrayed their nervousness in several ways, some cleaning their nails with the large blades of their pocket knives, others doing hopeless make-work tasks, such as wiping the dust off the headlights of the SUVs.

"I told you to come with me!" Riley roared at Achilles and Perly.

"I thought we established this already," Perly said. "We don't take orders from you."

"Well, I got someone here on the phone, maybe you'll take orders from him. This just came in for you." Riley handed Perly a satellite phone.

"Lyman," Perly said into the phone, rubbing his stubble noisily while he listened. "Yes…yes…yes, sir, right away." He clicked the phone off and handed it back to Riley.

"There's a Lear comin' into the landing strip here to pick us up," Perly said to Achilles. "We're bein' called back to Arlington ASAP."

"But our stuff!" Achilles said.

"Don't worry about it," Riley said. "We'll send some men to the motel to pick it up. How do you want it sent? In boxes or laundry bags?" He broke out laughing; he was so pleased with himself, and so glad to be rid of their foreign presence, that he simply couldn't hide his delight.

Dejected, Perly and Achilles slumped on a rattan couch in the shade of the portico. The SS men drifted off to await the arrival of the plane.

"Perly," Achilles said when they were alone, "who was that on the phone? Malcolm?"

"Yep. The governor of Ring Zero himself. Guess we're in some kind of big trouble, pal. Don't know why, but we're in big trouble. Remember what I said at lunch."

"What do we do when we get back, go straight to Malcolm?"

"No. He said to go home, get a little rest, and see him at 7:30 in the morning. There'll be a car sent around for us."

There was nothing to do but collect the new computers from the Ford Escort and wait for the air ferry.

CHAPTER ELEVEN

Riley managed to have their bags moved from the motel to the ranch before the plane arrived, so Achilles and Perly would at least be able to go home with their razors on hand. Achilles had worried about that, about meeting Malcolm, the governor of Ring Zero, without being clean-shaven. Such small worries, he knew, tend to crop up at big moments. He chided himself for not being more diligent concerning his supplies. He hadn't put his backup razor in place. Although he had taken the precaution, after years of dealing with misplaced luggage, of stashing a spare razor in his closet, he wasn't sure if he had put it in the closet of his apartment or the linen closet of his house, now occupied by Ollie North Two—Achilles had such a distaste for the man he couldn't even recall his real name; he spent a few minutes allowing himself to get angry all over again about the divorce, and how quickly Phyllis had remarried. After years of serving his country in his own behind-the-scenes fashion, he found it galling to be called "boring" and "not a player" by his own wife. A nice present for his new life at the Pentagon, she had given him.

It was now almost 6:30, and the setting sun highlighted the surrounding mountains with an impressive show of Georgia O'Keeffe colors. The distant whine of jet engines announced the arrival of the Learjet. With a takeoff this late, they wouldn't be getting back to Virginia until well past midnight their time.

"What are you thinking?" Perly asked.

"Getting mad at my ex all over again. Wish I'd never gone to that alumni party with you at your old frat house. A Columbia man should never marry a U. of Virginia woman."

"Keepin' your mind off the present, eh?"

"Why not? Seems like a good thing to do under the circumstances."

Perly tried to laugh, but could only manage a snort. He was plainly quite worried. "Hope they didn't send us a jiggered airplane."

"Do you think...?"

"Who knows? If we've created a problem for Malcolm I wouldn't put anything past him. How convenient, to lose a couple of agents in an airplane accident. 'So sorry, where do you want the body parts delivered?' You get my drift?" Perly, imagining his improbable scenario, laughed a deliciously malevolent laugh.

"I think I'll stick to fretting about Phyllis."

An SS man walked up to them, the same one who had picked them up the day before. Apparently they were his assignment.

"Time to go out to the strip," he said. "Your ride is here."

"Do you mind telling us your name?" Achilles said.

"What for?" The agent said, in a tone of genuine surprise.

"We thought we'd send you a card when we get back," Achilles said sarcastically. "'Wish you were here,' or something like that."

"Very funny."

"Actually, I like to know the names of the people I'm supposed to be working with. Or have worked with. Makes me feel better at the end of the day."

"Rudy," the agent said.

"No last name?"

"Rudy," was the answer. "Regulations."

"Rudy Regulations. What an interesting name."

"I mean it's regulations I can't," Rudy said, becoming increasingly irritated.

"I know, I know. I'm just having you on."

"How Brit of you. 'Having you on.' Why don't you talk American?"

"It's that evil East Coast influence. I've been to too many embassy balls, I guess."

Rudy was fed up with the banter. "Come on, let's go. Soon as the plane gets refueled, you're outta here."

As Rudy drove them out to the airstrip, Achilles wondered what lay in store the next day. Maybe Malcolm was so furious with some misstep they'd made that he'd have them shot in the Pentagon basement, Soviet style. Achilles could see Rudy watching them in the rearview mirror with detached interest. *Probably wondering what size caskets we wear,* Achilles thought.

———

Once the plane was airborne, Perly curled up on his banquette to take a nap. Achilles, too wired to sleep, decided to do some work, and unpacked his new laptop. The techies at Kirtland had set up the software the way he requested, installed a pre-charged battery, given him an airplane power adapter, and thrown in a wireless card for good measure. Achilles made a mental note to drop them a line, thanking them.

The first thing he wanted to do was access his backup server so he could download the pictures of the domino and the file that contained the cipher. But he couldn't get online for some reason. After several frustrating tries he rang for the steward, who came out of his nook behind the pilot's cabin with a pot of coffee.

"Don't need any coffee, thanks," Achilles said. "I'm wondering why I can't get an outside line. Can you have the pilot turn on the communications ports back here?"

"Sorry, sir," the steward said. He was a polite young man in his mid-twenties, wearing a plain light blue uniform with dark blue pocket flaps, cuffs, and collar. "This flight is sealed."

"Sealed?"

"No communications in or out, everything blocked, except those necessary for navigation and landing."

"By whose orders?"

The steward shrugged. "Don't know, sir. I was told to say, if you asked, that the flight is sealed."

Achilles fought to turn back the panic he felt rising up inside him. *I should wake Perly up and tell him,* he thought, but then, what good would it do? Perly couldn't change anything. Let him enjoy a few hours of blissful ignorance.

"Thanks," he said to the steward. "Maybe I'll take that coffee after all."

The steward poured a cup for Achilles, left it on the table, and returned to his post.

Achilles stared at the screen of his laptop in disbelief. The communications software blinked on and off, taunting him with the message *Unable to Make Connection.* Was Malcolm really that upset? What the hell could they have done that would make him that angry? Why the orders to black out communications?

The open dialogue box of the software insolently continued to blink at him. He quelled its insolence by closing the program. At least he could make that much go away. He was about to shut the laptop down and give up when he thought of a way to burn off his anxiety, do some other work that would help him solve the cipher.

What's to solve? came the taunting inner voice. *Don't you get it? You're off the case. As of tomorrow morning you're going to be retired, at the very least. What do you have to offer?*

"A lot, goddammit," he said aloud.

"Hunh?" Perly said, stirring on the banquette. He sat up partway. "You say something?"

"Just arguing with the computer. Cyber-muttering. Go back to sleep."

Perly was only too happy to comply.

Get a grip, man, get a grip, Achilles told himself. He loaded the word-processing software and made a blank table for working on the cipher. He would plug in the new numbers. The thought occurred to him that he had the hole card, if there was going to be a confrontation with Malcolm tomorrow. No one knew about the second message but Achilles and Perly. The SS didn't know it; the local police and sheriff didn't know it; neither the FBI nor the CIA knew it. Only the two of them from Ring Zero, two wild and crazy guys, to quote the old Steve Martin / Dan Aykroyd skits on *Saturday Night Live*. He'd have to be sure to safeguard the precious piece of paper when he got home.

For now he'd enter the numbers into the computer to see if they gave him any ideas. He pulled the plastic bag from his shirt pocket, put on some vinyl gloves, and gingerly removed the note from the bag. The cabin filled with unpleasant traces of dead-pony odor. Achilles choked briefly, then brought the bronchial spasm under control.

Perly partially woke up again. "Wha's that smell?" he muttered. "Hadley, did I take the garbage out?"

Achilles did his best to imitate Perly's ex-wife, whose voice he had heard many times carrying on around the backyard barbecues in Leesburg.

"Never you mind, sweetie," he sang out in his best falsetto. "Everything's okay."

Perly smacked his lips, snuffled a bit, and drifted back into his dream.

Achilles unfolded the note paper, carefully flattened it, and reinserted it in the bag with the numbers facing out. It was about the size of an index card. There were only four numbers: 33-02-50-16. *Damn,* he thought. *Only four?* Next to useless. He couldn't do frequency analysis. There wasn't enough to work with. Yet they must have some meaning; otherwise the killer, or killers, wouldn't have bothered stapling them to the pony's ear. Achilles dutifully entered the numbers in the table on his computer.

Wait a minute, he thought. Maybe this wasn't part of the message. It might be the key that would enable him to crack the larger cipher. That was why it had been left with the pony. Anyone who hadn't done enough groundwork on the case would never get to the pony, and would never have found the key.

Of course! Achilles nearly yelled, rather than thought. Here were four numbers: 33, 02, 50, and 16. And the brand on the pony's rump had four letters, the same letters as the brand on Stonewall's forehead: SODM. So 33 must equal S, 02=O, 50=D, and 16=M.

He was off and running. He had a key. Once he retrieved that other file from the backup server he'd be able to use the key to start unlocking the rest of the cipher. *How could anyone be so stupid as to give this away so easily?* he thought. Then he caught himself short: maybe the four numbers were a red herring left behind to tease him, make him think he had a key when he didn't.

There was nothing more he could do without the pictures and the file of the other cipher. Time to shut down for the night and get some rest. Soon he had joined Perly in jet dreamland, tossing fitfully on his banquette, dreaming of Phyllis calling him a cipher, which she knew was the worst insult she could hurl at him—not only a nonentity, but an indecipherable nonentity. Instead of resting, he thrashed violently, imagining himself beheading his ex-wife, jamming a domino in her mouth, and pinning a piece of paper to her navel that contained a code for the phrase *the cipher strikes again*.

CHAPTER TWELVE

Thursday, April 28, 1:00 am (EDT)

The lights at the Bull Run airport winked on long enough for the plane to land, then winked off before the men disembarked. A waiting car took them to their homes. During the last hour of the flight they had both managed to wake up enough for Achilles to tell Perly about the blocked communications, and catch him up on the key to the cipher. Although still concerned about the reason for the communications blackout, they felt in better spirits than they had when the flight started. At least, they agreed, they had some positive news to give Malcolm, and weren't going into the meeting empty-handed.

When Achilles got home he scanned the pony note, uploaded the file to his backup server, and downloaded the previous Stonewall files to his new laptop. He was too weary to do any real work, so he put the bag containing the note in a small Allenbury Pastille tin in the freezer to keep the dead-pony odor from ruining his food. It was past 3 a.m. by the time he got to bed.

The next morning the car came at 7 a.m. to pick him up. Perly, looking hung over, was already aboard, rubbing the stubble on his chin. No matter how often he shaved, Perly could never get rid of his stubble. Achilles had long thought his partner might have enjoyed a second career as a rock star, if only he had shown some musical talent.

"What's the matter?" Perly said. "You look hung over."

"I was thinking the same thing about you."

Perly laughed. "Guess it isn't every day we get hauled into a face-to-face with the governor himself."

Achilles pulled out a note pad and worked on the cipher while the driver picked his way through the rush hour traffic on I-395. Perly busied himself with a crossword puzzle. They were both too nervous for small talk, although neither one would admit it to the other. Finally the car swung into the vast parking lots of the Pentagon, depositing them at the South Parking Entrance. The hulk of the famous granite building loomed over them, reminding Achilles of the mesas in New Mexico—but this mesa, instead of being home to Indian holy sites, was the repository for the brains of the most lethal killing machine in history.

They went inside, flashed their badges through the scanner, and signed the destination sheet. The guard eyed them warily while the central ID computer checked their badges; then the automatic gate clicked open, and they went through.

Even this early in the morning the endless hallways were already hopping, with military uniforms everywhere, most worn by junior officers running files to meetings. Morning chatter spewed out of open doorways, intermingled with the smell of coffee being brewed. At last Achilles and Perly reached their destination: Ring Zero, Pentagon-speak for the central courtyard. They took an elevator down to the bunker basement, where they were to meet Malcolm in a room suspended by cables, jokingly referred to as the moon rover. The entrance door was at least three feet thick, lined with acoustic foam.

The governor's assistant, Mary Sue—a tall, attractive blonde wearing a black silk pants suit—greeted them outside the door. She was clutching a thin manila file to her breast.

"The governor is waiting for you," she said, smiling warmly. "Go on in."

The conference room contained a large metal table surrounded by tube-frame side chairs, all empty except the one at the far end. Several inactive video screens lined one wall. Mary Sue went to the head of the table and laid the file in front of the governor, Malcolm Evers, who was dressed in his customary baggy suit.

"Sit down," he said to Achilles and Perly, regarding them with a detached manner, neither friendly nor unfriendly. He was of medium build, with dark thinning hair and a careworn face that seemed to be losing its battle against gravity.

"Coffee?" Mary Sue said.

"Yes, please," the governor replied. He busied himself leafing through the file as Mary Sue went to a stand in the corner, poured coffee from a thermos into ceramic mugs emblazoned with the Pentagon seal, and handed them around. Perly and Achilles grasped at the mugs eagerly, taking big sips of the life-giving java, grateful for the opportunity to do something besides jiggle their knees nervously.

After what felt like an eternity, Mary Sue left and swung the giant door closed, rotating the airlock mechanism from the other side. Achilles heard a whoosh of air as the sealed internal ventilation system took over.

Now that they were safely encapsulated in their cocoon, the governor leaned back in his chair and sighed.

"I'm sorry for the theatrics," he said, taking a sip of his own coffee. His avuncular appearance brought to mind a neighborhood jeweler rather than the governor of Ring Zero; and indeed, he might well have masqueraded as a jeweler at some point during his career. Renowned as a master of disguise, he had once been fond of wandering the CIA campus incognito, testing to see if anyone would challenge him.

Malcolm had risen through the ranks of the CIA to the position of assistant director of the Covert Action Staff, and was highly regarded by both his troops and the higher-ups who make and break careers—so highly regarded, in fact, that the Pentagon, rather than hunt for someone to head their new top-secret operation, simply raided Langley. Malcolm had insisted on bringing two of his best field agents with him, which explained how he, Achilles, and Perly now found themselves in the moon rover at Ring Zero.

"So," Malcolm said, "as you might have guessed, I have a particular purpose in summoning you back here so precipitously. Unfortunately I felt it necessary to bring you here under blackout conditions. That's why I had your plane's communications blocked, so there could be no possibility whatsoever of any interceptions. Sorry for the inconvenience," he said directly to Achilles. Evidently the baby-faced steward had been part of the governor's pod, one of his private agents.

Achilles and Perly both relaxed. This had to do with the assignment. They weren't in trouble. They weren't going to be taken to the tenth sub-basement and shot, with jeering colleagues egging on the firing squad.

"Before I get into my reasons for this meeting," Malcolm went on, "do you have anything to report? Any progress?"

He listened thoughtfully while Achilles and Perly related the events of the previous couple of days. He took notes on a yellow pad as they talked.

"Do you have any idea where the helicopter came from, the one that moved the pony?" he said when they had finished.

"None," Perly said. "The SS couldn't figure it out either."

"So a big Chinook, or some other helicopter big enough to carry horses, came out of nowhere, loaded up at least one, maybe two of the critters, and dumped the pony's body into the mine shaft like a basketball slam dunk, and no one had any idea where this helicopter came from, no one saw it, no one heard it?"

"We were nowhere near the ranch at the time," Achilles said. "And the SS seemed to be directing their energies toward being furious with us."

"Not a surprise," Malcolm snorted. "The reorganization has changed nothing." He scribbled more notes on his pad. "The Indian who disappeared. Did anyone get his fingerprints from the sheriff?"

"Don't know," Perly said. "We didn't have time to find out," he added pointedly.

"The Indian's wife and the stable hand, no one has any idea where they went either?"

"None," Perly said, squirming uncomfortably. "Riley said they found Ray's pickup by the back gate not far from the mine, but we didn't have a chance to follow up."

More notes. "This domino," Malcolm said. "You say you took a photograph. May I see it?"

Achilles booted up his laptop and loaded the domino file.

"The picture's a little fuzzy," he said, turning the laptop toward the governor. "I shot it in a freezer full of vapor from people's breath, and the domino was inside a plastic box, but you'll get the idea."

"Interesting piece of carving. Where is it now?"

"The Secret Service took it."

"That means we'll never get our hands on it. Good thing you have that picture. What about the cipher? Any progress there?"

"The four-number cipher we found on the pony may be a key." Achilles pulled the Allenbury Pastille tin out of his computer case and handed it to Malcolm. "Here it is," he announced triumphantly. "We're the only ones who've seen it. SS doesn't know it exists."

Malcolm opened the tin and inspected the Ziploc-enclosed piece of paper.

"Good work. I'll send it to the lab." He put the paper back in the tin and snapped the lid shut. "And you say the brand on the pony was the same as the one on the secretary's forehead?"

"Yes sir, four letters, S-O-D-M."

Malcolm made some notes, then turned to Perly. "You said the groom told you about a ranch named the Double Six, in Texas, where the new horse came from. Have we checked into that?"

"Not yet. Maybe some of the termites in Research could find that out."

"Yes, naturally. That one should be fairly easy." The governor stopped scribbling for a moment, thinking deeply, tapping the eraser of his pencil on the pad, and then turned to the two men once again.

"The preliminary autopsy results on Secretary Kean just came in," he said, calling Stonewall by his honorific, "and the manner of death was quite simple: the Kevorkian system."

"Dr. Death?"

"The same. Not to say that he was involved. He couldn't have been. But whoever murdered the secretary did it with a lethal injection of potassium chloride. They didn't have the grace to provide him with a muscle relaxant, so he died in spasmodic agony." Malcolm seemed quite angry as he related these facts. "The business with the head, the branding, the body being dumped in a mine shaft, those were done for effect, to send a message."

"Send a message where?" Perly said. "Who's the addressee?"

"That's the big question. I have an idea, but I don't want to reveal it to others yet. I need you two to prove or disprove my theory."

"What is it?" Achilles said.

"It concerns this rubric, SODM. The letters you say might be the key to the cipher. Do you have any idea what they mean?"

"No. At first I thought there might be a connection to Iraq and Saddam Hussein, given the nature of the secretary's death."

"Somethin' jihadist," Perly said.

"Something jihadist is possible, and that's one reason the Pentagon and RZ have been brought in on the case. However, there are some complicating facts that point in other directions. For instance, the skull on the domino leads the trail of suspicion away from Islamic militants. They wouldn't use a symbol depicting a human form. They would have used the more geometric standard domino, with nothing on it but the number pips."

Malcolm paused, as if he weren't sure of what he should or could say next. Achilles thought he seemed visibly and uncharacteristically nervous. "For another thing," the governor continued at last, "the letters S-O-D-M stand for 'Society of the Domino Mask.'"

"Never heard of it," Perly said.

"No, you wouldn't have. It is highly secretive, even more so than the Knights Templar."

"And you think this secret society is behind the attack on the secretary?" Achilles said.

"Could be. But there is also an alternative possibility."

"You mean the secretary belonged to the society, and someone is out to get the members for some reason?"

"That is possible, yes."

"Is there any basis for this?"

"Let's call it a working hypothesis. I can't be any more specific than that."

Perly and Achilles remained silent for a moment. Presented with a problem to ponder, they were their old selves again, and their jiggling knees finally calmed down. *What is the governor trying to tell us?* Achilles thought. *Why is he being so coy?*

"So, what do we do next?" Perly said. "Go back to Taos?"

"No. This has become a bit more complicated."

"How so?"

"I need you to go to New York City."

"Why? What's the Big Apple got to do with Stonewall's—sorry, the secretary's—murder?"

"I'll tell you, but first, a few ground rules. Since there's a G8 summit being held at the Javits Center in New York this weekend, all the services are busy with that, and it's just as well, because I want you to operate on your own. You have to function like goblins running a black op in a hard-target country, and keep base contact to a minimum. No more company jets. You fly commercial, drive, or take Amtrak. No more set-tos with the other services, unless it is absolutely unavoidable. If there are real problems, of course, things that go beyond your scope to deal with, you'll have to let me know immediately."

"How can we reach you?" Achilles said.

"A go-between will be provided. When it's time, you'll be contacted."

"I don't get it. What's the reason for going goblin?"

"As I said, things have gotten a bit more complicated. Yesterday we discovered that there's been another murder."

"Another one?"

"Done in the same manner. The head severed, and a domino similar to this one stuffed in the mouth. The body thrown in an out-of-the-way place—in this instance, a dumpster near the construction site of the new Freedom Tower, with a piece of paper pinned to the navel. Everything the same."

"Who's the victim?" Perly asked.

"John Maguire." The governor waited as the name sank in, and the two men looked at each other in disbelief.

"Yes, *that* John Maguire. Chairman of the New York Stock Exchange."

CHAPTER THIRTEEN

Achilles and Perly came out of the Pentagon reeling. An unknown person, or group, was apparently out to assassinate some of the most powerful people in the country, perhaps in the world. First, the former secretary of defense—retired or not, he was an infamous symbol of immense power. Now, the chairman of the New York Stock Exchange.

"Do you have the same feelin' I do?" Perly asked Achilles.

"Best not to talk here. Let's grab some coffee and a roll at Starbucks. We need to catch our breath."

An official-looking black Buick pulled up in front of them and stopped. The driver got out, checked a piece of paper in his hand, and walked over to them.

"Achilles Smith? Perly Lyman?" he said.

"Yes," Achilles and Perly answered simultaneously.

"Hop in. I'm your ride."

"Didn't know we had a ride back," Achilles said to Perly as they got in the back seat.

"Neither did I. Thought Malcolm said we were on our own."

"You could let us off at the Starbucks over on Joyce Street," Achilles said to the driver. The driver grunted as he headed out of the endless Pentagon parking lot, showed his ID at the security barrier, and took a route north and west.

"Hey!" Perly yelled. "What is this? Where you takin' us?"

"Don't get excited," the driver said. "Karl wants to see you."

The divider between the front and back of the car slammed shut, and they heard the sound of doors locking. Achilles looked at Perly in consternation.

"What the hell," he said. "What's Karl up to? What do we do with this?"

"I guess we roll with it, ole buddy. I been wonderin' when he would surface. He used to be our boss of bosses, after all." Then he began to scratch his stubble.

Achilles had to stifle the urge to cross himself. He had never been religious, but his concern over being "abducted" by order of the CIA's DCAS—director of the Covert Action Staff, and Malcolm's former boss—was so great that he felt, in spite of himself, the need for a little boost from unseen forces. Maybe he had carried a bit of the pueblo back from Taos, and was hoping the mountain would smile on him.

For the next half hour they stared glumly at the countryside, each man lost in his own private thoughts, not wanting to say anything that might be picked up by the driver, who watched them closely in the mirror. He drove at a leisurely pace along the toll road to Dulles Airport, took the Wolf Trap Farm exit, made a U-turn back under the highway, and headed for the Wolf Trap Farm itself, a national park and performing arts center.

"Nice place for a meeting," Perly said, with a tinge of sarcasm. "Guess we're not good enough for a coffee in Karl's office anymore."

"He didn't want you two to log into the Campus," the driver said over the intercom.

Makes sense, Achilles thought. Standard black op procedure. A little stroll through the park enjoying the spring blossoms, who would be suspicious? And Karl's troops could keep an eye on the open approaches.

The driver pulled into one of the main parking lots for the arts center, a large wooden building surrounded by work crews cleaning it up in preparation for the summer season. The lot already contained several cars and trucks, some obviously belonging to the crews, others probably owned by people who had come to stroll in the adjoining park, and some no doubt from Karl's personal car pool.

"Brings back memories," Achilles said. "My daughter Jennifer got her first theater job here, working as a summer techie."

"Where is she now?"

"Doing something in New York. Not sure what. I don't hear from her that often. She's always on the road, I'm always on the road… You get the picture."

"Picture I have is of her dancing around the barbecue in your back yard. Hard to remember she's grown up."

The driver found a spot near the outbuildings of the arts center and opened the rear door for them. "Karl is waiting for you on the other side of the foot bridge."

"Karl" was Karl Himmelman. At the CIA he had been their "boss of bosses," as Perly put it: above them, above Malcolm. He considered himself second to none in the world of intelligence gathering, an estimation few people would argue with. An imposing man with permanently rosy cheeks and a stiff '50s-era crew cut, he had played fullback for Ohio State in his college days, and took great pleasure in skewering Perly for playing football with a "genteel" Southern team instead of a Big Ten powerhouse.

"Achilles, Perly," he said warmly, as they crossed the bridge. Then, out of habit, he reverted to black op mode and began speaking through taut, nearly immobile lips, to avoid detection by lip readers with telescopes. "Have a good meeting with Malcolm?"

"I, ah…we…ah…," Perly stammered.

Karl winked. "It's okay. I'm in the loop. How do you think I knew where to send the car?" He glanced around to make sure no one was in earshot. "Let's walk," he said, setting off along a path through the wooded park. The trees were in full spring blossom, and the robins and mockingbirds sang at the tops of their lungs. Other than a few people enjoying themselves on nature strolls the park was deserted, providing a secure environment for a meeting.

"So," Karl said, "you're working on the Stonewall case." He paused and noted with satisfaction the nervous glances exchanged by Achilles and Perly. "Malcolm briefed me yesterday. Did you really think he would—or could—keep me in the dark?"

"We hadn't given it any thought," Achilles said. "He didn't say anything to us about sharing."

"Which means," Perly added, "that without orders to the contrary, we can't share."

"I see." Karl thought for a minute as they continued on a path that looped back toward the bridge. "So he didn't give you any instruction concerning how you should deal with your former boss, who would surely be involved in the same case?"

"Nothing, not a word," Achilles said. "I promise you, Karl, we'd be the first to tell you if he said we could…"

"So now you are Pentagon sewer rats instead of CIA sewer rats, and your lips are sealed shut, is that it?" Karl said, his voice developing an edge of barely concealed anger.

"Karl, come on," Perly said. "If anyone knows about protocol, it's you."

Karl paused at the edge of the woods and gazed out over the parking lots. The limo, and the driver standing beside it, were specks in the distance.

Karl sighed deeply, like a teacher who has given up trying to get through to a recalcitrant student.

"This is so sad. This reorganization is proving every day that it's an unmitigated disaster. We might as well hand the country over to the ACLU and let them give it to the Arabs." He turned to the two men at his side and spoke softly, but with a passion Achilles had rarely heard in him. "I expected something like this. The minute the Pentagon raided my operation I knew we were in for trouble. I never thought I'd lose two of my best agents that way, but then, that's Washington. I shouldn't have been surprised."

He took a fork in the path that led down the hill toward the parking lot. "I already know more than you'd believe. I probably know things you won't find out for weeks. I thought it might be a simple courtesy for someone to tell me what trail Malcolm has set you on, so I don't duplicate his effort."

"What do you know?" Perly said.

"I should say I can't tell you, shouldn't I? Return the same favor I'm being given. But I'm an old-timer. I believe in helping my colleagues. I'll tell you this much—I know that Stonewall was beheaded, domino in his mouth, carving of a skull on the domino. Brand on his forehead reading 'SODM,' code attached to his navel, dead pony in a mine shaft. All of it. How could you think I wouldn't know? And you're going to New York next, to check out the John Maguire case, am I right so far?"

"Yes," Achilles said grudgingly.

"And Malcolm told you SODM stands for Society of the Domino Mask, am I still right?"

"Right," Perly said. "So since you already know everything, why do you need to pick our brains?"

"I just wanted to establish a line of communication. I don't trust memos and papers. You know me. I'm hands on. I want to hear it from the agents, and because of the Pentagon power grab, I find myself without agents in the field on this one. Well—never mind. Now that my worst fears have been confirmed and I see the nature of the game, I'll find other ways to function." Although Karl acted perfectly polite and friendly, Achilles sensed a tinge of menace buried in his voice, an indefinable spoor of threat.

As if to underline the threat, he went on: "When I was thirteen, I found out my father had been banging someone besides my mother. I tracked him on my bicycle, spent weeks scoping out where they hid their nest, and when I found it I beat him to a pulp. Then I ran away from home. The point being, in case you're wondering, that I don't let anyone get in my way once I'm out to do what's right."

They had reached the parking lot. "My limo will take you home, so you can pack and get going to New York. Happy hunting, guys." With that, Karl turned on his heel and went to the pool car that had brought him there.

"Not to be believed," Perly said. "I never expected the reorganization to cause this kind of chaos."

"Might be a power struggle that goes beyond the Pentagon and CIA. I've never seen either Malcolm or Karl so nervous. Maybe they're members of SODM themselves."

Perly digested that for a minute as they walked toward the car. "Could be you're right. And I don't like it, bein' caught between those two. Just the thought of crossin' either one of 'em makes me sweat. Wonder if this is gonna be Perly's last operation."

"We can't lose our focus," Achilles said, determined to put up a brave front no matter what his internal qualms and fears might be. "We have to concentrate on doing our job."

"Achilles—I'm not talkin' about some minor inconvenience to us doin' our job. I'm talkin' about somethin' far worse. I'm talkin' about death, Achilles. *Our* death."

The driver opened the rear doors of the car for them. They got in and lapsed into a silence that lasted all the way home.

CHAPTER FOURTEEN

By noon Achilles and Perly had repacked their bags and were sitting next to each other on Amtrak's Acela Express bound for New York, taking advantage of the forced inactivity to do some work on their computers. Perly had logged onto the Internet so he could look up the personnel of the First Precinct, which covered lower Manhattan. Achilles busied himself studying the Stonewall cipher. He had an instinct that whoever was behind these murders had a particular message to get out, and wanted to make the cipher just hard enough to slow analysis down, but not defeat it.

"We could start with Detective Captain Bernardo," Perly said. "Think I might know him. When I worked Trade Center One, he was a sergeant. Good cop—if it's the same guy."

"Perly, I'm trying to work on the cipher."

"Sorry." Perly resumed surfing and left Achilles alone.

Achilles went back to work, hoping to pry some information loose from the numbers before him. He decided to begin with the SODM message they had found on the pony: 33-02-50-16. Unfortunately, not a single one of those numbers occurred in the Stonewall cipher.

Damn, he thought. Nothing fit. This had all the makings of a nightmare, but he had to keep working at it. Decryption was a time-consuming, laborious process involving trips up endless blind alleys, and no one had ever found a substitute for brain time.

He struggled for over an hour, trying different sequences, cursing each time he failed. Much as he loved solving the puzzle of ciphers, he hated the frustration of not finding the answers quickly.

Perly shut down his laptop and glanced at the blur of tables on Achilles' screen.

"How's it goin'?" he said.

"Not good. Reminds me of a joke Wiksil played on me at Columbia."

"Wiksil?"

"My math instructor. No older than me. He must have jumped three grades in high school."

"Had one like him at UVa, but I slept through his classes."

"First day of the term, Wiksil went around the room asking where everyone came from. When I told him I had grown up in the Pacific Northwest, he said he had a special test for me. 'What mathematical progression,' he said, 'is expressed in the following sequence of numbers? 14, 18, 23, 28, 34, 42, 50, 59, 66, 72, 79, 86, 96, 103, 110, 116? You have ten minutes.' I sat there in front of the whole class, sweating like a jock, erasing, writing, crossing out. I could hear giggling all around me. Finally I gave up. 'One devised by the IRT,' he said. 'Those are the subway stops on the IRT 7th Avenue line from 14th Street to Columbia.' So the whole class had a good laugh on me."

"Must have been a nice bunch in that place. Prepared you for the life you're leadin' now, wouldn't you say?" He stretched, made himself comfortable, and hunkered down for a nap.

Recalling the moment in that class, Achilles felt a mixture of humiliation and anger, feelings that had been rekindled on this day as he sat on the Acela Express trying to master another sequence of numbers. Maybe Perly had a point: that humiliation, and his determination to overcome it, might well have led him to his career.

Back to the cipher. He had to try a different approach. For an exasperating half hour he pulled one tool after another from his kit: frequency analysis, substitution ciphers, Vigenère squares, Caesar shifts, and variations on those themes, all to no avail. The Stonewall cipher was simply too short to give him any clues.

"Perly," he said finally. "Help me out, here."

Perly was fast asleep. "Hunh?" he said, struggling into consciousness.

"Take a look at this." Achilles angled the screen so Perly could have a better view. "Do you see any pattern in these numbers?"

"Achilles, come on, I'm tryin' to sleep."

"I need some help, dammit."

"You're the cipher genius. You're the one who waves the wand and decrees that sense will appear out of nonsense. What makes you think I can help?"

"Fresh pair of eyes. What do you see?"

Perly pulled himself up in his seat and squinted at the screen. "6-44-41-15-64-6…. Looks like a Super Lotto pick. Nope, it's a quarterback's call. Tight end deep right." And that was it for Perly's contribution. Within seconds he had fallen back to sleep.

For now, Achilles was stumped. SODM and its sidekick, behaving like guilty children trying to cover up their misdeeds, did not give him any real information. He had to hope the cipher waiting for him in New York, the one found on Maguire's body, would give him more to go on.

He followed Perly's example and was soon snoring peacefully, his computer clutched to his belly.

CHAPTER FIFTEEN

The whoosh of air brakes being emptied woke the men up, alerting them to their arrival at Penn Station. They got their bags and trench coats down from the overhead rack, fought their way through mobs of people, and hailed a cab. Since this was a special assignment and they needed to be near their work, they had prevailed upon Malcolm to put them up in a hotel close to the Wall Street area. The RZ travel desk had booked them into the Soho Grand on West Broadway near Canal, only three blocks from the First Precinct. It had been built during the boom of the '90s, sported a red brick exterior, and had a two-level lobby decorated in faux Cast-Iron District style. They were happy to have a change from the usual Holiday Inn; the only glitch was their rooms being four floors apart, at the back of the building.

"Don't you have anything closer together, on the same floor?" Achilles asked the clerk.

"Sorry, sir, your reservations came in late, and we're totally booked because of the G8 summit."

They took what they could get: room 621 for Achilles, 1030 for Perly. Achilles wished he could have a view of the Hudson River, but then, he hadn't come to the city to indulge himself with views and sightseeing. After taking a little time to settle in, the two men walked the short distance to the First Precinct. The weather in the Northeast was being quirky this spring, with wintry squalls and hot muggy doldrums trading places frequently, sometimes within hours. Since that morning their beautiful Virginia spring had evaporated; the temperature had plunged and the sky clouded up, so they wore their trench coats in case of a sudden squall.

As they crossed Canal Street, Achilles was struck by the hole in the sky where the familiar twin towers of the World Trade Center had once stood. The towers, reviled as they had been when they were new, had become the emblem of the entire city, and seeing lower Manhattan without them unsettled him. The skeleton of the new Freedom Tower rising in their place did not compensate for their imposing bulk.

Several uniformed policemen stood outside the precinct, smoking and talking. The precinct house itself was a three-story gray stone building, situated on a street that swarmed with traffic coming out of the Holland Tunnel. Police cruisers had been pulled up on the sidewalk diagonally, making the street even more congested.

Inside, the reception foyer was lit dimly by institutional neon ceiling fixtures, with half the tubes blown out. Two suspects, their hands against a wall, were being patted down by a group of patrolmen at the far end of the room. To the left of the doorway a staircase led to the second floor, and to the right stood the duty officer's cage, protected by bullet-proof plexi.

The sergeant on duty, surrounded by papers on spindles and old take-out coffee containers, eyed Achilles and Perly with mild bemusement as they approached the cage.

"Lyman, Pentagon," Perly said, flashing his ID.

"Smith," Achilles said, differentiating himself from Perly by laying his ID politely on the countertop and sliding it through the opening to the sergeant.

"We're here on the Maguire matter," Perly said. "We'd like to speak to Detective Captain Bernardo."

The sergeant examined their IDs, then picked up the phone slowly, as if making a yoga stretch, and punched a button.

"They're here," he said into the receiver. He put the phone down and nodded toward the staircase. "Up those stairs, left at the top, end of the hall. They're expecting you."

"They?" Perly said.

"FBI's been camped out here all day. Meeting started at four. What took you so long?"

They could hear the sergeant chuckling to himself as they went up the stairs; apparently he thought he had made a funny joke.

A few beefy detectives heading out on assignment passed by, their adrenaline already up, bantering about the stakeouts they'd been assigned, the arrests they hoped to make. For all their bravado, and despite the size-18 collars and size-48 chests, they appeared visibly nervous. Three women accompanied them, dressed like prostitutes to serve as undercover bait—one Asian, one Hispanic, one white. They would be kept pretty busy in this neighborhood, Achilles thought. He gave thanks, as he regularly did, that he had never been on the front lines of daily police work.

He and Perly reached the conference room at the end of the hall. Perly gave a quick rap on the door and they entered a cramped room with a beat-up wooden table in the middle, which was surrounded by people sitting on chairs of various vintages. A freestanding blackboard, covered with unintelligible chalk marks, stood at one end of the room. A cork bulletin board plastered with notes hung on the wall at the other end. Barred windows lined the wall opposite the door, but they were so dirty it was impossible to tell what was outside—probably an alley strewn with discarded fast-food cartons and rat bones, Achilles reckoned. He noticed a faint odor, which he thought at first might be garbage, until an image of the stable in Taos flooded his mind and he realized the odor must be emanating from a stable nearby. It was horse manure.

There were six men and a woman seated at the table, dressed in civilian clothes. All except one gave the two newcomers tentative smiles of welcome. The one who did not was seated at the head of the table. A well-groomed man with dark, slicked-back hair and a thin '40s-style moustache, he gave the impression he was trying to re-create the William Powell look in *The Thin Man* series. His demeanor made his status plain: *I am FBI, not NYPD.*

"Late to the party, as usual," the man said. "I suppose that now you're here, you'll want to take over the investigation."

"Not at all," Perly said. "We're here to listen and learn. Mind if we introduce ourselves?"

"Excuse us a minute," the man said to the group. He got up and motioned for the newcomers to join him outside. He closed the door behind him and led them down the hallway a bit, out of earshot of the others.

"I don't want any freelancing," he said. "I don't want to see anything happen here like what happened in Taos."

"I see our buddies in the Secret Service are serious about the new mandate to share information," Perly said.

"This investigation is under my command."

"This gets so tiresome," Perly said, his voice dropping to his "official" octave. "I think that if you bother to call your superior and mention the letters 'RZ' in connection with us, you will be disabused of that notion. Now, could we have an introduction?"

"My name's Ramirez—Justino Ramirez. And I know all about your RZ clearance. I simply want you to understand that we can't be working at cross purposes. Someone has to coordinate this probe. The SS kept us out of Taos because Kean was a protectee. That won't happen here, I can assure you."

"Fine. We'll be sure to check in with you whenever we discover anything. And we'll ask the same in return. We didn't have any more fun in Taos than your SS buddies. Now, can we meet the others and get on with business?"

They re-entered the room. The others sitting around the table broke off their small talk and looked up expectantly.

"Folks," Ramirez said as he and the two Pentagon men settled into chairs, "this is Perly Lyman and Achilles Smith, from a new outfit attached to the Pentagon. The Pentagon is inexperienced at this stuff, so we'll have to help them along the best we can," he added, trying unsuccessfully to suppress a snicker. Perly and Achilles ignored him and nodded greetings around the table.

"This is Andrew Winters, my assistant," Ramirez said; pointing to the man at his right. Winters was a thin-faced black man with a discreet white beard.

"Next, assistant DA Mikhail Goldovsky. He's a Brighton Beach Russian, specializes in the Russian mafia. Is that a fair description, Mikhail?"

"*Da, gospodin*—yes sir, you bet," Mikhail retorted sarcastically. He was a muscular man, with sandy hair cut in the now-universal brush cut. He wore a tan suit to match. "Russians are the new Italians," he said to Achilles. "Mention the word Russian, and the next word is always mafia." He turned back to Ramirez. "What would the FBI do without its mafias?"

Ramirez continued his introductions unfazed. "Next, Detective Captain Frank Bernardo." Bernardo, a stocky man with dark hair and an open face, flashed a smile of recognition at Perly, then returned to scribbling in his case book.

Next, a trim Asian man. "Frank's assistant, Jeshua Lin." Lin nodded politely in their direction. "Specialist on the Chinatown mafia. We're covering all bases, you see. Only in New York can you do this." He turned to his assistant. "We love it here, don't we, Andy?"

"Yeah, the melting pot, in crime like everything else. First thing you gotta figure out is what ethnic group is involved, then you figure which gangs are fighting each other."

"Andy, we're not that far yet."

"Yes, of course, I was only stating a general principle."

Ramirez continued around the table. Next one up—heavy-set Yaley type, silver hair, blue pinstripe suit, hanky in the breast pocket—seemed distracted to the point of boredom, had no pad in front of him, and had not even bothered to pull a pen out of his pocket.

"Phil Levitan, counsel for the mayor's office. He's here to keep tabs on what we're doing. Don't want the Exchange getting upset and moving out of the city, isn't that right, Phil?"

Phil did not deign to answer with words. He nodded regally toward Achilles and Perly, then resumed his reverie.

"Next," Ramirez said, gesturing toward a slim man who had the ascetic appearance of a marathon runner, "the guy who's giving Phil the jitters: Brian Mooney, point man for the New York Stock Exchange. Head of their internal security."

One introduction remained: the woman sitting to the left of Perly.

"And last, but not least—sorry for the cliché, Lauren—is Lauren Vogel." Lauren nodded at them and smiled. She was attractive, with long dark hair faintly streaked by gray—but the gray struck Achilles as a sign of savvy rather than age. She wore a light blue silk pants suit. "Lauren," Ramirez went on, "is our liaison with the White House."

"White House?" Perly said. "Why the White House?"

"Why, indeed?" Lauren said smoothly. "Perhaps your sojourn in the desert has led you to forget about the G8 summit being held here in New York, beginning on Sunday. Don't you think we'd be inclined to take an interest in a sequence of events like this one? First, our ex-secretary of defense murdered, and now the chairman of the Exchange—those qualify as a national emergency, don't you think? The other participants in the summit are expressing some concern about their safety."

Ramirez, obviously uncomfortable with Lauren's presence, had begun to squirm in his seat while she spoke. Achilles could well imagine why. Not only did Lauren and Phil have the potential to get in his way, their very presence was liable to put him on the spot. Too much interest in the case among higher-ups.

"Now, on to basics," he said when she had finished. "Have to catch the new folks up." He opened a three-ring binder that lay before him on the table and shoved it their way. "There are the pictures. I assume, unless you're into forensics, that you don't need to see the actual body."

Perly leafed through the book, grimaced, and passed it on to Achilles. The condition of the victim's body parts was by now familiar, but no less gruesome for that. The word SODM had been branded on the forehead, as he expected. According to the statistics listed in a sidebar Maguire had been a giant of a man: six feet five inches, 240 pounds, in perfect physical condition. Not someone who could have been taken down easily.

"Any pictures of the domino, or the paper with the cipher?" Achilles said when he had gone through all the pages. "They're not in here."

"We've impounded the pictures and the items themselves," Mikhail said. "They're critical evidence."

"You don't even have a suspect yet."

"They're still critical evidence."

"I understand that. But they're also critical to me if I'm going to break this code. Do you think you could arrange to have some pictures released to me?"

"I'll look into it. It'll have to go to higher authority."

"I'll expect them by tomorrow morning." Achilles was losing his patience with the endless positioning for turf that cropped up in these situations, so he made no attempt to be polite. "We're at the Soho Grand Hotel, West Broadway north of Canal. I'm in room 621. Here's my cell phone number." He pulled his business card out of his wallet, jotted his hotel address on it, then flicked it at Mikhail, who missed the catch; the card slid on the floor, and Achilles had the additional satisfaction of watching him fish around for it beneath his chair.

"After all," Achilles went on, "little pieces of evidence like this can be just as important as severed heads and discarded bodies. Although I'm sure I don't need to remind you of such an obvious fact."

Mikhail glowered at Achilles. *Oops,* Achilles thought. *Mistake. Made an enemy. Might need his help later. Have to fix this when the meeting is over.*

"Actually," Ramirez said, pushing his chair back with a loud scraping sound, either to relieve the tension, or salvage his control of events, "we should all exchange cards. Be sure to do it when the meeting breaks up."

Then he went to the blackboard. "So here," he said, waving a piece of chalk in one hand while he erased the board with the other, "is what we know so far." He began drawing squares on the board. "This is the street grid around the Exchange and its office building. Maguire's office is here," he marked with an *x*. "The cleaning woman had come in about 9:15 p.m., saw the lights on, papers on the desk, as if he planned to come back. No sign of a struggle, but the situation was so out of the ordinary she called Internal Security. You take it from there, Brian."

Brian strode to the blackboard and took the chalk, making a couple of squiggles and arrows as he talked. "Our night duty officer got to Mr. Maguire's office at 9:20. Checked the main exits, determined that Maguire had not been seen leaving the building since the night crew came on duty. His wife called in at 9:30, wondering why he hadn't been on the 9:15 at Rye. She said they were due at a party in Westchester. He had told her he would be working late, something about a new listing, but we couldn't find anything of that sort logged in his calendar. We called in some help from the NYPD immediately. Here, Frank, you take over."

Frank Bernardo ambled to the board, jingling the change in his pants pocket. He picked up the chalk and began adding to the marks on the board.

"This is the area between the Exchange and Battery Park City," he said, still jingling change with his left hand as he wrote with his right. "Over here, this big area, is the new Freedom Tower. We called in all available troops to help with the search. The precinct didn't have enough men, so we sent out calls to Midtown South and Headquarters. We looked everywhere, searching the Exchange first, of course, then the alleys between buildings, kept fanning out, looking in all the likely places…"

"Frank," Ramirez interrupted. "The change. You keep rattling the change in your pocket. It drives me crazy."

"Sorry." Frank pulled the offending hand out of his pocket and went on drawing arrows. "Finally, Sergeant Pignatero saw signs of blood outside a dumpster at the Freedom Tower construction site, right here on lower West Broadway," he said, drawing an *x*. Apparently unable to prevent himself, he had started jingling his change again. "And he found the head nearby, over here, in a trash can." Another *x*. "The sergeant put in a call to the desk. The desk called me. I called Midtown South to let them know…"

Ramirez couldn't stand it anymore. He stomped to the blackboard, took the chalk away from Frank, and placed it in the chalk tray.

"Thanks, Frank." Everyone around the table heaved a sigh of relief. They would have been there all night, listening to the jingling change and the minutiae of Precinct One's activities.

"So that's where the body had been buried," Ramirez finished, brushing the chalk off his hands and sitting down. "Underneath the junk in the dumpster. And the trash can containing the head was in the doorway of a foreman's trailer, near the construction walkway along Vesey Street. The head itself had been wrapped in a clear plastic garbage bag. Frank called in the medical examiner, who determined that the cause of death had been a lethal injection of potassium chloride. And they found the domino in his mouth, and the string of numbers written on a note pinned to his abdomen." He paused, searching Achilles' and Perly's faces for reactions, but they had put on their best RZ virtual masks, refusing to broadcast what they might know.

"So, near as we can determine, the business with severing the head had been done for effect, unless Maguire was into satanic rituals," Ramirez continued. He looked at his note pad for the first time. "Let's see if there's anything else—oh, yeah. We checked with his secretary, and with the Exchange staff. Secretary didn't know of any bookings. Day security saw him leave at 5:30, just before they went off duty—he said he'd be back in an hour or so, didn't give any destination. No one saw him with anyone—that's it. Anything you two guys want to add?" he said to Achilles and Perly. "Anything from the other case that might help us with this one?"

Perly looked at Achilles, and they came to a private understanding: they would share only obvious facts. They both sensed that this room held many potential dangers—too many new people, with unknown agendas. Achilles and his partner had to be even more careful here than in Taos. The Secret Service was an enemy they could count on, set in its ways, its protocols known to anyone who worked with them. Same for the two FBI men here. But the rest of them—as Perly talked, Achilles glanced around the table and ticked them off:

A local district attorney, a Russian at that, holding back critical information.

A detective with the NYPD who had probably studied at the Columbo school of "How To Act Stupid In Order To Trap Your Quarry."

His assistant, still an unknown, but someone with connections to Chinatown.

An Ivy League lawyer representing the mayor.

The security chief from the Stock Exchange—eager, no doubt, to keep the CEOs with Exchange listings from panicking. Not to mention the millions of viewers of CNBC.

And a rep from the White House. What section? Press? Chief of Staff? International Relations? National Security Council? His first goal would be to book dinner with her so he could find out. He and Perly had to learn what was coming down from the top.

Achilles was so lost in thought that he hadn't been listening to Perly briefing the others.

"...Method of death the same. Brand on the forehead, the same. Domino in the mouth, a note pinned to the navel, everything the same. We obviously have a serial killer of powerful people—someone who must be one of them, travels in their circles, is able to arrange private meetings with them."

"Well, I guess we have a lot of work to do," Ramirez said. "Andy and I are going downstairs with Frank to go over witness statements. The rest of you can go to your corners and do what you have to do. We'll reconvene here, 8 a.m. tomorrow. Everyone agree?"

A mutter of approval rolled around the table.

While the others picked up their papers and put on their coats, Achilles went over to Mikhail to apologize.

"Sorry for being so brusque. I get frustrated when I can't get the stuff I need to do my work."

"Not a problem." Mikhail took Achilles' hand and shook it vigorously—almost too vigorously, coming close to breaking knuckles—and then slapped him on the back. Achilles noted that Mikhail was wearing a striped red, white, and blue tie, which could have been a patriotic gesture for the USA, or for Russia, whose flag had the same colors, but a different pattern. He stored the observation in his mental data bank.

Outside the station house the conferees had a little ceremony of exchanging business cards. They seemed reluctant to part company, even though they knew they'd be tired of each other before long, and would move on to new assignments in any event. It was akin to what Achilles had heard from Jennifer about the theater business: an intense feeling of "belonging to family" during a run, and then off to a new show, a new family, no memory of the old one. *Need to call her while I'm here,* he thought. He hadn't seen her in a long time.

After exchanging pleasantries, they began to disperse in separate directions. Achilles wanted to book a dinner with Lauren, and she appeared to be hanging back. He sidled up next to her.

"Dinner?" he said, at the exact same moment Perly made the same proposition from her other side. He and Perly scowled at each other; then the three of them broke out laughing.

"I was hoping for at least one invitation," she said. "Two is even better. And besides," she whispered, looking around to make sure the others were out of earshot, "I have pictures of the domino and the paper they found on Maguire's body."

CHAPTER SIXTEEN

"Let's go to the hotel," Perly said. "The restaurants around here will be full of cops. We can talk more freely in the hotel lounge, right, Achilles?"

Achilles nodded his assent.

"Done," Lauren said.

The three walked up Varick Street toward Canal, with the prison-like fortress of the AT&T building towering over them to the east. To the west, the Holland Tunnel swallowed legions of cars and trucks. The workday was over for the financial district, and the streets teemed with activity. The weather had turned squally, and the wind picked up plastic bottles, old newspapers, and shreds of truck tires, flinging the litter along the sidewalks and streets, slamming it into cars and pedestrians indiscriminately. Conversation was impossible; they had to turn around and walk backwards to prevent the flying grit from chiseling holes in their eyes. As Achilles swung about, he noticed Mikhail standing on the pedestrian overpass that looped above the tunnel entrance, looking down at them. *Something funny going on with that boy,* Achilles thought. *Have to watch out for him.*

When they reached the hotel, they went up the Industrial Revolution iron staircase to the central lounge, which stood between the restaurant and the bar. An attractive young lady greeted them.

"Drinks or dinner?" she said.

"Drinks out here first," Perly said. "Then dinner."

The hostess showed them to a spot with three easy chairs surrounding a round table.

"The waiter will be with you in a moment," she said, laying drink menus before them.

Jazz resounded through the space, provided by the hotel's DJ service, extraneous sound that would normally have annoyed Achilles no end, but in this situation served a useful purpose, because they didn't have to worry about being overheard. There were several other early drinkers in the lounge, denizens of the financial center.

The waiter, a youthful male who resembled a chorus line dancer, attended to them immediately. Achilles ordered a glass of house red wine; Perly ordered a Scotch and water; and Lauren opted for a margarita. Curiously, she asked for the glass to be brought on a saucer. *Fastidious,* Achilles thought.

With the housekeeping details settled, Perly went into action.

"What division?" he asked Lauren.

"What division of what?" Her eyes sparkled with life, and despite the few streaks of gray hair, she had the flinty energy of youth about her. She was probably in her late thirties, early forties at the most. "Division of labor, long division, third infantry division? I don't understand the question. Could you be more precise?" She also, apparently, loved to spar.

"Perly means, what part of the White House staff," Achilles said. "You'll have to forgive us. Even though we're from the civilian side, we live in a military building. We find ourselves slipping into their terminology."

"Ah," she said.

"So," Perly said, "are you with the president's staff, or on loan from another agency?"

"Gentlemen, please. How would you like it if I started probing into your work at Ring Zero?"

"How the hell do you know about that?" Perly said, his eyes darting nervously around the lounge.

"I rest my case," she said, grinning.

Their drinks came, brought by a busboy. They hoisted the glasses for a toast, then took their first soothing sips.

"Anyway," she said, "let's talk about what we learned today. And didn't learn. First, I suppose you want to see these." She reached into her copious leather shoulder bag to pull out a manila envelope, extracted a sheaf of 8x10 photos from it, and passed them to Perly, who split the packet and gave some to Achilles.

On top of Achilles' pile lay a gruesome picture of a domino inside the opened mouth of John Maguire's severed head. These were forensic photos passed on from the medical examiner's office, the very photos Mikhail had thought he'd suppressed. The domino was similar in design to the one in Stonewall's mouth, but it had a different number—the 2-5—and the carved character portrayed a citizen of some far-away place and time, probably a European merchant or adventurer, a man with long, flowing hair, wearing a cavalier's hat.

Achilles made a mental note to track down this set of dominoes. Stonewall's death's-head had apparently been picked for more than its shock value; these dominoes were extraordinary, and there might be some clues in the costumes adorning the characters.

The next picture was of the abdomen, with the piece of paper still attached. Achilles moved quickly to the following photo, which showed the paper spread out and flattened. Finally, he could get at the next part of the code. Numbers again, as he expected: 42-22-60-45-12-06-21-53-44-16-65-12-63. He took out his scratch pad and wrote them down.

"Here," Perly said, passing his packet of photos across the table. Achilles exchanged packets with him and went through the new set. These pictures showed the dumpster and the area around it, then a body bag being removed from it, the head being unwrapped—gruesome police photos in full color, repulsive and fascinating at the same time.

Something caught his eye in the one of Maguire's body being removed from the dumpster: a mounted policeman in the background, dressed in a hard helmet and leather jacket, watching the operation. Nothing unusual in that. New York teemed with mounted police, and Achilles had smelled a stable during the meeting at the First Precinct. Probably the precinct had its own stable—he'd have to inquire about that tomorrow. The odd thing about this particular policeman was his dark glasses, because this picture, like the others, had a date and time stamp in the bottom right corner. Why was the cop wearing shades at 3 a.m.?

They finished examining the photos and handed them back to Lauren.

"Notice anything?" Perly asked Achilles.

"These are pictures that were not in Ramirez's notebook. And there were a couple of other things. We'll talk later."

"Not sharing?" Lauren said. "Don't trust me?"

"It's not that," Achilles said. "Even with this jazz playing, we might be overheard." Although, to tell the truth, there was an element of mistrust involved, but he didn't want to say so.

Lauren slid the photos into the envelope and returned it to her bag.

"Mind if I ask," Perly said to her, "how you managed to get those, with Mikhail hell-bent on suppressing 'em?"

"Mikhail is a junior DA. With a case this important, he's a pretty small fish. Getting these was quite easy for someone with the right phone book." She fished in her bag for a minute and brought out another, smaller envelope.

"And now," she said, "for some other business." She pulled a piece of folded 5x7 notepaper from the envelope and handed it to Perly, who unfolded it and read it. He clenched his jaw and narrowed his eyes slightly, refolded it, and passed it on to Achilles.

Achilles unfolded the paper and read it.

Do not react. I am Malcolm's messenger. Lauren.

Achilles stifled his natural reaction with some difficulty, then passed the paper back to Lauren, who crumpled it up, removed her margarita glass from its saucer, took a sip, and put the crumpled paper in the saucer.

"But…," Perly began.

She brushed his hand gently to hush him. Achilles thought he saw a look pass between them, but he couldn't be sure; the moment passed too quickly.

Lauren reached into her bag again, pulling out a small bottle that could have been a vial of eye drops. She extracted some liquid and squeezed a drop onto the paper, which curled and writhed slightly at first, like a worm that had been cut in two, and then vanished without a trace. Achilles was truly impressed, not just with the technology, but by the way she had handled the issue of being in a non-smoking city where ashtrays wouldn't be available.

"And there's more." She pulled out another piece of 5x7 paper and handed it to Perly.

Same routine. Perly unfolded it, read it, refolded it, and passed it on to Achilles.

Message from Malcolm—

There are currently two ranches named Double Six, one in Texas and one in California. The one in California breeds Thoroughbreds, and they have no knowledge of a Quarter Horse named Persimmon, or of any other Quarter Horses, for that matter. The one in Texas breeds cattle exclusively. In other words, Kean did not buy his horse from a ranch in Texas.

Achilles and Perly looked at each other with raised eyebrows, having decided that was the limit of reaction they could show openly. Achilles crumpled the paper for Lauren and handed it to her, and she dispatched it as she had the other one.

"Any more?" Achilles said while they watched the paper do its worm dance and then vanish.

"That's all for now. And I'm hungry. Let's move on to more sociable talk."

They finished their drinks and moved into the Grand Bar, which was actually the restaurant. When they saw the prices on the menu, they were dismayed.

"We can't keep comin' here," Perly said to Achilles. "Malcolm will have our hides."

"We'll find some places in the neighborhood. Or we'll go to Chinatown and Little Italy. We won't go hungry, that's for sure."

So they each ordered a $70 prix fixe dinner and a couple of bottles of wine for the table, pushing the thought of taxpayer wrath to the backs of their minds. Their conversation drifted to various long-finished Cold War assignments, which were now safer to discuss. Perly, in particular, displayed considerable nostalgia for those days. Or, more likely—so Achilles thought— he was trying to impress Lauren, who had been too young to participate.

Achilles read the dynamic correctly. When they had finished, and paid the bill on the house tab, Perly leaned across the table in conspiratorial fashion while Lauren went to the ladies' room.

"Achilles, you won't mind if I take Lauren to her hotel, will you, ole buddy? She's only a few blocks down, at the Tribeca Grand."

"No problem," Achilles said, hoping his hurt feelings didn't show. Not that he was angry with Perly about pursuing a woman. This competition of theirs for female favors was a long-standing one, and had lost both of them their wives. Sometimes Perly came out on top, and sometimes Achilles did, yet in the moment being the rejected one did not sit well.

"I'll go upstairs and study the code," he added, trying to make Perly feel guilty. "Maybe I'll call my daughter. I should see her before things get too crazy."

Perly smiled and stood up as Lauren returned. "All set. Let's go."

Achilles walked them out the hotel entrance, then waved them off down West Broadway. He felt like the house monitor of a fraternity.

He had probably drunk too much wine to do much justice to the code, but he was determined to give it a try before he went to bed. He took the elevator to the sixth floor, and headed toward his room.

Leaning against the door jamb, waiting for him, was Mikhail.

CHAPTER SEVENTEEN

Achilles made a quick decision to pretend he had been expecting Mikhail to drop by.

"Pictures already? That was fast."

"I aim to please. There won't be time tomorrow." Mikhail followed Achilles into the room and went to the window, taking in the view of the street while Achilles double-locked the door and prowled the wet bar.

"Drink?" Achilles said.

"Snapple."

"Snapple? No alcohol?"

"You expected me to ask for vodka, straight up, I suppose. Another Russian cliché. Sorry to throw a wrench in your cliché machine, but I grew up in the USA."

Achilles poured himself a Heineken, the ubiquitous wet-bar beer, and handed Mikhail a bottle of Snapple. "Bit sensitive about this issue, are you? Little porcupine quills all over."

"I suppose so. Being talked down to by the likes of Ramirez is hard to take. By the way, even though I'm Russian, I do drink from a glass."

Achilles laughed and handed him a glass. Mikhail settled into an easy chair by the window, poured his Snapple into the glass, and took a sip. Then he opened his attaché case and pulled out a manila envelope, which he handed to Achilles.

"There are your photographs."

"Thanks." Achilles placed the envelope on the desk. "Does Ramirez know?"

"Know what?"

"That you're seeing me alone. Did he send you?"

"Of course not. Quite the opposite. He told us before you arrived that we are not to cooperate with you. He wants the FBI to handle this, not the Pentagon."

"So that's why you watched us from the overpass as we were walking up here with Lauren? How soon does Ramirez get the report that she's breaking his rule?"

"He can't control her and he knows it, but he thinks he can order the local police and DA's office around, and he's not shy about expressing himself."

"That answers the second part of my question—sort of. But you skipped the first part. Why were you watching us from the overpass?"

Mikhail shrugged. "Just curious, I guess."

"Curious? Curious as in Curious the Cat, or as in Someone Says to Follow Them?"

"No one ordered me to do anything. And you're turning into another Ramirez. You federals act as if you own the store and everyone else is a clerk."

"Sorry again. Don't mean to be overbearing."

"At least you had the decency to apologize, back in the conference room."

"No problem. I do my best to maintain cordial relations with co-workers."

"Especially when you might need them later."

"You know how it is. One hand washes the other…" He let the thought drift off. Mikhail did not respond, and the conversation lapsed into a moment of awkward silence. "So," Achilles continued, "you like to freelance." He stopped Mikhail from objecting. "It's okay, I like to freelance too. Only way to get anything done."

Mikhail relaxed a bit, and Achilles took another sip of beer. He didn't really need any more alcohol after what he'd consumed before and during dinner, but now that he'd opened the bottle he didn't want to waste it. And drinking helped buy him moments to think.

It was time to open the envelope and look at the pictures. Although the thought crossed Achilles' mind that the DA's office might try to throw him off by giving him faked pictures, he saw nothing out of the ordinary. These were identical to the ones Lauren had shown him and Perly. Maguire's head, the mouth gaping, with the 2-5 domino in it. The domino itself. The two pictures of the piece of paper. The extraction of Maguire's body from the dumpster, the head being removed from its bag. Achilles feigned deep interest, since it was important to make Mikhail think he hadn't already seen the pictures. So he grunted, *tch-tch*ed, and made *hmn, interesting* sounds at intervals.

"Pretty bad mess," he said as he put them back in the envelope. "Thanks for these."

"You're welcome."

"Do you have any theories?"

"We're totally baffled. Of course, considering the power and position of the man, he could have had any number of enemies, especially after a huge stock market crash like the one we experienced recently. If this were a totally isolated incident, we'd be looking for a disgruntled investor or hedge fund manager, or some such thing. Now that there's this other case out in Taos, nothing to do with the financial markets—hard to say where to begin. What about you? Do you have any theories?"

Ah, thought Achilles. *The real reason for the visit. Wants to pick my brain.*

"We're driving blind, in a pea-soup fog, on an empty tank. Whatever similar clichés come to mind. Someone, obviously, had it in for at least two very powerful people, which leads me to think there may be more victims on the way. Beyond that, we don't have a clue."

"No contact with anyone in Taos who might provide a wedge?"

Achilles had to make another quick decision. He and Perly, on their own, simply didn't have the resources to be everywhere at once. They needed some more eyes and ears. They had to turn to some locals at some point. He decided to test Mikhail.

"There were, actually. Doubt you'd come across them here in New York, but who knows?"

Mikhail took a notebook out of his briefcase, fished a gold Cross pencil from the breast pocket of his suit jacket, and waited, pencil poised.

"An Indian, name of Sam Rains," Achilles said. "He found Kean's head while he was hunting rabbits, reported it to the Taos County sheriff. The sheriff detained him as a material witness, then released him. Rains called us, said he wanted to talk to us. While we were going to meet him, someone trashed our motel rooms."

"Sam Rains doesn't sound like an Indian name. How do you know for sure he's an Indian?"

"It's normal practice for them to take two names. They have a name in their native tongue, which they use among themselves. They have another name, usually Anglo or Spanish, which they use in dealing with outsiders. The local authorities use the non-Indian names."

"What happened at your meeting with him?"

"Didn't have one. He was a no-show. We want to get our hands on this guy, ask him some questions. For one thing, we need to know how he found out who we are and where we were staying."

"The Taos County sheriff must have taken fingerprints. I'll give them a call. Anything else?"

"Sam had asked us to meet him late at night, at his pueblo. When we got there we were met by a delegation led by the chief, whatever he's called these days, guy by the name of Francisco Orozco. Long story short, after two trips to the pueblo we discovered that Sam didn't really come from there, but had a wife who did. He may have disappeared right after the sheriff released him, or after he called us. He may or may not have returned to the pueblo to pick up his wife, because she's gone missing too. And he may or may not have some information about Kean's death. He could be anywhere, including dead, and the same goes for his wife. We figured she must know something if she's alive, at the very least something about him. We want to talk to her, big time."

"Do you know her name? Can I assume her last name is Rains?"

"Can't assume anything. I don't know it. They wouldn't tell us."

"Did you ever think of going to court for a warrant?"

Achilles chose to ignore the slight. He had handed out plenty, and didn't want to get into a game of one-upmanship.

"We made threats along those lines, but they blocked us with talk about tribal sovereignty, same line they took with the sheriff. We didn't have time to work any of that out. We got called back East for this."

Mikhail scribbled furiously, apparently trying to write complete information rather than quick notes. After a couple of minutes he finished his Snapple, put the glass down, and resumed his writing pose.

"Is that it?" he said. "Anything else?"

"Kean's groom. Name of Ray Muller."

"What about him? Why is he of interest?"

"He owned a pony that was also killed, left near the mine where the SS found Kean's body. Apparently the pony had been used to carry the body to the mine from the ranch house. Muller maintained that someone had taken the pony without his knowledge. And there was another horse, belonged to Kean himself, that simply disappeared. The groom's story had inconsistencies we thought should be checked out, but he disappeared too."

Achilles left out a few details, such as the paper stapled to the pony's ear, the brand on its rump, the transfer of its body to the mine by helicopter. What he had given would be good test information. He'd see if the DA's office could actually deliver on a basic job like finding a few missing "persons of interest."

Mikhail finished his notes, put his pencil back in his pocket, and the notebook back in his case.

"Thanks for the leads," he said. "There's no way of knowing if these people will have any useful information about the Maguire murder, which is my jurisdiction, but it never hurts to compare cases." He stood up and stretched. Achilles thought he was about to leave, but instead, Mikhail went over to the wet bar and eyeballed its contents. "Mind if I have something alcoholic now?"

"I thought you were a Snapple man."

"Snapple when I take notes and need to keep my wits. Afterward, vodka, when I can allow myself to relax. You see, I'm a true Russian after all. I couldn't possibly let you down when it comes to fulfilling my role in the Universal Cliché."

Achilles laughed. "Sure, help yourself."

Mikhail found two mini-bottles of vodka and a clean glass, and returned to his seat. He opened both bottles and poured them simultaneously into the glass, holding them between the fingers of one hand, then tossed them into the trash. He took a huge gulp from the glass, nearly draining it.

"Much better. I hate that sweet crap."

"I'm not going to try keeping up with that performance."

"Don't expect you to." Mikhail finished off the glass and started nibbling on some pretzels he had found on top of the bar. "I know I sound thin-skinned about being of Russian descent, but our minority status here is so peculiar it makes us defensive."

"Any more peculiar than Ramirez being Hispanic? Or Winters being black? They've got plenty of gripes."

"Has to do with the perceptions the older generation brings with it, I guess. My parents had to claw their way out of the Soviet Union. My father was a musician, defected on a tour."

"There was a lot of that."

"Yes, you bet. People hoped and prayed their children were talented in the performing arts—classical, not rock, it wasn't allowed. Being a performer was one of the only ways to get out of the country and be able to defect. Then, as the number of defections grew, the KGB started punishing the family members left behind. Threw them out of their apartments, sent them from big cities to small villages, or worse, shipped them to camps.

"We were lucky. Father managed to get us all out later, during the time your government was putting maximum pressure on Brezhnev to allow Jewish emigration. My brother and I were little kids, I don't remember that much about it, just a lot of crying and carrying on when we left Moscow."

"You say your father is a musician. What does he play?"

"Did. He's dead."

"Oh. Sorry."

"Do you really care what he played? Most people in this country think it's some sort of laughable hobby."

"No, I'm really interested. My daughter works in theater."

Mikhail looked at his empty glass, looked at Achilles, and raised his eyebrows in a silent question. Achilles nodded, signaling *Sure, go for it,* and Mikhail fetched two more mini-bottles, which he promptly subjected to his special treatment. This time, at least, he took smaller sips when he was through pouring.

"Played," he said, continuing where he had left off, "yes, played. He played the violin. A wonderful musician. A fabulous violinist. I woke up in the mornings hearing the sounds of his practicing. Late at night, when he came home from a performance, my brother and I could hear him practice the next day's repertoire. All my memories of my youth are filled by the sounds of a violin being played by my father."

"Must have been tough for him, coming here, finding work."

"Actually, not so. There was a network, an organization, that helped Soviet refugees find housing and jobs. His biggest complaint was about the horsehair."

"Right, horsehair," Achilles said, regretting his earlier expression of interest. His attention had begun to drift. He wanted to get to work on the cipher, and hadn't really planned to have a drinking session with a new buddy.

"Strings and horsehair, horsehair and strings, he talked about that more than the actual music. He loved the strings that were made here, but he couldn't get Siberian horsehair for his bow because of U.S. trade restrictions. It drove him mad."

"Very important issue," Achilles mumbled through his exhaustion. "To a violinist, I'm sure."

Mikhail looked at his watch and snapped out of his reverie. He hurriedly downed the rest of his drink. "Time to go. My wife will be out searching for me on the boardwalk if I don't get home."

Achilles walked Mikhail to the door. Mikhail enveloped him in a big Russian hug, and then turned on his heel. Achilles watched him striding down the hallway, his back straight, not a trace of a wobble in his gait.

CHAPTER EIGHTEEN

Finally he was free to study the cipher. But first, he wanted to call Jennifer. Her answering machine picked up. *Blast,* he thought. *She's still at the theater.* He always managed to forget that she worked late most evenings. He left her a message giving her both his cell phone and hotel numbers, suggesting they get together for lunch or dinner during the next few days.

Then he turned to work. He fired up the laptop, pulled out his scratch pad, and pondered how to plug the Maguire numbers into the computer table. His first problem would be deciding the proper sequence. Did this cipher correspond to a complete new message? The second part of a longer message that began with the Stonewall cipher? Or should it be placed third, with the pony cipher serving as a link?

His first rule, one he had to repeat constantly to himself: *Start somewhere, dammit.*

He settled on treating Stonewall as cipher one, first part of a longer message. The pony code he put aside; his instinct insisted it was a key of some sort and not part of the main message. The Maguire cipher would be part two of a longer message. So he expanded his table and inserted the numbers. He now had the following sequence:

Stonewall

6	44	41	15	64	6	12	4	3	63	34	43

Maguire

42	22	60	45	12	06	21	53	44	16	65	12	63

But something didn't jibe. In the Stonewall cipher the numbers six, three, and four had been written 6, 3, and 4; but in Maguire the number six was written 06, with a leading zero. He checked the pony cipher, and it agreed with the Maguire: the number two had been written 02. He had to wonder why. What purpose would be served by changing format? No code-writer would change the format of the numbers without a reason. Then he remembered he had actually seen the pony and Maguire ciphers, but Paul the SS man had read the Stonewall cipher aloud to him in the freezer at the ranch. He hadn't been allowed to look at it. He must get his hands on that cipher! That would be his first message to Malcolm through Lauren: send him a picture, not a transcription, of the Stonewall cipher.

Temporarily stymied, he put the cipher aside, fished his magnifying glass out of his computer case, and inspected Mikhail's picture of the domino. He wondered where this kind of carving, of a cavalier-looking man with flowing hair and a big-brimmed hat, might have come from. The dress and facial expressions were so specific that someone, somewhere, must have a record of it. He went back to the laptop and loaded the picture he had taken of the other domino. The death's-head on the double six really had an expression, if such a thing were possible. It had the same specificity of time and place as the cavalier on the 2-5. Maybe he could find these dominoes himself on the Internet. If not, he could ask Malcolm to have the termites at the Pentagon chew on this particular log.

Then, just to round out the evening and burn off the Heineken, he made a quick pass through the rest of the photos. His stomach turned when he saw Maguire's head being taken out of its bag; he put that one aside and found himself looking at the picture of the body bag being pulled from the dumpster. He was about to turn it over and go on to the next one when he felt a perplexing disquiet, a sense that the details weren't quite right. He inspected and reinspected it, but couldn't make out why anything in the picture would set off his alarm bells. It just didn't jibe with the picture Lauren had shown him earlier. Since he didn't have that one in his possession he couldn't compare them side by side, so he had to rely on his memory.

At last the anomaly bubbled to the surface: the cop on horseback. This picture looked identical to Lauren's, taken from exactly the same angle. He was sure of that much. It had the same time and date stamp in the lower right corner. The same burly men from the medical examiner's office held the body bag in the same position on the lip of the dumpster. But there was no cop on horseback anywhere to be seen.

Achilles picked up his magnifying glass again and studied the print closely, looking desperately for some sign of tampering, but he couldn't find any. He broke into a cold sweat. This must be a doctored print of the extraction. That explained the delay. Mikhail had needed time for some Photoshop geek in a back room to take out the cop and fix the background so Achilles would never know the cop had existed.

"Christ!" he shouted, furious with himself for giving information to someone new, someone he hadn't checked out. A beginner's mistake.

Then he had another, more disconcerting thought: what if Lauren's print, not Mikhail's, had been altered? What if someone had inserted the cop? That might explain the shades. In their hurry, they might have copied a picture of a cop taken in the daytime and pasted it into the nighttime shot, but forgotten to remove the shades. Why would anyone want to insert a horse cop into a picture if one hadn't actually been on the scene? Why go to that kind of trouble? And besides, this photo came from a set that hadn't been in the original portfolio Ramirez showed them. They could have left this one out altogether, and nobody would have been the wiser. Why would two people each show him a different version of a picture that could simply have been suppressed? This had to be a deliberate plant, but who had done the planting, and why?

Achilles kicked his chair over and paced furiously. At times like this he really hated digital technology. His job had been difficult enough with pictures airbrushed the old way. Nowadays it was next to impossible to tell an authentic photo from a fake.

He must reach Perly. He pulled out his cell phone and dialed Perly's number. Two rings, then the rollover to mobile voice mail. Unusual for Perly to have his phone off.

"Perly," he managed to say calmly, "give me a call will you, old buddy? It's Achilles. Thanks."

On the off chance Perly had struck out with Lauren and gone to his own room, Achilles tried there next. Voice mail again.

He would have to try Lauren's cell phone. He found her business card and dialed the number. Same result: a voice mail prompt.

Damn, he thought. "Uh, Lauren," he said in his best goblin voice, "this is Achilles. Sorry to bother you. If Perly's with you, could you have him give me a call, please? Soon as he has a chance. Thanks."

He clicked off, more furious than ever. Of course. They must be hot at the game of making love—to be more accurate, at this stage it should be called making discovery—and they did *not* want to be interrupted.

He had one last recourse. He went to the phone book to find the number of the Tribeca Grand, then saw it listed on the tourists' guide next to the phone as a sister hotel to the Soho Grand. He quickly dialed the number.

"Tribeca Grand," responded a sleepy voice.

"Vogel. Lauren Vogel."

"Do you have a room number?"

"No, I don't."

"One moment, please."

He waited and waited. No ringing sounds. As he was about to hang up, he heard a click. "Lauren?" he said.

"This is the operator. What room, please?"

"Vogel. Lauren Vogel."

Long pause. Then: "Spell the name, please."

"Vogel. V-o-g-e-l."

"The first name?"

"Lauren! Lauren!"

"Is that with an 'o'?"

"L-a-u-r-e-n!!"

"One moment, please."

Another interminable pause. Finally, a ringing sound. Then a generic "happy lady" voice mail prompt: "The guest you are calling is not in at the moment. Please try again later, or you can leave a message when you hear the tone."

"Lauren," he barked into the phone. "This is Achilles. I've discovered something really important. I need to hear back from either you or Perly ASAP. Pay attention to the blinking light on your phone, please." He slammed the receiver down.

More pacing. *Stop,* he told himself. *Calm down.* No doubt someone would have an explanation for the anomalous photographs. He looked at Mikhail's version again. No. Impossible to come up with any explanation that made sense. Either there had been a cop on a horse wearing shades at 3 a.m., or the cop never existed, and someone at the medical examiner's office, or whoever had given the pictures to Lauren, thought it would be a funny joke to add one.

Damn! Someone! Call!

On cue, his cell phone rang.

"Hello!" he barked.

"Uh…uh…" A female voice, but not Lauren's.

"Who is this?"

97

"Uh, is this Achilles Smith?"

Suddenly he recognized his daughter's voice. "Jennifer! I'm so sorry. Just in a bit of a swivet."

"Should I call back later? Is this a bad time?"

"No, no. I want to see you. Let's set up a time."

They made a date for dinner between the Saturday matinee and evening shows, two days away. She was stage managing a tour of the Bolshoi Ballet at the Koch Theater in Lincoln Center, she told him.

"Russians," he said. "Everywhere I turn, Russians."

"I'm sorry?" she said, not comprehending.

"Nothing, honey. Ignore your old man. Saturday it is, then, stage door, Koch Theater, 5:30 p.m. I'll call if there's a problem, but there shouldn't be."

"Great, Daddy. See you then." She gave him her cell number and the stage door number, told him to call the stage door if he needed to reach her during a performance, and then hung up.

He waited and paced for what seemed like hours, but didn't hear from Perly or Lauren. The thumping sounds and wailing noises from a karaoke bar behind the hotel helped neither his mood nor his ability to concentrate. He made a few stabs at working on the cipher, but kept returning to the photo of Maguire's body on the lip of the dumpster, trying to divine the meaning of the missing horse cop. Unfortunately he was too excited about his discoveries, too angry at Perly, and too annoyed by the karaoke bar, to make any progress.

Succumbing to exhaustion at last, he collapsed on the bed still clothed, and fell asleep.

CHAPTER NINETEEN

Achilles awoke with a start in the middle of the night. He couldn't tell if he had heard a noise, or experienced a nightmare. Whatever had done the damage, he was unable to go back to sleep, so he flopped in the easy chair. His gaze turned to the scene outside—the ghostly aura of street lamps glowing in the humid atmosphere, the headlights of vehicles traveling north on Sixth Avenue. Above the rooftops he saw a spring squall moving in; within moments, sheets of rain began splattering against his window and bouncing off the streets and sidewalks. Maybe a thunderclap had awakened him.

Feeling dazed and disoriented, he decided he could use a stroll, squall or not, so he put on his trench coat and headed out.

An eerie radiance greeted him when he got off the elevator; pinpricks of light, like so many stars reflected in a pond, were diffracted through translucent glass discs embedded in the steel treads of the lobby stairway. He nodded at the night concierge, went through the doors to the street, and stood under the marquee soaking up the delicious smell of the spring rain. This was what he needed—fresh air. The air in hotel rooms always felt stuffy, laden with the vapors of foam rubber and plastic.

He looked at his watch—2:30. Maybe he should go to the Tribeca Grand and bang on Lauren's door. No—his anger had dissipated; best to leave the lovers alone. No one could do anything at this time of night anyway.

He didn't want to go back to his room, so he set out to look for a late-night bar, and found one around the corner—the Lucky Strike. He was about to go in when he changed his mind. A walk. He really did need a walk, not a sit-down session in a bar full of noisy revelers with a glass of booze staring at him.

His thoughts returned to the mystery of the horse cop. Why not check out the dumpster? Maybe he could pick up a few clues by poking around on his own. He turned on his heel and walked south on West Broadway, headed for the site of the new Freedom Tower. The rain had stopped, but a veil of misty drops still hung suspended in the air, something lighter than rain but heavier than fog. This was really a great night to be out alone, he thought. The atmosphere and the deserted streets gave New York the feel of a small town.

He crossed Canal Street and continued down West Broadway for several blocks, allowing himself to imagine, in the foggy nighttime sky before him, the silhouettes of the old Trade Center providing beacons to lead him on. Then the vision soured. The very buildings around him seemed to have eyes; a few lights in each building blazed away into the mist. The whole neighborhood bristled with menace. In his mind he could hear planes slamming into the towers ahead, the screams of people jumping from the heights, the roaring infernos. The new building would never overcome the legacy of that day, no matter how many years had gone by. He struggled to shake the images off; instead of looking up, he looked down, following the variegated path of the pavement, which showed its age wherever patches of old brick peeked out from under the asphalt.

At last he reached Barclay Street. Bernardo's x for the location of the dumpster had been on West Broadway, between Barclay and Vesey. Vehicular traffic had to stop at Barclay, because the area further south had been shut down for the duration of the construction. Two patrolmen sat in a squad car parked at the corner, doing sentry duty. Achilles could feel their eyes boring into his back as he went past an unoccupied guard shack; within a few yards he had come across the dumpster, situated directly under a street light and cordoned off by yellow tape with black letters that read, "POLICE LINE DO NOT CROSS," no punctuation. Achilles thought he could sense the spirit of John Maguire joining the chorus of Trade Center victims, demanding justice.

As he approached the taped-off area, one of the patrolmen got out of the car and hailed him.

"Excuse me! Sir! Please do not go near that area! That's an active crime scene!"

"Oh, sorry," Achilles said. A moment of indecision. Should he identify himself, seek access to the site so he could get a closer look? No—they would report back to the precinct, and the report would filter up to Ramirez and

Bernardo. Not that he had any fear of confronting them. He simply didn't want the bother of explaining his actions, so he played dumb.

"What happened here? Somebody throw out illegal garbage? Hah-hah."

"Sorry, can't say. Aren't you out a bit late for this neighborhood?"

"In town on business, staying at the Soho Grand. Couldn't sleep. Unfamiliar room, strange hotel, you know how it is." *Truth always works best,* he chuckled silently to himself. "Just came out for a stroll."

The officer relaxed. "Well, okay. Just watch out. Pretty deserted around here."

"Thanks." Achilles quickly scoured the ground and the dumpster itself with his eyes, seeking some evidence that a mounted trooper might have been there. Nothing really looked out of place. If it hadn't been for the squad car and the yellow tape, no one passing by would have given the dumpster a second thought. The ground around it had been swept clean by the forensics teams, and the rain had certainly finished the job. The photo had been taken at an angle, facing the dumpster from the southern side, so the horse cop had been on the northern side. In daytime the cop would have had sky and buildings behind him. Trying to reconstruct the view now, Achilles could see streetlights, some of which would have been blocked by the cop and the horse, but others might not. That would be one thing he could check.

He found it difficult to imagine that a mounted trooper would have been in this deserted area at three in the morning. Even though the precinct had put out a call for personnel to search for Maguire's body, the idea of the call going out to the cavalry didn't make a lot of sense. They were utilized for crowd control. He would have to raise this issue in the morning, discreetly, not at the meeting—maybe talk to Frank Bernardo or pay a visit to the stable, find out if any troops had been sent out on the search.

He turned around and walked back north. He wouldn't be able to get down to the construction walkway, not with NYPD sentries watching, and he couldn't flank them by taking Barclay west, because it had been cordoned off also. He concluded that he'd seen enough. The neighborhood was such a jumble of new foundations and partially finished buildings that he felt like a space traveler wandering into a moon colony under construction.

A few yards north of the squad car, he saw a brief flash of reflected light coming from a spot near a curb, caught in a passing headlight: a metal object, maybe a flattened tin can. Curious, he strolled over for a look. There were no streetlights in this spot, and it took him a moment to relocate the object. Then he saw it: a horseshoe. Proof! Proof there had been a horse cop here! His heart began to race, and he had to force himself to calm down. What could be unusual about a horseshoe? He already knew that a squad of mounted police patrolled this area. Occasionally one of the horses was bound to throw a shoe. Why get excited? Who could say the shoe hadn't been thrown a week ago?

But he couldn't resist. The shoe beckoned to him, demanding his attention. Not enough light, not enough time to study it here. And the sentries behind him might see. He turned to look at them, so he could judge his timing. The driver was napping, and the one who had accosted him was sipping from a container of coffee. He leaned down and quickly picked up the shoe, stuffing it into the big pocket on the inside of his trench coat lining, then jammed his hands in his pockets to impersonate a man huddled against the cold, and walked briskly toward Canal Street and the hotel.

He wanted to get back immediately, put the maximum amount of distance between himself and the screams of the Trade Center victims who, joined by the more recent ghost of John Maguire, insisted on following him like the Furies pursuing Orestes. They stayed on his trail until he reached Canal Street.

The entire experience had disoriented him, and he found the relentless spirit of the Furies actually frightening. No wonder Orestes had gone mad. Achilles was supposedly inured to such things, but every once in a while, especially on rainy nights like this, the demons who visit children's nightmares wandered off course and showed up in his mind too. He needed some distraction to drive them away, and being around other people would help, so he went back to the Lucky Strike. The bar area was fairly small, packed with rowdy city stags hunting for does. They made such a racket with their adenoidal bellowing, arguing over which team would win the pennant in the coming baseball season, that he sought a quieter space, a table in the back room. He dropped his trench coat on the banquette and sat next to it, facing out to the room.

A pretty waitress came over, all smiles. "Kitchen's shut down. Bar closes in half an hour."

"Okay." He ordered a bottle of Brooklyn Lager.

Achilles could sense the horseshoe in his coat beaming its energy at him. He fumbled through the mass of cloth, searching for the shoe, then thought better of it. He didn't want to inspect it in a public place. It was probably nothing—a mere token from a different world, one in which horses still had some use. It would end up being a souvenir on the wall over his dresser back in Arlington. His beer came, and he gratefully descended into the oblivion common to loners in bars, listening to the various arguments and discussions going on around him, silently taking sides, picking the winners and losers, indulging in the harmless fantasy of wondering which women would leave with which men. He thought of Perly and Lauren making discovery together, and became furious for a moment. Why Perly? Why not Achilles? No matter how old he got, he could still be capable of sexual envy. Why? Why now? Would he ever outgrow it? Should he ever outgrow it?

"Last call," the waitress announced as she scooped bottles and glasses off tables.

Hoping one more hit would put him to sleep, Achilles ordered another beer and tossed it down. The game of listening to other people's arguments had played itself out. He threw some cash on the table and got up to leave. On his way out of the bar, the waitress caught up with him.

"Sir! You forgot this." She was holding the horseshoe. "It slipped out of your pocket when you put your coat on."

"Oh," he mumbled. "Didn't notice. So much noise. Thanks."

For the first time he took a close look at the horseshoe. She had handed it to him with the business side face up, the side that touched the ground as the horse walked. The sole of the shoe, so to speak. It had twelve raised metal dots on it, six on each side of the arch.

The double six.

CHAPTER TWENTY

Suddenly wide awake, Achilles rushed to his room, ripped off his trench coat, and turned on the lights. He sat down at the desk with the horseshoe and studied it. Although he was no expert on horseshoes, clearly this one corresponded to the hoof prints he had seen in Taos. The message he and Perly had just received from Malcolm said the termites could find only two ranches named Double Six in the country. Where could these horses be coming from, then? Was the Double Six a fictional ranch, or located in some other country, possibly the Mideast, where they also love their horses? But why would an Arabic horseman name his ranch the Double Six? Considering the friction between the Islamic world and the West, no citizen of an Islamic country in his right mind would give his ranch a name that had a Western ring.

He felt the metal bumps on the shoe: rough to the touch, heavily worn, made of some abrasive material. Maybe they weren't simply for decoration. He had never seen anything like them, but that didn't mean they couldn't have some practical use. That would be another thing for him to do after the meeting: find out who put shoes on the police horses, ask the farrier some questions about these metal dots.

Damn Perly! Of all the nights for him to go AWOL with a woman.

Achilles pulled the digital camera out of his computer case and took pictures of the horseshoe, went online, and uploaded the pictures to his backup site. He couldn't take any chances with these. Then, too riled to sleep, he reexamined the photos Mikhail had brought him, now that he had seen the site. There were no signs of tampering. Putting the photos aside, he returned to the code, but it still refused to give up its secrets. Finally, with the sky lightening at dawn, his head slumped on the desk and he fell asleep, inadvertently using the horseshoe for a pillow. When the hard pillow had given him a headache strong enough to wake him up an hour later, he looked in the mirror and saw that he had impressions of the raised dots on his forehead.

He shuddered, and hoped they weren't a precursor of something more deadly, like the SODM brand.

After a quick shave and shower, he packed the computer, put the horse-shoe in the case, and went downstairs for breakfast. He wanted a plain and inexpensive breakfast—ham, eggs, coffee, not the fancy stuff they served in the hotel—so he asked at the front desk for some help, and they told him of a diner around the corner on Sixth Avenue that fit the bill.

Breakfast, four cups of coffee, off to the meeting. He had given a passing thought to calling Perly or Lauren again, but decided against it; he would let them squirm at the meeting.

Achilles strode briskly toward the First Precinct station house, taking in the sights along the way. The sky had cleared, blessing the city with a beautiful spring day. On a side street just below Canal he noticed a building with a sign over the door that read "Animal Hospital." This could be a good place to ask about farriers in New York City. The animal husbandry community, he knew, was a tight one. He preferred not to ask the precinct men unless he had no other choice. He looked at his watch. Almost eight. A couple of minutes to spare. Why not?

The hospital had just opened. A woman stood behind the raised counter, scrubbing the Formica and getting set up for the day.

"Hi," Achilles said. "I'm wondering if you could help me."

"Glad to." She was middle-aged with a round pockmarked face, wearing a none-too-stylish pants suit covered with filaments of animal hair.

"I'm wondering where to get a horse shod around here."

She raised her eyebrows. "Horseshoeing is not exactly our line."

"I expected as much, but I thought you might know someone."

"You should try up in midtown, along the West Side Highway, where the hansom cab operators stable their horses. They'd be better able to tell you."

"What about the precinct down here? They have horses, don't they?"

"Yes, but they have their own farrier. They don't use outsiders."

"I see." He turned to go, then thought of another question. "Do they ever have your vets treat their horses? Or do they have their own vets too?"

The woman stared at him suspiciously. "You're asking a lot of funny questions about the police. Why don't you go on over there and ask them directly? I'm sure they'd be glad to tell you."

She's still suffering from post-9/11 jitters, he told himself. Before the attacks on the Trade Center he would easily have received answers to questions like these. No more.

"Okay," he said, feigning nonchalance. "Actually, I was headed there to do just that. I thought I'd check with you first, on the off chance…"

He let the thought drift away enticingly, and left.

Now in danger of being late, he picked up his pace, arrived in a few minutes at the station house, and had to go through the drill of showing ID and stating purpose to a new desk sergeant. Approaching the conference room, he could hear the drone of a voice through the closed door, the jingle of change: Frank Bernardo giving another report.

He knocked on the door and entered without waiting for a response. "Sorry I'm late." Bernardo paused for a moment while Achilles got settled. Someone had played musical chairs and rearranged the seating. Perly and Lauren, looking sheepish, sat across the table. In the chair Achilles had occupied the day before sat a new face: an astoundingly beautiful woman, who turned and smiled at him warmly.

"It's all right," Ramirez said. "We just started." He nodded toward the newcomer. "Frank is catching Ms. Timothee—Timofeev up on current events. She's from the SVR. Go ahead, Frank."

Achilles took the only seat vacant, an empty chair next to the woman. Her papers covered the space in front of him on the table, but she obligingly scooped them out of the way so he could have a clear space. Catching a glimpse of her notes, he noticed she had written them in Cyrillic. *Another Russian,* he thought.

As Frank droned and jingled his change, Achilles pondered this new wrinkle. Why was the SVR, the successor to the foreign espionage branch of the KGB, represented at the table? What interest could they possibly have in these murders, and why would the SS, the CIA, the FBI, and the Pentagon let them in on meetings? Why hadn't Malcolm told him about this? He looked over at Perly and Lauren, seeking enlightenment. They both shrugged. The Russian woman next to him kept scribbling industriously, apparently writing down every word Frank said, although Achilles couldn't be sure, since his ability to read Cyrillic script had atrophied with the demise of the Cold War.

Frank finally finished and sat down.

"Any questions, Ms. Timofi-ev—eev—sorry, how do you pronounce your name?" Ramirez said.

"Ti-mo-fee-EV-na," she articulated patiently, with hardly a trace of an accent. "But call me Galina. It saves us time." Her voice sounded smooth and silky, with a sonorous timbre reminiscent of a church bell. She could have been one of the famous Russian mezzo-sopranos Jennifer had told Achilles about.

"Great, thank you," Ramirez said to her. "Do you have any questions?"

"Not at the moment."

"Achilles? Since you came in late?"

"Ah…well…nothing I can ask at the moment."

"You're wondering why the SVR is here?" Ramirez said, prompting an uptake of breath around the table. "Let's be open. We're professionals here, and we all understand about protocol. I received a call last night from Washington, informing me that the Secret Service wanted Galina, here, to join us. Since the presidents of Russia and the U.S. are spending Saturday together at Camp David, and are flying up to the summit together on Sunday morning, there is a strong interest in coordinating any operations that might have an impact on the security of the summit. My orders are to provide complete cooperation. Beyond that, I know nothing."

"But…," Achilles protested.

"The recent tensions? Forget about them for now. The big guys have kissed and made up, so now the drill is for the rest of us to cooperate and make nice. Does that about sum it up?" he said to Galina.

"Perfectly, I think," she said in that beautiful voice. Achilles, hopelessly smitten, felt like turning himself into a cat, jumping into her lap, and purring.

"Now, also as a result of that call from Washington, I have another announcement to make," Ramirez said. "Congress, in its usual inimitable fashion, is getting into the act. The Senate Select Committee on Intelligence is holding a closed session this afternoon, and they want to know where things stand on this investigation, among other things. I have to fly down to Washington ASAP and be there when our director testifies. So, unfortunately, I have to leave you for the rest of the day. Andy will be covering for me until I get back, which should be in time for the Saturday morning meeting. Andy, why don't you take over now?" Ramirez pushed his chair back, put on his coat, and left to murmurings of "Goodbye" and "Safe trip."

Andy launched into a speech he had obviously prepared ahead of time. "I just want you all to know I'm honored to be working with you. I know this is a tough and gruesome case, same as Taos, but we've got to keep working all-out to crack these things. We can't let ourselves be distracted by the hoopla going on with the G8 summit. Now, has anyone found anything out since we met yesterday? Anything to report?"

Achilles wanted to put in a word about the horseshoe. He also wanted to mention the discrepancy in the photographs. But his internal alarm bells held him back. Best to keep his report to a safer topic.

"Mikhail brought me the photos I requested," he said. "Thank you, Mikhail." Mikhail nodded and smiled benignly.

"Anything interesting? Were you able to scope anything out?" Andy said.

"Nearly identical technique to the one used in Taos. Even the same set of dominoes, which, I should add"—he felt safe saying this much—"are from a unique set, with figures carved on them in relief. Most dominoes have flat surfaces, only the numbered dots stamped on them. These seem to be some sort of antiques, or special issue jobs." He addressed Mikhail. "Maybe you could have one of your photo experts extract the domino from the rest of the picture, so people wouldn't have to look at poor Maguire's head," he said, cleverly—he thought—laying a trap. "Then you could distribute the picture to give the troops an idea of the appearance of these dominoes. If we could find a store or gallery that sells them, it would be bound to lead us somewhere fruitful." *Thrust.*

Mikhail took some notes, then looked at Achilles. "What about the domino in Taos? Isn't there already a picture of that?" *Parry.*

"Yes," Achilles said, cursing the parry. He hadn't wanted the probe to go in that direction. "But I took the picture in a freezer, and they had stowed the domino in a plastic box. It's not really clear enough to be useful to troops on the street, looking in store windows." *Counter-parry.*

"Does the Secret Service have a better picture?" *Riposte.*

"I have no idea. They enjoy impounding things even more than the Manhattan DA's office." *Counter-riposte.* "I was lucky to get the picture I did."

"Could we see it?" *Second counter-riposte.*

"It'll take a minute. I have to boot up the laptop." Achilles pulled his computer out of its case and turned it on. While they waited for it boot up, Andy kept going around the table.

"Phil, anything from the mayor's office?"

"No, nothing. Except to emphasize that the mayor is very concerned about the murder of such a prominent person. Especially considering the publicity about this murder bumping up against the G8 summit."

"I need to second that," Lauren said from across the table, her voice sounding husky and tired. Achilles thought he caught a little whiff of discovery; he wondered if the others sensed the new dynamic between her and Perly. "The White House is highly concerned about this case and the Kean case. Phone calls are coming in from the other governments involved in the G8. Some of them are beginning to express real doubt about holding the summit here."

"Please assure the president," Andy said, "that everyone at the G8 will be completely protected."

"He has every confidence. But the perceptions…"

"Understood. But maybe he should be expressing these concerns to the two gentlemen from the Pentagon."

Now even Andy feels free to get snippy, Achilles thought. "We're on the case," he said irritably. "I stayed up all night with the damned thing."

"Really?" Andy said. "And all you have to report is an antique domino? What about the cipher? Aren't you the code-breaker?"

At this point Achilles really started to boil. "Look. This is Friday. I've been cross country twice since Tuesday morning. I didn't see the first cipher until late Tuesday. I'm not even sure I'm looking at the complete cipher yet. You don't crack these things in twenty minutes."

"Agreed," chimed the gorgeous Russian voice of Galina. "It is very difficult work." She smiled at Achilles. "I do some of this kind of work, too. Perhaps we can work together."

"That…that…might be a good idea," Achilles said, not wanting to get snared in an SVR trick, but not wanting to turn down some real help, either. Especially if it provided him a chance to jump into that lap and purr.

"We can talk about it later," she said.

"Great." He glanced at Perly. *Ha,* he thought. *Now look who's jealous. Keep your White House staffer. I'll go with the exotic Russian.*

"China, too," an unfamiliar voice said. It belonged to Jeshua Lin, Frank Bernardo's assistant, speaking for the first time. His voice had a surprisingly authoritative ring.

"Excuse me," Andy said. "I don't follow."

"China is concerned. These murders are getting huge play in Chinatown, and back in the home country. China is not in the G8, but it is in the G20, and it is sending monitors to this summit. They are wondering if the summit should be moved or cancelled." Lin's English enunciation, Achilles noted, was spotless. On the phone no one would guess his Chinese background.

"Well," Andy said. "We have our jobs cut out for us. We know this will be tough, but we have to move quickly. You can tell the mayor, Phil, that we're expending every effort. Same message for the White House, Lauren."

"Oh, thank you," Lauren said, sarcastically.

Brian Mooney, the security chief from the New York Stock Exchange, finally spoke up. "Everyone here is ignoring the obvious. Why is there such a fear to discuss it?"

"I don't follow," Andy said. "What are you talking about?"

"I'm talking about Islamic terrorists. This must be another phase. They wanted to take out Secretary Kean to get revenge for Gulf War Two. They take out Chairman Maguire to roil our markets—a way of creating chaos and confusion in the Western economies and political structures that is more subtle than what they did on 9/11, but just as effective."

"That is why the Pentagon is here. Gentlemen?" Andy said, looking at the RZ men.

Perly spoke up. "Anything is possible."

"Don't give me that 'anything is possible' crap," Brian said. "I'm talking about probability, not possibility."

"Brian," Lauren said soothingly, "we can't allow ourselves the luxury of jumping to conclusions. There are domestic political considerations."

"When they point another plane at the White House, maybe then you'll pay attention," he said bitterly. The room lapsed into an awkward silence. "Sorry. I know I'm a bit out of order. I used to be on the security staff at the Trade Center, and I lost friends there. This is starting to look like some kind of run-up to another hit."

"Both the Pentagon and the CIA are scouring the world—with the FBI's help, of course," Perly said, nodding to Andy. "We got to believe we can head somethin' like that off."

"Too late for my friends," Brian said. "Or Mr. Maguire."

"Do you have any more information about his last movements?" Andy said, trying to defuse the tension.

"One of the traders, on his way to the subway, saw Mr. Maguire hailing a cab at Cedar Street and Broadway. He had left the Exchange by the side door, the one on the corner of New Street and Wall Street. The guard said he acted quite cheerful, whistled 'Call to the Post' on his way out."

"'Call to the Post'?" Galina said.

"The bugle call they use at the race track. Mr. Maguire, like a lot of us, loves—loved—the horses. He often whistled that on his way to the track."

"Makes sense," Achilles said. "The odds on horse racing are better than the odds on stocks, as we've been reminded recently."

Brian snorted. "Some people still think it's a good way to invest."

"You mean horse racing?"

"Gentlemen, please," Andy said, rapping on the table with the cap of his pen. "Is there anything else, Brian?"

"Not really. After he got in that cab he simply vanished."

Achilles' laptop had long since booted up, and while they were talking he had opened the file with the picture of the Stonewall domino taken in the freezer.

"Mikhail," he said, turning the screen so Mikhail could see it, "there's the picture of the Kean domino. I think you'll agree it's not useful for putting in the hands of the troops."

Mikhail looked at it closely, then shrugged in resignation. "You're right. I'll see what I can have them do at the office to extract the domino from Maguire's picture."

Touché, Achilles thought. Exactly what he had been seeking: proof that the DA's office had Photoshop geeks in the back room altering photos. Not that he really needed proof. Every agency had such a back office, staffed by former owners or employees of bankrupt photo studios. Yet hearing it tossed off so matter-of-factly provided a nice confirmation.

At least, so he thought until his inner voice yanked his chain. *Yes,* it said, *but he didn't act the least bit defensive about it. Don't you think he would have, if the horse cop photo had been altered?*

Shut up, Achilles nearly said aloud.

"May I?" Galina said. Achilles rotated the computer so she could see. She studied the picture closely. "Interesting. I might have seen some dominoes similar to these in Leningrad—sorry, St. Petersburg. At the Hermitage. Or maybe some other museum. I'll send a message back."

"That would be great," Achilles said. "If we could only track these things down…"

"Anything else?" Andy said. Receiving no response, he stood up and cleared his papers. "Then I think that's it for this morning's meeting. I suggest we reconvene at 5:30 this afternoon."

Achilles shut down his laptop, and everyone else stood up, stretched, chatted—the normal meeting-is-over routine. Achilles had to intercept Perly, so he could talk to him. But he was momentarily distracted by Galina.

"When would you like to talk about the cipher?" she said.

"Why not right now? After I catch my partner and have a word with him."

"That would be nice." She was actually tiny, he noted, now that they stood face to face. She wore her long russet hair in a bun, and seemed ageless. Mother Russia stood before him—the Russia of Tolstoy, Pushkin, and Chekhov.

Mikhail came over and entered into a spirited discussion with Galina in Russian. Achilles realized he had missed Perly.

"Perly!" he called, racing out into the hallway.

CHAPTER TWENTY-ONE

Achilles caught up with Perly on the staircase and sheepdogged him into a nook by a Coke machine.

"Perly, I need to talk to you."

Lauren joined them. "What's up?" she said cheerfully.

"Look, Achilles, I'm sorry I didn't get back to you…," Perly began.

"Never mind that. I've got to talk business with you."

"What's up, guys?" Lauren repeated. "Can the girls play too?"

"Lauren, please excuse us for a minute. I don't mean to be rude, but I really need to talk to Perly alone."

Lauren dropped the friendly façade and stomped out to the street.

"What the hell did you do that for?" Perly said.

"This is important, dammit!" Achilles realized he had raised his voice, looked around to make sure no one had noticed, then quickly told Perly about the photos Mikhail had dropped off, and the horseshoe with the dots.

Perly furrowed his brow and whistled. "Let's go out and get Lauren. We need another brain on this."

"But what if it's her photo that was doctored?"

"Then she needs to know that."

Emerging from the precinct, they saw Lauren across the street, talking to Galina.

"Girls bonding," Perly said.

"I want to drop by the stable in back and ask a few questions," Achilles said.

They got the women's attention and motioned for them to join them.

"I'm really sorry, Lauren," Achilles said, once she and Galina had crossed the street. "But sometimes…"

"It's all right," she said, not convincingly. "Forget it."

I've lost her, he thought, but he had to plunge on nevertheless.

"I need to drop by the stable. I have a couple of questions I want to ask the guy in charge. You want to come with me, or go off on your own?"

"I'm game," Lauren said.

"Galina?" Achilles said.

"Of course."

Achilles noted with satisfaction that the warmth she used in addressing him caused Perly considerable discomfort.

They walked the few feet to the stable at the back of the station house. Laid out in a narrow space the width of an alley, it was a clean, well-kept facility with ten stalls, five on each side of a central aisle, and 100-pound bags of oats stacked neatly near the doorway. A metal crowd control barrier kept the horses in and the curious public out.

Two men worked behind the barrier, both wearing the uniforms of the equine squad. One busied himself grooming a horse tethered in the aisle between stalls, which stood quietly, entranced by the crowd of two-legged creatures passing by on the sidewalk. The other cop, apparently the officer in charge, adjusted the reins on a bridle while he kept an attentive eye on the grooming. When Achilles and company approached his barrier, he half-smiled, half-frowned, as if to say, *Hi, don't touch my horse.*

"Hello," Achilles said, flashing his badge.

"Oh, hi," the cop said, seeing that this was not just a curious tourist.

"My companions and I are working on the Maguire case. I'm sure you've heard of it."

"Heard of it? Everyone has a theory."

"Really? What's yours?"

"He was just in the news, a couple of weeks ago, wasn't it? Something about how much jack he made? I think it was a bungled kidnap job. Like that big shot they buried alive up by the West Side Highway."

"Hmm." Achilles glanced at the others, wondering if Galina could track New York cop jargon. "I'm hoping you can help us with this," he said to the cop, pulling the horseshoe out of his computer case. "Does it look familiar to you? Would any of the NYPD horses be wearing a shoe like this?"

The cop turned the shoe over in his hand and inspected it. "Ryan," he said to the other cop. "C'mere and take a look at this."

The two men inspected the shoe, shaking their heads.

"Nope," the first cop said finally. "Not one of ours."

"What's your name again?" Achilles said.

"Abe."

"Abe, you're sure this isn't an equestrian squad shoe?"

"Positive."

"Could it be from a hansom cab?"

"Nah, they use rubber pads, nothing like this."

"Then how can you be sure it isn't from the equestrian squad? Nobody would be riding for pleasure down here by Wall Street."

"I'm sure because we don't use that many dots."

"That many? You mean you use dots?"

"Oh, yeah, standard procedure. Borium dots welded to the shoe. They give the horse better traction on pavement."

"So, how many dots are normal?"

"Four. Two on each side. But this, six to a side—too many. May not hurt, but it seems like overkill."

"Do you know any farrier around here who might put on this many dots?"

"Might be one, but we have our own farriers. None of them would."

"Do you know of any other farriers around the city, someone who might work for the hansom cab outfits, for instance?"

"Funny you should ask. I don't, but you're the second guy in two days to ask that."

Achilles could hear an intake of air from Perly.

"I'm the second? Who was the first?"

"Some guy with a western accent. Kind of a drawl. Not from the city. Said he worked as a hostler for some big shot, needed to find a farrier in town. I told him that very thing, go hunt the hansom stables over by the river. Or maybe he should check out Belmont."

"Did he tell you his name?"

"Nah, I don't think so. No, wait a minute. Maybe he did. Yeah, he did. When he first came up to me, he made some small talk before he sprang the question. Said his name was Ray."

CHAPTER TWENTY-TWO

Achilles thanked Abe and led the others across the street so they could talk.

"What is it?" Galina said. "Who is this Ray?"

"Kean's groom in Taos," Perly said. "He disappeared just before we got called back here."

"We need to go somewhere we can have a powwow," Achilles said.

"I'm hungry," Perly said. "Didn't have time for breakfast."

"What's powwow?" Galina said.

"Conversation," Achilles said. "Strategy session."

"There's a place to eat—over there, on the corner," Perly said.

"No," Lauren said.

"Why not?"

"Too close to the precinct. It'll be full of cops, remember? Let's go to the Franklin Station Café, near my hotel. No cops, guaranteed. And we can sit outside."

"Done," Perly said.

Perly and Lauren walked ahead, talking animatedly. Achilles hung back with Galina.

"I have a few questions to ask you before we go any further with this joint discussion," he said.

"You're wondering why SVR is involved, and not PSB."

"Well, yes, that's one of them." After the KGB had been broken up, the PSB had been established as the Russian equivalent of the U.S. Secret Service, charged with protecting high government officials. The SVR was supposed to be comparable to the CIA, restricted mainly to foreign intelligence gathering. Achilles had not wanted to ask the question at the meeting. The answer might not be appropriate for local ears.

"I will explain everything," she said. "When we reach the restaurant."

Perly and Lauren had already found a table when Achilles and Galina got there, perfectly situated on the short leg of a triangle at the junction of Varick and West Broadway. Only a few tables had been set up outside, and this early in the day those were unoccupied, since the air still had a nip to it. Being outside with the traffic noise would provide a good cover against prying ears.

The busboy came with water, followed by the waiter, offering to tell them the daily specials, which they waved off. They ordered omelettes and coffee for everyone, and then got down to work.

"First thing I want to straighten out," Achilles said to the others, "is why the SVR has been sent to work on this case with us, instead of the PSB." He hated being this blunt; he found Galina impossibly attractive, yet business had to be business. "Tell me where I'm wrong, Galina, but it seems to me, if your government wants someone here because of a concern over your president's safety, they've sent the wrong unit."

"You are wrong in several ways. First, although there is element of presidential protection in our government's interest in these murders, the events raise other issues also. Our bureau has greater mandate to work with foreign agencies than PSB. We can go beyond simple issues of protecting the president."

"Sounds okay so far. But it still doesn't fully address my question."

"Second," Galina went on, "we are not entirely sure we can trust our own PSB."

She paused, waiting for that statement to have the expected effect, which it did. Perly choked on his mouthful of water. Lauren helplessly opened and closed the clasp of her bag; and Achilles took refuge in a nervous habit of rearranging the silverware when he couldn't think of anything to say.

"Should I continue?"

"Yes, please do," Achilles said.

"We have been led to understand that you reported airlift of horses in Taos. A helicopter lift, in which unidentified persons deposited one dead horse in a mine shaft, and probably ferried another, live horse to points unknown."

"As of today, I'd say to New York City," Achilles said.

"Quite possible."

"But that still doesn't tell us why the SVR is involved, or why y'all don't trust your own PSB," Perly said.

"I guess you have not been told of joint maneuvers."

"Joint maneuvers? What joint maneuvers?" Achilles said. He and Perly exchanged panicked glances. What had Malcolm not told them that he should have?

"As a favor to his government, your retired secretary of defense, Mr. Kean, agreed to let a remote section of his ranch be used for joint extraction maneuvers operating from corner of Air Force base nearby, involving your Secret Service and our PSB. For first time in history, the U.S. administration authorized Russian military helicopter to operate in American airspace, and use the Secret Service codes for verifying a friendly aircraft."

"What extraction?" Achilles said. "I don't follow."

"And why'd they need his ranch?" Perly added. "The military's got plenty of their own playgrounds."

"Extraction of the presidents, in case there is some kind of trouble. Extracting them from a hot spot if it is overrun by demonstrators, or any such event that might come up. And they chose his ranch because they wanted to keep presence of Russians secret, even from your own troops. Preparation for the summit, you see."

"But a Russian helicopter operating in our air space?" Achilles said. "Impossible. We've been at each other's throats ever since you sent troops into Georgia."

"You haven't been following events. Problems are settled. Some things are more important than a spat between a great power and a pesky flyspeck on its border."

Their food came, and they made small talk by commenting on the nice weather while the plates were being placed on the table. When the waiter and the busboy had left, Lauren spoke up.

"But that doesn't tell us why the PSB can't be trusted."

Achilles forced himself to take some bites of omelette while he listened.

"Because of what we learned about the horses being airlifted out. Yesterday, your governor called our adjutant general on the hot line. I am normally assigned to our mission at U.N. My superior filled me in on situation last night, and told me to attend this meeting today. I have received full clearance from your own governor, if that means anything to you."

"It does, most certainly it does," Achilles said. "But—pardon me for being thick in the head today—I still don't understand why you don't trust your PSB."

"Russian helicopter being used for joint maneuvers was Mil Mi-17, one of our large transport helicopters, flown by PSB crew. We think it did airlift of horses, but the crew denies any involvement. We suspect they aren't telling the truth. We are afraid there may be some plot, some attempt made on the lives of one or more dignitaries at G8 summit, and SVR wants to make sure PSB helicopter is not part of that plan."

The other three sat in stunned silence for a few moments as they digested this piece of information. Silence, that is, in the sense that no one at the table did any talking. There was plenty of noise around them, with cars and trucks on the street, airplanes and helicopters overhead, sirens wailing a couple of blocks away. At this one table, however, on the sidewalk of the Franklin Station Café, an outside observer would have thought four enemies had tried to patch things up at a brunch, and the reconciliation had failed.

Achilles was furious with Malcolm. The governor must have known about those maneuvers. Why had he made such an issue of questioning his two agents over the helicopter, if he knew about it all along? Or, if he hadn't known, what did that mean? How could he have been so far out of the loop on something that important?

Perly broke the conversational gridlock first. "Anything else? The fact there's been joint maneuvers doesn't explain the sudden intense interest y'all are showin' in a couple of murders. I can understand your interest in protectin' your president. But what do these murders here in the U.S. of A. have to do with that?"

"I'm getting to that," Galina said. "What really caught our attention were the common elements."

"What common elements?" Achilles said.

"Common elements present in murders," she said, pulling out a cigarette and lighter. "Prominent people, severed heads with dominoes in their mouths, letters branded on forehead, ciphers pinned to the navel." She lit the cigarette and blew a cloud of smoke into the air.

"This is for the three of you only. You see, Taos and New York City are not the only places to have such murders. We have had two just like them in Russia."

CHAPTER TWENTY-THREE

Once again they sat in mute astonishment, listening to the chorus of neighborhood sounds. Galina smoked and sipped her coffee, waiting for the others to come back to life.

"Well," Lauren said at last. "This has been an instructive morning. We've learned that a hostler named Ray is floating around New York City looking for someone who knows how to shoe a horse, and we've learned that the Russians are coming. What do we do next? Any suggestions for positive action, or do we go back to our corners?"

"I think," Achilles said, "that maybe you and Perly should take this horseshoe to the precinct, have Frank Bernardo send out the word to his troops, tell them to check out farriers, stables, anything of that kind in the city, so we can track down who else Ray might have approached. If we can find the farrier, then we'll find the horse that threw the shoe. And my bet is the horse's name will be Persimmon."

"And what about you?" Perly said. "What are you going to do?"

"Galina just told us there are more ciphers. I need to put them together with the ones we have already and get busy. I have a feeling that time is running short. I don't like the way this is progressing."

"I can help you," Galina said.

"You mentioned that before. Are you a cryptanalyst?"

"Let's say—how do you put it in your universities? I made a minor in ciphers."

The other three laughed. Now that they had overcome their astonishment, they moved quickly: downed the rest of their coffee, which by now had turned cold, but who cared; tried to finish the omelettes, but those had solidified into rubber; paid the bill, and left. Achilles took the horseshoe out of his computer case and gave it to Perly, who stashed it in his own case.

"Don't leave that with the cops," Achilles said. "They'll probably hand it over to Mikhail."

"What's wrong with that?" Lauren said.

"I'm not sure he can be trusted."

"But at the meeting you thanked him for bringing the photos to you last night."

"What I didn't get to tell you, because we had bigger news just now, is that there's a discrepancy between the photos he gave me and the ones you showed us. Soon as you're through at the precinct, come to the hotel room and I'll show you what I mean. Do you have your photos with you?"

"Yes."

"So let's hop to. See you back in room 621." Then he remembered the cipher. "No, wait. Lauren, I need you to send a message to Malcolm. I need a picture, or an accurate transcription, of the cipher they found on Mr. Kean."

"Don't you have that already?"

"A Secret Service man read it off to me. I never saw the actual piece of paper. I need those numbers, every digit that's in the cipher, including any leading zeros."

"Okay, got it." Lauren and Perly went up Varick toward the precinct, and Achilles and Galina walked north on West Broadway to the hotel.

"Do you always take charge in this manner?" Galina said.

"Not usually. Perly is normally the one on lead, but we take turns, and he was a bad boy last night, made himself unavailable with important intel coming in. So I have to fill in the gaps for him."

"Bad boy? What did he do?"

"I shouldn't say. It's personal in nature. You'll figure it out."

Galina laughed. "Oh, you mean he spent the night with Lauren. And you call him a bad boy. Well, if he was bad boy, she was good girl. Even spies should be allowed to have a little pleasure once in a while."

Achilles sensed with relief that he might get a few moments of pleasure himself, a break from the stress of the intense work. He steered the talk back to business in order to conceal his upwelling excitement.

"I noticed that you had a bit of conversation with Mikhail when the meeting broke up. Did you learn anything interesting?"

"No, not really. We merely exchanged pleasantries, seeing if our families might have known someone in common."

"And?"

"No links. His family lived in Moscow. Mine came from Novosibirsk, in western Siberia, middle of the country in Soviet days, but now, with the breakup, it's on the southern border of Russia, not too far from Kazakhstan. Almost as if the city had moved."

They had reached the hotel, and took the elevator up to Achilles' room. He pulled out his laptop and turned it on.

"Want anything from the wet bar?" He desperately wanted a drink himself, but didn't dare. He was already running on pure adrenalin and, considering his lack of sleep over the past three nights, couldn't take the chance of tossing down alcohol this early in the day.

"No, thank you." She had pulled a small device from her bag that resembled a remote control for a television set, and was punching various keys, then making sweeping motions around the room with the device held at arm's length.

"What are you doing?"

"Checking for bugs."

"Yours, or ours?"

"Both." She turned the device off and put it back in her bag. "The service is getting lazy. We should have had this room bugged before you checked in."

"How can you be so open about this? Are you trying to make me trust you, or throw me off guard?"

"Achilles, I can't tell you how important this job is. Both our careers are on the line, whether you know it or not. In fact I would say, both our lives are on the line. Now, let's get down to work. Show me what you have."

He opened the tables of the ciphers on the computer and showed them to her, then handed her the pile of Mikhail's photographs. She looked at them quickly, her lips pursed. Then she pulled a large manila envelope out of her bag, took some photographs and papers out of it, and handed them over to him one by one, explaining each in its turn.

"First murder victim. Killed three weeks ago. Head was left outside Kremlin. Homeless people found his body in Moscow sewer."

Achilles looked at the photo. A severed head. A bald man, his face in a grimace, his mouth propped open by someone's hand so the photographer could get a good shot of the domino inside. And the Cyrillic letters ÓОДМ branded on his forehead.

"So these are the Russian letters for SODM."

"Yes."

"Should I know this man?"

"I would hope so, but not necessarily. He was Yuri Grubkin, chief economic adviser to the president. What do you call it in the U.S.—the head of the Council of Economists, or whatever."

"Better watch yourself. You're starting to talk Yankeese."

She laughed and handed him the next photo, of the domino itself: the 2-3. It had come from exactly the same set as the Stonewall and Maguire dominoes.

"You say you might have seen these in a museum?"

"Not might have—did. I said 'might' for benefit of others. The dominoes are from the Hermitage, in St. Petersburg."

"Could someone steal them from the museum that easily?"

"They didn't need to. Reproductions are for sale in gift shop." She handed him the next photo, a close-up of the victim's navel, with the paper containing the cipher still attached.

Next, a photo of the paper itself, flattened out, showing the cipher. Similar to the ones Achilles had already seen.

"Has anyone tried to crack this cipher?"

"Yes. To no avail. No one has had any luck yet."

"Your whole service is working on it?"

"Of course. The president doesn't take lightly the loss of his chief economic adviser." She handed him another photograph. A new head, a different victim. "This one is truly interesting. Killed two weeks ago."

"Interesting in what way?" Other than the difference in the victim's features, he couldn't see anything more or less striking in this photograph than the one of Grubkin. The domino in the mouth, the brand, the paper—everything the same except for the number of the domino, a 1-5.

"Nikolai Atlantov, an industrialist. He owned big part of Russian resources—oil, gas, nickel, diamonds, gold. Boatmen found his body floating in a canal in St. Petersburg. His head was discovered by a cleaning woman in orchestra pit of Mariinsky Theater."

"One of your robber barons."

"Precisely. What we call oligarchs."

"What makes him truly interesting?"

"The new president has been putting great deal of pressure on oligarchs. Grubkin devised new policy, by which the government is trying to break their hold on the economy. Two of them have gone into exile, and two more are in jail. But this one, Atlantov, who controlled most of the natural resources, had been spared the pressure. He was only one of Yeltsin's oligarchs to survive the Putin era."

Achilles whistled. "I see where you're headed. You think one of the exiles is exacting revenge."

"Possibly. That would be most obvious explanation. There are others. It could be one or several of the old Red Directors. They used to run industries the oligarchs took over. They had been most important men in the Soviet Union, but are now old, impoverished, very bitter, maybe nothing to lose by taking their revenge years later. Then there is also this." She handed him another piece of paper, not a photograph. It contained a table written in her florid Cyrillic.

"I need help with this. I don't read Russian that well anymore. Out of practice."

"Translation is on back."

"Oh." He turned the page over and saw the same three-column table in English. She had written a series of two-digit numbers in the left column; a name in the middle column, beside each number; and in the right column, after each name, an explanation of the person's position in the world hierarchy. The names were not listed in alphabetical order; rather, they followed the order established in the left column, starting with zero, written 00, and progressing in an unusual sequence to the last number, 66.

Kean's name had been placed last on the list, next to 66. Maguire's name occupied the space next to 25. And the two Russians were on the list as well: Atlantov after 15, and Grubkin after 23. Achilles studied the table, looking at the other names. Some he recognized as heads of state from major countries, such as the president of France; the chancellor of Germany; the prime minister of the U.K.; the presidents of the U.S., Russia, and China; and the king of Saudi Arabia. Others were industrial or trade leaders, such as the CEOs of major multinational corporations, or the heads of the International Monetary Fund and the World Trade Organization. In addition, there were a few media people, such as the publisher of the *New York Times*, and the head of a worldwide cable news network. These were names that would show up on the "short list" for Georgetown parties—a list of the world's most powerful people. Twenty-seven names in all, although there should have been twenty-eight; because, oddly enough, no name occupied the space next to the 00.

"This is quite a list," Achilles said when he had finished.

Galina took the sheet back and looked at it. "What are you making of number order? There is 00, which has no name by it, then 01, 02, and so on, up through 06. Then 11 through 16, then 22 through 26, 33 through 36, 44 through 46, then 55 and 56, and then 66 by itself."

"Just like the old IRT subway joke."

"I don't know this joke."

"Never mind. It's too hard to explain. I would say this is a list of dominoes. The numbers are the sequence of dominoes as you would lay them out on a table. Do you get where I'm headed?"

Galina beamed. "But of course. It is on page in Cyrillic. These people are members of *Obshchestvo Ot Domino Maska*. In English, the Society of the Domino Mask."

CHAPTER TWENTY-FOUR

Achilles heard a knock at the door. When he answered it, Lauren and Perly burst in. Lauren kicked off her high heels and fell on the bed next to Galina, as if they were sisters or roommates in college. Perly set the horseshoe on the desk, then flopped in a chair by the window.

"Frank's on the case," he said. "He's puttin' the word out to all the precincts—find farriers."

"Needless to say," Lauren said, "the first thing he had to do was explain to the communications unit what the word 'farrier' means, so they could explain it to the troops. We had Abe, the stable cop, with us. He got quite a laugh out of the whole thing. That's what took us so long." She pushed herself upright. "I'm dying of thirst. What's in the wet bar?"

"For you, club soda," Achilles said.

"You're going to tell me what I can drink?"

"I think you need to sit tight for a minute and listen to what Galina has to say."

Perly and Lauren listened raptly while Galina repeated what she had told Achilles. By the end of the recitation, Lauren was tapping her nails on the night table next to the bed, and Perly was out of his chair, pacing and scratching his stubble.

"Well," Perly drawled at last. "You're really the proverbial Russian doll, aren't you? One goodie after another, all nestled nice and cozy inside each other."

"I'm sorry. I have to tell you what I know."

"What I don't understand," Perly said, "is why Malcolm didn't tell us any of this."

"Tell us what?" Achilles said. "The Russian murders, or the cast list of the society?"

"Both. Why's he holdin' out on us?"

"Maybe," Lauren said, "and I hate to admit this in front of an agent from SVR—he isn't holding out. Maybe he doesn't know."

"How could he not know?" Achilles said. "That's impossible."

"Not," Lauren said.

"Okay," Perly said, "out with it. What are you sittin' on, besides a mattress? Why didn't Malcolm know about this?"

"He didn't know about the Russian murders, because only the Russian government knew. And they didn't pass the intel on to us until today. I suppose that like us, they checked it off as something local at first. Am I right, Galina?"

Galina nodded.

"And he didn't tell you about the list because he couldn't," Lauren continued. "He didn't know the full story. He knew about Kean being a member of the society, and he knew about Maguire, but he didn't have the whole list."

Achilles quickly looked over the list again. "And we don't have the full list either. There's no name associated with the double zero."

Galina shrugged. "We could not find out the name. Either double zero is vacant, or it is person unknown."

"And what is the purpose of this society? What do they do?" Perly said.

"It is informal. It doesn't have any real power, not as an organization. It is group of people with influence who maintain regular contact with each other, to make sure their various governments and economies are proceeding in right direction. Something similar to your C Street house in Washington, but international."

"Informal, indeed," Achilles harrumphed. "No wonder they want to be secret. Imagine if the anti-globalization protestors found out about this."

"Lauren, how are you so sure Malcolm wasn't in the loop?" Perly asked.

"Because I didn't know, and Malcolm gets his information from me."

"What? Are you tryin' to tell us you're higher up the food chain than the governor of Ring Zero?"

"On certain things, yes. Anything involving the president's membership in private organizations, yes. The only way Malcolm would have found out would have been through a leak from the NSC staff, and that wouldn't happen, not even in the new kinder, gentler White House."

"So that raises the question," Achilles said to Galina, "of why you would have this information, but the CIA, the Pentagon, and the FBI wouldn't."

"I think answer is quite simple. SVR is more able to get information than your U.S. services. You already know that. If winner of Cold War had been decided by a race between KGB and CIA, we won by meters."

"You can spare us the plugs for the good old days of the KGB," Perly said. "We're talkin' about now, and the SVR."

"What I am saying," she continued, enunciating carefully to break through the interruption, "is that things have not changed very much for us. Even though Russia is more open than Soviet Union, we are still not that open. Head of the SVR is not dragged in front of demagogues in the Duma to explain everything he does. The press sometimes gets hold of an embarrassing fact, but more often not. And when they do, there are still unpleasant consequences for them. To us, your press are mad sled dogs, barking and yapping for next piece of meat."

"That's because we haven't cottoned to your system of sendin' masked troops to raid offices whenever the press criticizes the government," Perly said.

Galina glowered at Perly. Achilles could see her face flushing with anger, so he moved quickly to shut off the gas.

"We shouldn't be getting into sidebars about things we can't control. Please, Galina, keep going."

After taking a moment to calm herself, Galina cleared her throat to speak again. "Just to say, as short as possible, we have more room to operate." Her voice had regained its normal resonance and modulation. "We are able to find out more. And most important," she said directly to Perly, "maybe our president, because of all previous, trusts us more with information. He had no problem sharing this with us, once he knew about the murders."

Achilles, Lauren, and Perly headed simultaneously for the wet bar.

Galina laughed. "I'll take one too."

"Only beer," Achilles said. "It's too early for the hard stuff."

He pulled out four Heinekens, opened them, and poured the beer into glasses, passing each glass around as he filled it. When everyone had been served, they touched glasses.

"Cheers," Perly said.

"*Za nas,*" Galina said. "To us."

"So," Achilles said to Galina, returning to the society, "if you know who's in this Society of the Domino Mask, you must know when and where it started."

"We think seventeenth century, Netherlands. These figures on the dominoes are caricatures of Dutch burghers, who were fighting each other at same time they were struggling for independence from Spain. One group created secret society to escape notice of their enemies. Obviously the society passed through different hands, migrated to different countries, in years since. It is self-propagating. I have sheet here, dominoes without carving, that SVR thinks might represent the structure."

She took a paper from her bag and handed it to Achilles, who studied it while Perly and Lauren looked over his shoulder.

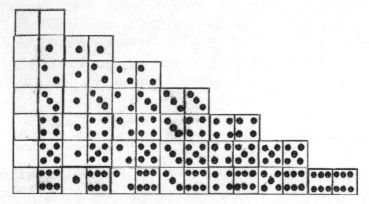

"Are you sure this is the right orientation?" Achilles said. "This puts Kean at the bottom of the heap. What's it supposed to mean?"

"That is what we have to find out. We don't know which domino represents top person, and we don't know process of selection."

Lauren's cell phone rang.

"Vogel here." She listened silently and took notes while the party at the other end talked, responding with "uh-huh" and "hmm" once in a while, but otherwise did not participate in the conversation. Finally she snapped the phone shut and put it back in her bag.

"Well," she said to the expectant three, "that was interesting. Message from Malcolm. But not Malcolm himself."

"Is that so unusual?" Perly said.

"Not completely. Not in and of itself. But today it is. First, I'll tell you what I'm supposed to pass on to you. Sam Rains's wife showed up at the Taos County sheriff's office."

"Yes!" Perly and Achilles shouted simultaneously, giving each other high fives. At last, a real breakthrough.

"And what did she say?" Perly said. "Did they get anything out of her?"

"She was being held captive at the pueblo by the tribe."

"Why the hell would they do that?" Achilles said.

"She had brought trouble and disgrace on them. They really can't tolerate federal interference in their affairs. Her actions had encouraged the federal government to question members of the tribe, and they punished her. She eventually managed to break away."

"What was the disgrace? Marrying outside the pueblo? I thought Sam came from Isleta, a related pueblo."

"That's what the tribe wanted outsiders to think. They were so ashamed of what she had done that they didn't want to publicize it. Actually, he's from the far North. Alaska, probably. He's Yupik, not Isleta."

"Yupik?" Perly said. "Never heard of 'em."

"You probably call them all Eskimos," Galina said, "but the Eskimo are really Inuit. There are other tribes. Yupik is one of them."

"How do you know that?" Perly said.

"You forget about Bering Strait. We have same tribes in Russia."

"So, go on," Achilles said to Lauren. "What else did she say? Has the sheriff tracked Sam's prints down?"

She paused to check her notes. "They have prints, but haven't been able to match them to any IDs."

"Damn!" Achilles said. He had just remembered the photos, which only a few hours ago had been the most important thing of all to him. "While we're on Sam, I have to show you something. Lauren, do you have the photos we looked at last night?"

"But I have more…," she said.

"I've got to show you these. It's really important."

Lauren paused, as if deciding whether to comply, and then pulled the envelope of photos out of her bag and gave it to Achilles. He quickly extracted the one of the horse cop, got the companion photo from Mikhail's batch, and walked around the room holding the two photos side by side, so each person could compare them.

Perly whistled. "Nice job, whoever did it."

"Looks like one of our old KGB photos, when they airbrushed disgraced commissars out of reviewing stand," Galina said.

"Lauren?" Achilles said. "Any ideas?"

"I know my photo came from a highly reliable source. I can't say the same for anything that came from the DA's office."

"Why would they want to zap the cop?" Perly wondered.

"Talking about Sam made me think of it," Achilles said. "I wonder if this cop might be Sam."

"Why would it be Sam?" Perly said.

"Perly, think. Ray Muller and Sam Rains disappear within hours after we show up at Stonewall's ranch."

"Who is Stonewall?" Galina said.

"Sorry—Kean," Achilles said. "That's our nickname for him." Continuing with Perly he said, "Now, Ray Muller, or so we think, shows up here in New York, asking the guys from the mounted unit where he can find a farrier. And we have one picture of a horse cop at the site of the dumpster where they found Maguire, a picture taken at 3 a.m., with the cop wearing shades. And we have another picture, same place, same time, no cop. This cop's face is a bit swarthy. Don't you think that might be Sam? Wearing shades to hide his identity?"

Perly whistled again, sat in his chair, and took a long swig of beer. "And who would be tryin' to hide the fact?"

"Exactly. Where does Mikhail fit? Messenger, or participant?"

"I still have more…," Lauren said.

"Lauren, sorry, one last thought," Achilles said. "I just realized—I forgot to ask you and Perly to have the guys at the precinct review their log, see if any mounted units were assigned to the search for Maguire, or if any of them might have been around at the time his body was being extricated from the dumpster."

"We'll have to go back now, ask 'em about that," Perly said.

"We could call," Lauren said. "The Lord has invented telephones, you know."

"Very funny. I have a couple of other things I want to talk to Bernardo about. I like bondin' with the local police, let's put it that way."

"Now, is everyone through?" Lauren said. "Can I finish what I have to say?"

"Of course," Achilles said. "Sorry, I didn't mean to hog the floor, but I've been sitting on the news about these photos since 2 a.m."

"Well, here's another one for you," Lauren said. "I guess it's my turn to play the Russian doll. I haven't told you the rest of the message I just received."

"Let me guess," Perly said. "Somethin' about Sam?"

"No. This is really quite bizarre. You know that the Senate Select Committee on Intelligence is supposed to be holding a hearing on this matter as we speak."

"Yes, what of it?"

"And that the directors of the FBI and CIA had been called to testify."

"Yes. And?" Perly said.

"Did you know that the witness list included Malcolm?"

"No."

"Well, it did. And now the committee has adjourned early, without taking testimony. The senators are furious."

"Why?"

"Malcolm was a no-show. He sent an assistant with an excuse that he had fallen ill. They can't locate him at the Pentagon or at home. It seems that no one in the U.S. government knows where Malcolm Evers is."

CHAPTER TWENTY-FIVE

Perly's mind was quickest to jump to the next step.

"What about Karl? Where's Karl?"

"No word on that," Lauren said. "And I didn't think to ask."

"Karl is our former boss at the CIA," Achilles said to Galina, who was looking from one person to the other, clueless. "And he used to be Malcolm's boss too."

"We better get going," Perly said. "I think Malcolm's rule about not callin' home is inoperative. Lauren and I will take care of that business at the precinct. You and Galina, y'all better get to work on the cipher. It's gettin' a little hairy around here, and I don't like not knowin' what these messages say."

"Right," Achilles said.

Perly and Lauren packed their things and left. Achilles sat at the desk with the paper Galina had given him and studied the list of names.

"I'm not sure what to make of this," he said. "I don't know if it's relevant to the cipher. I need the ciphers the police found on your murdered Russian gentlemen. Could I see them?"

Galina searched in the envelope that had held the sheets about the domino society, and pulled out another sheet.

"Here," she said, handing it to him. "Each cipher has twelve numbers."

Achilles looked at the sheet. The numbers had been listed in neat handwritten script—*good thing Russians use Arabic numerals, at least,* he thought—with a separate line for each cipher:

> 34-11-04-35-33-00-22-03-26-13-06-53
>
> 12-41-01-24-05-42-33-53-32-60-42-12

He noted that the numbers between zero and nine were written with leading zeros.

"The leading zeros," he said.

"What of them?"

"Are these accurate transcriptions? Did the numbers from zero to nine have leading zeros, or did someone add those later?"

"I believe these are accurate transcriptions."

"So what we don't know is the proper order of the messages."

"I think we put them in logical sequence, following sequence of the murders. That would mean the Grubkin cipher first, Atlantov second, your Stonewall, as you call him, third, and your Maguire fourth."

"And we have to decide where my little four-number cipher goes, the one I found on the pony."

Galina hadn't heard about the pony cipher, so Achilles had to take a few minutes to explain that to her.

"I think we leave it aside," she said when he finished. "It may be a key, or it may be what you call a red herring."

"Do you have another phrase for it?"

"Mink in heat," she said, giggling girlishly.

"Why 'mink in heat'?"

"Serves same purpose. In England, they drag red herring across trail of the fox to throw dogs off scent. In Siberia, live mink in heat does the same. Dogs can't follow anything else after they come across that."

Achilles decided not to follow where she seemed to be leading, and opened the cipher file on his laptop. He concluded that, given the predominance of evidence so far, the numbers below ten must all have had leading zeros, so he proceeded accordingly, plugging the new numbers into the file. He now had three lines with twelve numbers each and one line with thirteen:

34-11-04-35-33-00-22-03-26-13-06-53 (Grubkin)
12-41-01-24-05-42-33-53-32-60-42-12 (Atlantov)
06-44-41-15-64-06-12-04-03-63-34-43 (Stonewall)
42-22-60-45-12-06-21-53-44-16-65-12-63 (Maguire)

"Next, we have to determine the language," she said. "Do the numbers represent letters in English alphabet, or Russian? Or, even worse, are messages from Russia in Russian, and from your side in English?"

Achilles groaned. "Or, to confuse us more, they might have reversed them, and given you the English messages and given us the Russian." He got up and paced.

"Please. I hate pacing." She pulled out a cigarette and lit it.

"This is a no-smoking room. There are no ashtrays."

"You Americans and your no-smoking rules." She picked up her beer glass, which was still full of flat, stale Heineken, walked to the bathroom, dumped the beer in the toilet, and christened the glass as an ashtray. She puffed furiously on the cigarette, a serious Russian cigarette with deliciously foul-smelling tobacco. Achilles, an ex-smoker, vacillated between the impulse to get sick and the equally compelling urge to join her. Instead, he switched the fan of the room ventilation system to "high" and turned on the exhaust fan in the bathroom, cursing modern hotels and their sealed windows. Then he returned to his pacing.

"If you're smoking, I'm pacing," he said, doing his best to imitate her Russian version of English. Galina laughed and leaned back on the bed. For a moment he almost forgot the task at hand. He had an urge to pull more booze out of the wet bar, slide under the covers with her, light up one of her Russian cigarettes, pour vodka on her belly—which he assumed was as well-formed as the rest of her physique—and lap the vodka up, one tiny puddle at a time.

"Achilles?"

"What?"

"Stop dreaming about having sex with me. We have work to do."

Achilles, completely flustered by this extraordinary woman, plunked himself down at his desk and tried to concentrate on the cruel numbers that stared at him, self-satisfied and gloating in their inscrutability, but he couldn't get the image of the vodka and Galina's belly to leave his mind.

A light tap at the door interrupted his reverie. Achilles opened it, and was surprised to see a hotel bellman standing outside.

"I'm sorry, sir," the bellman said, "but this is a non-smoking floor. The other guests are complaining."

"My guest is from a foreign country. She doesn't understand our rules. I've turned all the…"

"I'm sorry, sir, but the manager says…"

A sudden firestorm of Russian invective exploded from the bed, rolled around the minor obstacle of Achilles' body, and landed full force on the uncomprehending ears of the poor bellman.

"I don't know what she's saying," the bellman said, "but if you could only explain to her…"

"She's saying she's not going to vote for the mayor in the next election."

"But I thought you said she's a foreigner…"

"Right, they vote more than we do." Achilles tried to close the door.

"But sir…," the bellman persisted, holding the door open.

"Look, I really don't have time for this now. I have important work to do. I'll put my head office in touch with your manager, if it's necessary, and they can work things out between them." Achilles shut the door firmly in the bellman's face.

"Great explosion of curses," he said to Galina. "Someday, when we have time, you might teach them to me. I'm sorry for the disruption. American hospitality." Any thought of romantic byplay had dissipated by now, and he returned to working mode. "On to the cipher. When this job is done and over, my memory banks will call up Russian tobacco and lines of numbers, in that order."

"Not me?" Galina said, now fully engaged in acting coquettish. "Shouldn't I be number one?"

"Cut it out. You're sexy and attractive, no doubt about it. I'll put you number one on the list of memories in my memory bank, if that'll make you happy. But as you just said yourself, we have to get to work."

She abruptly sat bolt upright, all business. "Just testing. I wouldn't want to work with a man who is so easily seduced."

She lit another cigarette, and they began exploring the possibilities of the cipher in earnest. They settled on a simple approach, based on the assessment Achilles made after Taos that whoever had devised the messages wanted the cipher to be tough, but not so tough that it would take forever to crack. The mastermind of these murders was trying to send a specific message, and in order for it to reach its intended audience, he had to create one that someone else could decipher. Achilles wrote the numbers in one continuous string, using the order Galina had suggested, listing the messages chronologically.

"Forty-nine numbers," Achilles said. "We can work with these, do some frequency analysis. What do you suggest? English or Russian?"

"Our wizards have had no luck in Russian. I think we should try English."

"It would go faster with a key." His eye fell on the membership list for the society she had given him. "The word SODM might be a key. Or this entire list could also be the key. The numbers in this cipher all look like potential domino numbers."

"But there are only twenty-eight dominoes, and the message has forty-nine numbers."

"But some of them are repeated. If we take out the repeats, we might get down to twenty-eight. And then, using frequency analysis, we can translate the most common numbers into the most common letters. In English, the most common letter is E, so the most common number should be the one representing E."

After a couple of hours of counting numbers, rearranging them, trying to get them to line up in some logical fashion, they were both baffled, frustrated, and hungry. The forty-nine numbers could not be reduced to twenty-eight. Removing duplicates meant the cipher contained twenty-nine unique numbers: maddeningly close to twenty-eight, but functionally useless, unless some correspondence could be found between the extra number and some unknown part of the alphabet. Russian?

"Refresh my memory. How many letters in the Russian alphabet?"

"Thirty-three."

Achilles gave up. Frequency analysis was not working, but his empty stomach was.

"It's time for a break. I'm going down to the deli on Grand Street to get some sandwiches. What's your pick?"

"One American habit I enjoy. I want a hot pastrami on rye, lots of mustard."

"Right. Drink?"

"Club soda and coffee. We need to keep alert."

"A woman after my own heart."

"In meantime, I'll rest for a minute."

He knew full well she'd be checking in with her handlers for orders, but that was to be expected. He let himself out of the room and took the elevator downstairs. When he reached the staircase that led from the elevator bank to the lower lobby, the hotel manager, cued by the bellman, came from behind his desk and approached Achilles. The manager was a tall, elegant, gentlemanly type, the kind who used to be common manning hotel front desks, but had become a rarity.

"Sir, ah, Mister Smith, may I speak to you, please? It'll only take a minute."

Damn, thought Achilles. *They just can't let go of this smoking business.*

"Look," he said, "this is important work I'm doing at the moment. I really can't be bothered with New York's damn fool smoking laws…"

"Sir, I understand your position, but…"

"Did the bellman give you my message?"

"He did, sir, but it's not necessary for your home office to call, please understand, I still have to follow the local ordinances…" He could see Achilles swelling up with anger. "Wait, I have a practical suggestion, very easy, won't cause any disruption, just give me a chance to explain."

Achilles brought himself under control. "Okay, I'm listening. Please make it fast. We're on a quick lunch break."

"We have another room, a corner room, high floor, really a beautiful room, faces northeast, you'll see the Empire State Building lit up at night, the skyline, much nicer room, and it's a smoking room, your friend can smoke all she wants, if you would just let us move you there…"

"Done. When I come back from the deli, I'll give you the high sign, and you can send your men to move me half an hour after that."

"Thank you, thank you, Mr. Smith. Thanks for your cooperation."

The manager withdrew to his post behind the desk, visibly relieved to get the anti-smoking hounds off his back.

Achilles strode out to West Broadway and took a deep breath of air. The day was really a beautiful one. Too bad he couldn't be out on the riverside walkway, strolling arm in arm with Galina, planning a spectacular night on the town. Instead he had become a temporary cipher drudge, condemned to a small, smoky hotel room, with the beautiful day mocking him through the glass of his windows.

He swung up to Grand Street and walked across to the deli. When he reached the far corner, a homeless man—a staggering, disheveled derelict, reeking of alcohol—bumped into him rudely.

"Sorry, so sorry," the man said. He could barely stand. "You got some change?"

"No, I'm afraid not." Another distraction. Achilles wanted to get back to the room, eat, crack that code. The man persisted.

"C'mon, please, help a fella out. A man's gotta eat. Can't you spare some change? A buck? A couple bucks?"

"No, dammit!"

Achilles sped up to put some distance between himself and the derelict, entered the deli, and placed his order. While he waited for it to be prepared, he went out on the doorstep for a breath of air, and saw the homeless man wander off around the corner. Achilles nearly had a change of heart, thinking he should have had the generosity to share a bit with someone so unfortunate. *Maybe I'll give him my loose change,* he thought.

"Order's ready!" yelled the counterman.

Too late to do good works for the derelict, who had vanished from sight.

Achilles went back inside to pay up and get the food. When he pulled his money clip out of his pocket, a stray piece of yellow paper fell to the floor. He hadn't remembered putting any such paper in his pocket. *What the hell is this?* he thought. He picked it up, unfolded it, and read the message scrawled on it in pencil, with tight little letters:

You and Perly. Meet me tonight at 8 p.m., colonnade at the foot of Albany St., on the river walkway.
Malcolm

CHAPTER TWENTY-SIX

Malcolm! The derelict had been Malcolm in disguise, and he had shoved the note into Achilles' pocket! Achilles raced out of the deli onto the street.

"Hey! Mister! Your food!" the counterman yelled after him.

Achilles ran up to the corner and looked north on West Broadway, the last direction he had seen the derelict taking. No sign of him. Ran north for two more blocks, stopping at each corner to scan the side streets, but still no sign of Malcolm. He had evaporated.

Thoroughly winded and dejected, Achilles trudged back to the deli.

"Thought you weren't coming back," the counterman said. "I was about to put this stuff away."

"Sorry. Had to catch up with a friend. He walked away with my lottery ticket."

"Oh, gotcha. No wonder you lit outta here."

Achilles paid for the food and took it back to the hotel. The manager, eagerly awaiting his arrival, waved expectantly.

"Half an hour," Achilles said.

The manager called the bellman over to the desk and began giving him instructions.

"You took your time," Galina said when he came back into the room.

"Wanted to give you enough time to make a full report to your handlers."

"What's wrong? You seem winded."

"Nothing. I'm all right. A thief tried to pick my pocket, and I made the mistake of running after him. He didn't get anything." He opened the deli bag and started pulling out their food. "We need to eat up, then I have to pack. Hotel staff is moving us to another room."

"Why?"

"They are really on a tear about the smoking. They've offered me a better room, higher floor, where smoking is allowed, and I've accepted it on your behalf, so you won't feel constrained." He handed her sandwich to her, followed by the can of club soda and container of coffee. She gazed at him quizzically, holding the transfer of goods in a state of suspended animation. "No, I'm not being sarcastic. We have work to do, and if smoking helps you think, I'm all for it. And I don't want any more interruptions."

Galina smiled and put her lunch on the nightstand. "Thank you."

Slowly, surely, an element of trust had begun to enter their relationship. He may not be able to tell her about Malcolm being in town, but at least he could look after her comfort.

They had just finished eating when there was a knock at the door. Achilles opened it, and three bellmen presented themselves.

"Give me a minute," he said. "I have to throw my stuff together."

He could see the bellmen eyeing Galina appreciatively while they waited.

Achilles followed a strict rule on road assignments: be ready to leave on ninety seconds' notice. He lived, literally, out of a hanger bag and suitcase, even stashing his toothbrush there every night, so he threw the few loose items into his luggage, packed the computer, and signaled the bellmen to proceed. They loaded the luggage on a cart and made their way to the elevator bank. Achilles followed, carrying his computer, with Galina walking beside him. As they entered the elevator, he could feel her slip a hand into the crook of his arm. He steeled himself against another upwelling of desire that threatened to derail him, if he let it.

The bellmen tried their best to keep their eyes off Galina, but were helpless in her presence. Not that she flirted with them; her innate sense of royalty pulled their attention to her like a magnet, yet she managed to ignore them as if they didn't exist, even though each one towered over her.

Fourteenth floor, room 1485. The promised view of the Empire State Building. It really was a better location, even though the furniture, the bedding, and the drapes reeked of cigarette smoke. He would probably get sick from it, but *what the hell,* he thought, *all in the name of country.* He turned on the fans, then rebooted the laptop so they could get back to work.

"I need to call Perly, tell him we've moved." He dialed Perly on the cell phone.

"Lyman," came the quick response.

"Perly, it's Achilles. How are things going at the precinct?"

"Almost finished. Great bunch of guys. I've got some goodies for you—but not on the phone."

"Right, that's why I'm calling, so you know where to find me. Galina wants to smoke, so the hotel has moved us to a different room. We're in 1485 now. Opposite corner of the hotel." He wanted to tell Perly about Malcolm's note, but couldn't in front of Galina.

"Got you. We'll be there in a few."

The computer finished loading its applets, and finally Achilles had a usable screen. He opened the cipher file and took another look at the work they had done before the lunch break.

"First thing I want to do is see if the short pony cipher is a key to the long cipher."

The pony cipher read: 33-02-50-16. If 33 stood for S, 02 stood for O, 50 stood for D, and 16 stood for M, then the long cipher, with the key letters plugged in, would be:

34-11-04-35-**S**-00-22-03-26-13-06-53-
12-41-01-24-05-42-**S**-53-32-60-42-12-
06-44-41-15-64-06-12-04-03-63-34-43-
42-22-60-45-12-06-21-53-44-**M**-65-12-63.

He quickly calculated by what percentage each letter occurred in the message—S, four percent, O and D, zero percent, M, two percent—and compared the results with his frequency table for the English alphabet. According to it, both S and O should occur between seven and eight percent of the time, and both D and M should have a frequency of three to four percent.

No match. Either the pony cipher wasn't a key, or the key was trickier than it appeared. Or, perhaps, the key was in one language and the main cipher in another.

"Damn," Achilles muttered.

"Yes?" Galina had been waiting patiently for him to finish.

"No correspondence. Four percent frequency, zero percent, zero percent, two percent, when it should be seven, eight, three, four percent. It's not working."

"Let me see."

Achilles paced while Galina sat at the computer and pondered the cipher. After a few minutes she leaned back and lit a cigarette.

"This is not worth pursuing. I suggest we concentrate on the table that has membership of the society, and use those domino numbers. That seems more promising to me."

"Fine. In fact, why don't you take over for a while? The neurons in my brain have wrapped themselves around each other and can't find a clear path to anything." He flopped on the bed and let himself slide into a state of relaxation while Galina hunted and pecked at his keyboard.

Malcolm would be furious, he thought as he drifted off to sleep. Letting an agent from the SVR have free access to an RZ laptop—the very concept was unthinkable. He'd be fired, sent to prison for compromising national security. If he wound up in jail, at least let it be for a good reason, like taking the enemy agent to bed with him. Would anyone in the Ring believe he had met his end by snoozing on a bed while a foreign agent hunted and pecked at his laptop, sitting at his desk three feet away? No one would accept such a palpably unrealistic story...

A knock at the door roused him from his trance.

"Perly," he muttered, too spent to get up.

"Stay, I'll get it," Galina went to the door and opened it.

Perly and Lauren burst in as before, out of breath and excited.

"Nice room," Perly said.

"Stinks," Lauren said.

"Yes, Moscow sewer gas is injected into Russian tobacco," Galina said. "Leaves unmistakable trail in case we are kidnapped."

For half a second they believed her. Then all four of them laughed.

"Beer," Perly said.

"Seltzer," Lauren said.

They raided the new wet bar and poured themselves drinks.

"Well?" Achilles said. "What news from the front?"

"Frank has his tentacles out, trackin' down farriers," Perly said. "So far, nothin'. And he's made calls to every mounted unit in the city, to see if anyone had troops downtown that night. Precinct One did not. Frank says it wouldn't be normal for another precinct to send MUs into One's territory, but it's not out of the question—lot of calls were put out that night. Take him a while to find out. But that's not the big news."

"What is?" Achilles said.

"Follow-up to Lauren's report. Since Malcolm has gone AWOL, his instruction not to call home is inoperative, like I said. So I called Mary Sue at Ring Zero. I figured if anyone had some news she would, and she responds to my charms."

"Wait a minute," Achilles said. "I need my own beer. Galina?"

She shook her head *no* and glared at him disapprovingly, but he opened one anyway.

"Okay, spill it," he said. "I'm all ears."

"Well, here's what the Senate committee and the White House didn't get told. Karl came to visit Malcolm late yesterday afternoon, and they had a blowout, a major scream-war, in Malcolm's office. People could hear 'em havin' at each other through the door—then Karl comes bustin' out, says somethin' threatening to Malcolm—I'll piss on your grave—like that." Perly stopped to take a swig of beer. Lauren paced nervously at the window, waiting for him to get on with the story. Achilles and Galina also waited, spellbound.

"So then," Perly said, after taking down half the glass, "Malcolm calls in Craig, his chief of staff, for a conference. Briefs him, then calls the director of national intelligence. Late last night the DNI sends out a memo to the heads of all the clandestine services." Perly took another swig. "Lauren, you got the paper?"

She walked over from the window to her bag, which she had deposited on the easy chair by the door, and pulled out a piece of paper.

"We had Mary Sue fax this to us at the precinct," she said. "Sorry for the security breach, but we stood over the fax machine so no one else could read it."

She handed Achilles the paper.

"Good God," he said as he read it.

"What is it?" Galina said. "What does it say?"

"Karl has been put on administrative leave. He's been locked out of his office and is forbidden to enter any high-security areas of the government."

CHAPTER TWENTY-SEVEN

"So we got to figure out what to do," Perly said. "We're on our own, at least for now."

Achilles had to make a decision. Should he discuss Malcolm's note openly with Perly, in the presence of the two women, or should he take the risk of arousing their suspicions by pulling Perly into a sidebar? The rules of risk assessment ran though his head, like lemons and cherries in a slot machine: you have to decide who needs to know, who can be trusted, and whether the people who can be trusted are the same as the people who need to know.

Malcolm obviously wanted his whereabouts to be a closely kept secret, even from Lauren. Supposedly she was part of his inner circle, but perhaps Malcolm feared that once she knew he was in the neighborhood posing as a derelict, she would put her White House position first and have him rounded up. So that left her out of the loop, at least for now. Galina, with her efficient Russian friends, might already know Malcolm's whereabouts. She might have been informed by telephone while Achilles went to the deli. But, era of cooperation or not, he felt no obligation to be the one who told her. This was RZ internal business, and the SVR had no need or right to be informed.

Then there was the issue of Malcolm himself, and the fight with Karl. One or both of them had gone off the deep end. Clearly an entrenched rivalry existed between them, which had come to a head for some reason—now, of all times, stranding a team in the field on a critical mission. Malcolm, at least, had made an effort to reach them. Yet did that mean he could be blindly trusted? What if he had been involved with these murders himself? Maybe he was a member of the society; he could even be the missing name, the 00 on the list, Karl had found him out, and Malcolm had swept in with a preemptive strike. In which case Malcolm could be using Perly and Achilles to forward his own private agenda.

But the same could be said of Karl. He could be the one up to black tricks, and Malcolm had found him out. How could Achilles and Perly, here in New York, trying to keep an investigation together, possibly sort all this out? For now, they could do nothing. They'd have to wait for the meeting with Malcolm, see what he had to say. And Achilles would have to find some way to update Perly about Malcolm's note without letting the women know.

"Achilles," Galina said. "Are you daydreaming?"

"Sorry," he said, snapping out of slot machine mode. "Trying to sort out the next move."

"Come up with anything?" Perly said.

"Uh, not yet. What I do know is that there's nothing we can do about a power struggle taking place above our pay grade. Maybe we should get ready for the 5:30 meeting at the precinct, and we'll figure out what to do after that." He might get a chance to pull Perly aside during the walk to the precinct. Or Lauren and Galina might go to the ladies' room together. "For now, I guess we should show you what we've managed to do so far with the cipher."

He had them gather around the computer screen and explained to them the variations on a theme that constituted his and Galina's attempts to crack the cipher.

"We've decided to leave the pony cipher to one side," he said as he finished.

"What's the next step?" Lauren said.

"Where were you headed, Galina?" Achilles said.

"Membership list of the society. I think list of dominoes is the key. Here, let me show you." She pulled a pad out of her bag and set to work drawing a quick grid. "Forgive me, Achilles. I work better with pencil and paper."

"Your choice."

Galina drew some characters in her grid, and then showed it to the rest of them.

"Here," she said. "Starting with double zero, going through double six, assign a letter to each domino. Double zero is A." She filled in the blanks the rest of the way down the grid. "Zero one is B, and so on, up through double five, which is Z."

"What do you do with the 5-6 and the double six?" Achilles said.

Galina chewed on the eraser of her pencil. "Maybe they're jokers, wild cards. Or maybe they stand for numbers instead of letters."

"But that only leaves room for two numbers. Maybe there's some kind of Caesar shift. The double zero at the beginning and the double six at the end could be the wild cards or punctuation marks, and the letters start with the zero one."

Lauren and Perly looked at each other in dismay.

"So nice that the two of you have somethin' in common," Perly said. "Lauren and I are goin' to my room to make some calls. We want to see what more we can find out about the putsch back home."

"Fine," Achilles said. "Not everyone can get excited about ciphers."

"You said that, ole buddy. I didn't."

Perly and Lauren roared with laughter, then headed for the door, cackling. Before they reached it, Lauren's cell phone rang.

"Vogel here." She sat in the chair by the window, took out her pad, and jotted down some notes while she listened. As before, she had little to say, just kept scribbling frantically on her pad. At one point she mouthed "sorry" to the others.

Finally, she signed off and snapped her phone shut. "We have a fix on Sam Rains's fingerprints. Anchorage police had them on file. He was picked up seven months ago for illegal entry, and released on bail—paid by a local businessman. The court scheduled a hearing for late March, but he didn't show up."

"Illegal entry?" Perly said. "From where?"

"Russia. He came across the strait, did some island-hopping with a wave-skipping smuggler, you know, single-engine planes flying under the radar, all that. ICE had a tag out on this particular smuggler, so Sam got caught."

"Amazing. ICE actually caught somebody."

"ICE?" Galina said.

"Immigration and Customs Enforcement," Perly said. "Used to be called INS."

"What does the businessman say, the one who provided bail?" Achilles said.

"They can't locate him. Closed his business and left."

"What was the business?"

She paused to look at her notes. "Tourist trinkets. Native American goodies, scrimshaw. Also some Army-Navy surplus, both American and Russian. Now here comes the best part. The businessman's name was Sam Rains. The person we know as Sam Rains has a Russian name. Yuri Pribilof."

"Made up," Galina said. "He took most obvious name possible. If he had been going in other direction, he would have called himself John Smith." Achilles gave silent thanks to his mother for her foresight. "He must be Siberian Yupik," Galina continued. "Do they have his Yupik name?"

"Our people are in touch with your people to find out," Lauren said. "We don't have it yet."

"Well, we're out of here," Perly said. "Lauren wants to fresh up before the 5:30 meeting, right, Lauren?"

Lauren looked at him fondly, and then they were gone.

Achilles and Galina returned to the cipher. Achilles studied Galina's chart, comparing the numbers on it to the numbers in the long cipher.

"This looks encouraging," he said, "but there's another problem with it, in addition to the mismatch of twenty-six letters to twenty-eight numbers."

"Which is?"

"Some of the numbers in this cipher go the other way. For instance, the fourth number is 35, which would be the 3-5 domino; but the twelfth number is 53, which has to be the same domino flipped. The same domino would have to stand for two different letters—or the code-writer simply flipped the numbers and used two numbers for the same letter, in order to confuse us."

Galina furrowed her brow, chewed on her pencil, and went back to work. "So we expand the table," she said, filling in blanks as she talked. "Two lists of dominoes. One we have already. The other, with numbers reversed. Doubles are on both lists, same number on each end of the domino."

"So instead of twenty-eight dominoes, there are fifty-six. Now we have room to add digits. But there are no names to go with the reversed numbers."

"Achilles, there must be second list of names," Galina said quietly, without looking up from her work. "And if you take out doubles—I don't mean take them out altogether, but you count them once, not twice—if you add up possible combinations of numbers, after you reverse the dominoes, there are forty-nine. Forty-nine combinations. And there are forty-nine letters in the cipher." She could barely contain her excitement. "I think this is the right approach."

Achilles took the sheet from her and looked at it. She had arranged the lists in two different sequences. The duplicated doubles were not assigned letters on the second list.

"This is good," he said. "Let's see what happens if we add zero through nine at the beginning, then run the letters." He drew an empty table on his computer and plugged in the boxes according to her new plan. When he finished, he showed it to her:

00	01	02	03	04	05	06	11	12	13	14	15	16	22	23	24	25	26	33	34	35	36	44	45	46	55	56	66
A	B	C	D	E	F	G	H	I	J	K	L	M	N	O	P	Q	R	S	T	U	V	W	X	Y	Z	0	1
00	10	20	30	40	50	60	11	21	31	41	51	61	22	32	42	52	62	33	43	53	63	44	54	64	55	65	66
	2	3	4	5	6	7		8	9	A	B	C		D	E	F	G		H	I	J		K	L		M	

"I think we should pursue this," she said. "It looks promising."

"All right. Let's get to work. We can test it against the pony cipher."

"I thought we had given up on that."

"If this works for the pony cipher, it should work for the long cipher. It's probably there as a test."

Adopting her pen-and-paper technique, he wrote down the numbers of the pony cipher: 33-02-50-16. "According to the chart, number 33 should be an I. And number 2 should be the digit 2. Number 50 is a W, and 16 is a C." He threw down the pencil in disgust. "This is hopeless."

"Let's try it on the longer cipher."

"What's the point? If it's this far off on the pony cipher, how can it possibly work on the long cipher?"

"I have an instinct. I just feel this is right approach. You take last twenty-five numbers, the Kean and Maguire ciphers. I'll take one through twenty-four, Grubkin and Atlantov."

They retired to their different spaces, he to the desk, she to the chair by the window, and began scribbling ardently. Galina was so excited that she forgot to smoke, which was a welcome relief to Achilles. Within a few minutes they had plugged in the characters, and put their two sets of numbers back together:

J-7-4-K-I-0-D-3-H-9-6-1-8-A-1-F-5-E-I-I-D-X-E-8-6-M-A-
B-O-6-8-4-3-J-J-H-E-D-X-N-8-6-Y-I-M-C-M-8-J.

"Garbage," Achilles said. "Nothing but garbage." He checked his watch. "We'll get back to this later. Right now we need to go over to the precinct for the meeting. I'll buzz Perly."

"Achilles, wait. I need to make a call before we go. I think there may be clues in second list of names."

"Checking with your home team to see if they have it?"

"They would have told me. I need to have them start looking for it. You go ahead and call Perly."

While he arranged to meet Perly and Lauren on the sidewalk outside the lobby, Galina spoke to her handlers to start the search for a second list. Then they packed up to leave. Achilles had to wait a moment while Galina reorganized her bag and put on a new set of earrings.

"What's wrong with the old earrings?" he said.

"They're hurting me."

"Why not wear no earrings?"

"Not possible. A woman must have earrings."

Finally she had put herself in order, and they went downstairs.

————

"Funny thing happened after we left you," Perly said on the way to the precinct as they walked behind the women.

"What was that?" Achilles said.

"I went out to the deli for a sandwich. Ran into a derelict—really aggressive. Had to fight him off."

"That so? Did he try to pick your pocket?"

"Yeah," Perly said. Achilles could tell that Perly was dying to tell him something, but couldn't.

"Did he get anything?"

"No. Chased him a block or two, and then—don't know how to describe it—he vaporized, almost. Disappeared."

"That guy is working the neighborhood," Achilles said with a wink. "I had the same thing happen earlier."

Perly winked back. They could relax about one thing, at least. They knew they had both received the same message from Malcolm.

CHAPTER TWENTY-EIGHT

"I hate to bring this up," Perly said to the other three as they approached the precinct, "but we have to decide how much we want to dish out at this meeting."

"Don't you think we should keep what we know to ourselves?" Achilles said.

"I agree," Lauren said.

"Not so fast," Perly said. "There's the business of those two photos, and the cop on the horse. Bernardo is sure to say somethin' about the search for farriers, and he'll talk about any mounted unit assignments. Frank likes to share. That stuff comes out whether we want it to or not, unless we get to him first and ask him to wire his jaw."

"And he'll want to know why we want him to keep quiet," Lauren mused.

"You got it. And that'll singe our whiskers, 'cause the first thing he'll do is tell Ramirez we're tryin' to keep evidence to ourselves."

"I thought you worked with him before, on WTC One," Achilles said.

"I did, and he's a good cop, but he goes by the book."

"Maybe," Lauren said, "we should actually take the opposite approach. Since we think Mikhail is up to funny stuff with the doctored photo, we should try to smoke him out."

"I like that," Perly said.

They had reached the corner across from the precinct.

"Galina? You haven't said anything," Achilles said.

"I think it's obvious. We have to reveal some things. Those things Frank Bernardo knows already—the photographs, the horseshoe—we can bring up. But there are some things we should not mention, especially the Russian murders, or the hearing at the Senate closing early, or the fact that your Malcolm Evers is here in New York, disguised as a homeless derelict."

Achilles and Perly looked at each other, astounded.

"What?" Lauren said. "Would you repeat that, please?" Her cheeks reddened with anger, and her lips were compressed like a stern Victorian schoolmarm's.

"Oh, I think the two gentlemen know it already, am I right, Achilles?"

Achilles refused to answer. He averted his eyes and shrugged helplessly.

"Galina, what are you talking about?" Lauren demanded.

"We have saying in SVR. When we follow a man, we know everything it is possible to know. We know where he sleeps at night and what he eats for breakfast. I'm sorry, but if the four of us are to work together, we must be completely open. If we are not, we will fail at our job. Have I made my point?" she said, smiling sweetly at Achilles.

"Let's go to the meeting," Achilles harrumphed.

"You two have a lot of explaining to do," Lauren hissed to Perly as they crossed the street.

"That must have been some phone call you had while I was at the deli," Achilles said to Galina.

"It was—informative."

The desk sergeant, used to them by now, waved them upstairs. The others were just gathering around the table as they entered. To Achilles' surprise, Ramirez had already returned from Washington.

"Justino," Perly said. "We thought you…"

"The hearing adjourned before it started," he said curtly. "I'll talk to you later, after this meeting."

"Aren't we missing some people?" Achilles said. "Jeshua Lin, where's he?"

"He's up at the Chinese mission, dealing with their security for the summit. They're getting increasingly nervous, especially since their mission is so close to the Javits Center."

"What about Phil Levitan?"

"He's with the mayor at City Hall. They're holding a press conference to discuss the summit. Now, anything to report?" He looked at Achilles. "How's the hunt for the code going?"

"We're making progress, but it's slow. We're not ready to go into details yet."

"I suppose we'll get the details when it's too late, after there's been another murder." Ramirez made some notes on his pad, ignoring the furious energy directed his way by Achilles. Then he turned to Bernardo. "Frank?" he said, in his best business-as-usual manner.

"These folks here have found out some useful information," Bernardo said. "A doctored photograph showed up of Maguire's body being taken out of the dumpster. There are two versions of the same photo. In one, there's a trooper from a mounted unit in the background. In the other, the trooper has been erased out."

Achilles pretended to focus on Frank, but kept an eye on Mikhail across the table so he could see his reaction. He had stopped writing real notes and taken to doodling on his pad.

"So we are going through the records to determine if any horse troopers were on duty in the area that night," Frank continued. "We know for sure there weren't any from Precinct One. I should get a full report from the other precincts later tonight."

"Okay," Ramirez said, looking at Brian. "What about you, Brian, do you have anything?"

"Wait a minute, there's more," Frank said, passing around a photograph of the horseshoe Achilles had found. "This is a picture we took this morning—it's of a thrown horseshoe, origin unknown. It has the traction dots we use in the NYPD for our mounted units, but the number of dots is not consistent with NYPD practice."

"Where did this shoe come from?" Ramirez said.

"Achilles, here, found it near the dumpster," Frank said.

"And I still have it," Achilles said. He noted with satisfaction that Mikhail's doodling had become agitated, as if he were trying to spear a fruit fly with the lead of his gold pencil.

"You couldn't bring it to Andy?" Ramirez snapped at Achilles.

"I thought the easiest thing was to show it to Frank's stable men. Quickest way to get an answer about NYPD practice, don't you think?"

Ramirez was obviously furious. He bore down on his pencil with so much pressure that he broke the point. "So you have a horseshoe with bumps," he said to Frank. "May or may not be NYPD."

"Definitely not NYPD," Frank said.

"Okay, it could be from a hansom cab."

"They use rubber padding on their shoes, not borium dots," Achilles said.

"Now you're the horseshoe expert too," Ramirez said.

"I'm simply telling you what Abe, downstairs, told us."

"Anything else on the shoe?" Ramirez asked Frank.

"That's it for now," Frank replied.

Ramirez grabbed Andy's pencil and continued to write notes, but he quickly broke that one also. "Brian!" he barked, hurling the pieces of pencil at a trash basket. "Do you have anything?"

At that moment, Phil Levitan entered. "Hello, everybody, sorry I'm late."

The others murmured hellos, except Mikhail, who continued his agitated doodling and did not look up.

"Interesting thing came up at the mayor's press conference," Phil said as he took his seat.

"Brian's about to give a report," Ramirez said.

"This'll only take a minute. One of the reporters from Fox asked if we knew anything about the Senate hearing down in Washington breaking up early."

"What? How the hell did they find out about that? It was supposed to be a secret briefing."

"You know Fox," Phil said. "The point is, they asked the mayor if he knew why the head of the new Pentagon secret service didn't show up, and they wanted to know how that might affect the security at the G8 summit."

All eyes were now focused on Achilles and Perly, waiting for an explanation.

"Why are y'all lookin' at us?" Perly said. "We're as whapped as the rest of you."

"We've been here, working on this case," Achilles said. "The Ring Zero switchboard doesn't call every agent in the field to explain that the governor has or has not testified before a secret Senate hearing."

"Did the press give a reason for the mystery man not showing up?" Perly asked Phil.

"How would they know?"

"Seems to me," Perly said, "that since they most always know things before we do, they might be one up on that too."

"They said he called in sick. That got a big laugh."

Ramirez, who had become increasingly fidgety during Phil's question-and-answer period, shoved his chair back noisily and gestured toward Perly and Achilles to come with him.

"Gentlemen, ladies, would you please excuse us a minute?" He held the door for the RZ men, then followed them into the hallway.

"What gives?" Perly said when they were well out of earshot of the room.

"I thought we had this discussion during the first meeting," Ramirez said. "Didn't I tell you guys, no freelancing?"

"And I thought I made it clear that we don't take our orders from you," Perly said.

"Who do you take them from, then? Your boss is missing, nowhere to be found. It appears to me, gentlemen, that you are fish out of water. Without a proper reporting structure, without superiors who can forward your information to the right channels, you're not much use in this investigation. I think your time here is done."

"Not so fast," Perly said. "Until we get told contrariwise by someone who has the authority, we follow the last set of standing orders we received from Malcolm. You don't slide the ice under us that easy."

"We'll see about that. In my opinion, you're a detriment to a working investigation, going outside normal accountability and procedures. For now, I have no choice but to continue as before, at least until I can straighten this out with Washington. I can tell you that my recommendation will be to separate you from the investigation."

"Were we a detriment when we discovered a fake photo and a discarded horseshoe, both of which your hotshots in blue jackets missed?" Achilles said.

"You didn't coordinate," Ramirez said. "I told you we must have full coordination."

"So," Perly said, "let me see if I got this straight—the act of coordinatin' nothing is more important to you than findin' actual information, does that about say it?"

"Cut the shit, Lyman. You know damned well what I mean."

At that moment the door to the room opened and Mikhail came out, carrying his attaché case. "Please excuse me," he said. "I just got a message from the office. I have to go."

"Tomorrow, 8 a.m.," Ramirez said.

"Absolutely, I'll be here." Mikhail threw Achilles one last glance before he went down the stairs.

"We'll go back in now, and continue the meeting," Ramirez said. "But bear in mind that the phone call may come at any moment, removing you two from the investigation."

"Someone's got to appoint an interim governor," Perly said. "*If* the word is that Malcolm's really AWOL. Maybe he's actually sick, in a hospital bed somewhere, have you considered that possibility? Until we hear otherwise we follow Malcolm's orders, you get me, Ramirez?"

"And Justino," Achilles said. "There's another thing. Without us, you don't break the cipher."

"Fuck you and your cipher," Ramirez said as he headed back to the room. "In fact, maybe *you're* the cipher. You aren't producing squat anyway. By the time you figure it out we'll already have the answer some other way."

Achilles was boiling with rage. Perly stopped him from going into the room, and pinned him to the wall.

"Keep your head, man, keep your head," Perly said. "Don't let him diddle you that way."

"Bad as my ex," Achilles fumed. "I had to come to New York to meet up with Phyllis again."

"Relax, ole buddy, breathe deep." Perly had his hands on Achilles' shoulders, applying a gentle pressure that slowly calmed his partner down.

"Are you coming?" Ramirez bellowed from the room.

"I'm okay," Achilles said to Perly. "Let's leave it. We can get Lauren's people to stomp on him later."

Perly smiled and slapped Achilles playfully on the cheek. Then they returned to the room. They couldn't hide the fact that they were both steamed. The FBI man and the RZ men had now become full-blown enemies. Achilles felt relieved to see the friendly eyes of Galina searching his, trying to judge from his demeanor what had taken place in the hall. Another irony, he thought, similar to the one he had clocked back in the hotel room, when he was losing consciousness on the bed while she tapped away on his laptop: in this version, the face of an SVR agent made him happier than the mug of an FBI colleague.

Time to lighten things up, he thought. "Phil," he said, "I've had an issue come up, and I'm wondering if you could speak to the mayor about it for me."

"Sure. What is it?"

"The smoking laws. Our Russian friend, here, likes to smoke. She can't find anywhere legal in New York City to light up. Could you explain to His Honor that he's on the verge of creating an international incident, ask him if he can put in some exemptions?"

"Impossible. He's committed. The health lobby would crucify him."

"Ask him if the health lobby is bigger than the Brighton Beach Russian lobby."

Everyone laughed, except Ramirez. Then, back to business.

"Okay," Ramirez said. "Enough joking. We were waiting for Brian to give us a report."

"Yes," Brian said. "I think we've found something significant. We went up to Scarsdale to interview Mrs. Maguire. She found some stuff in her husband's desk that might be relevant to the investigation—notes about buying a horse, meeting the seller the following week, which happens to be the week he was murdered. But no specific date or time."

"So you think," Ramirez said, "that when he left the Exchange without telling anyone his destination, that's what he was doing?"

"It's a possibility. The guard said he heard him whistling 'Call to the Post' when he left the building, remember? Mrs. Maguire told us he had talked for years about actually owning a horse, not just betting on them. She disapproved, and argued with him about it. So he kept things like that secret from her."

"This is just great," Ramirez said sarcastically. "I can see the news zipper at the bottom of the TV screen: 'Maguire Murder: Went to see a man about a horse.'"

Everyone laughed except Galina. "I don't understand," she said.

"Old joke," Achilles said. "In the days when people still had manners, men used that phrase in mixed company when they had to excuse themselves to go to the toilet."

"So," Ramirez said with finality, "is there anything else?"

"One more thing," Lauren said. "We have a fix on Sam Rains's fingerprints."

Achilles cursed under his breath. He would have relished seeing Mikhail's reaction to this news—he was supposed to be checking on Sam Rains's fingerprints himself. Too late. He had left already. As Lauren recounted the facts about Sam, his fingerprints, and his illegal entry, Achilles drifted off, thinking about what Mikhail might know, or how he might be tied in with the wrong side of this situation. Perly was similarly occupied, so Galina jolted them both when she spoke up with an assertive, adamant tone.

"I wish to speak here for my service, the SVR," she said to Ramirez. "We are grateful for the cooperation and assistance from your side."

"No problem," Ramirez said. "Always glad to help. Who knows? Maybe we can bring back the good old days of World War Two."

"Yes, but World War Two became Cold War," Galina said. "Let's hope that doesn't happen again."

"Probably up to your side. Try staying out of Georgia. That would help." Before she could respond, Ramirez turned to the others. "Is that all?"

"But wait," Galina said sharply. "I am not finished."

Ramirez, thwarted at every turn, hunkered down in his chair and tapped his pencil on his tablet.

"What I want to say," Galina said, "is that I have developed very good working relationship with these two gentlemen, Mr. Lyman, Mr. Smith, and with Miss Vogel from your White House." Achilles noted with satisfaction that Galina put a great deal of emphasis on the words *White House*. "And I hope, for the duration of this—emergency, I guess we must call it—for the duration, I hope to continue working with them. My service would not be pleased if I lost time establishing some other relationship, especially when time is of the essence, as your people like to say."

Ramirez snapped his pencil in two. "Fine. We'll take it under advisement."

As the meeting broke up, Ramirez hung back to talk to Andy, Phil, and Brian. Frank Bernardo told Perly and Achilles that he had nothing further to report, but he'd call the minute he had any news.

Once they were safely across the street, Achilles let fly with the burning question of the moment.

"How, in God's name, did you know what happened out in the hallway?" he said to Galina. "Were you just guessing?"

Galina smiled and said nothing.

"Come on, Galina, level with me. I mean, it was great to have your backing, but how did you know?"

"Don't be so sure it was great," Perly said. "Could singe our whiskers. Maybe the FBI can convince somebody the SVR is too eager to have us working on the case."

"Don't worry about that," Lauren said. "Why do you think you're here? Why do you think I'm here? The FBI couldn't even catch that fugitive millionaire wanted for rape a while back. A bounty hunter found him first."

"Okay, okay," Achilles said. "But none of this answers my question. Galina, how did you know?"

"Have you looked at your change recently?"

"Not since the deli."

"Pull it out, take a look."

Achilles retrieved his pocket change. A couple of nickels, three dimes, two quarters, some pennies.

"A few pieces of small change," he said.

"That quarter," she said, pointing to one of them. "Take closer look."

Achilles brought the quarter up close and inspected it. He could see nothing unusual about it.

"It's just a quarter."

"Okay," she said, taking off her right earring. "Now I hold quarter, and you put earring next to ear."

Achilles handed her the quarter, took the earring, and put it next to his ear.

"Hello, Achilles," he heard Galina's voice saying in his ear as she spoke softly with the quarter close to her mouth. "Do you understand now?"

Achilles laughed, and passed the earring around to the others.

"Great trick," he said, when they were through playing with Galina's portable bug system. "But what happens when I spend the quarter?"

"We deactivate it. Then plant new one. Plenty more where that came from."

They made their way back to the hotel, so they could lay plans for dinner. Achilles was mindful that he and Perly had to meet Malcolm at 8 p.m. Since the women now knew the truth about Malcolm, the two agents would have to arrange a short break from the group, so they could keep their appointment.

CHAPTER TWENTY-NINE

By the time they had reached the hotel, Achilles could feel the rumblings of hunger in his stomach.

"Why don't we eat now?" he said. "It's already 6:30, and Malcolm told Perly and me to meet him at eight."

"What about me?" Lauren said. "I thought I was supposed to be his contact."

Achilles shrugged. "If you didn't get a note from him, I guess you're not included. We'll ask him about you."

Lauren exhaled loudly, compressed her lips, and resorted to snapping her bag open and shut in agitation.

"There's a Tandoori restaurant over there, on the corner," Perly said, trying to shift the focus from Lauren's place in the pecking order. "Let's eat there. You eat Indian, Galina?"

"If they have some food not too spicy, okay."

Dinner did not go well. Lauren continued to fume over the slight of being excluded from a meeting with Malcolm. Galina, sensing that the other three had a problem to work out, remained silent and picked at her food, which obviously didn't agree with her in any case. Eventually, after an awkward hour of desultory small talk, they settled on a plan for the evening. Lauren, nursing hurt feelings, wanted to soak in her tub at the hotel. Galina needed to change clothes. Since they still had urgent work to do, they agreed to reconvene at 10 p.m. in Achilles' room, so the men could give a report on the meeting with Malcolm; then Achilles and Galina would work on the cipher, and Perly and Lauren could follow up with the precinct about mounted units and farriers. Frank Bernardo had given them twenty-four hour contact information.

As they came out of the restaurant, Achilles put his arm around Lauren's shoulder.

"Everything okay?" he said.

"No—but we'll discuss it later. After I've had my own chance to talk to Malcolm." She wriggled out from under his arm and walked ahead of the others.

"I might as well drop my laptop off at the room," Achilles said to Perly. "No need to carry it everywhere."

"You kidding? You think Malcolm won't want to see where you are with the cipher?"

"I'll pick up Galina's paper and show him that. And we should ask the concierge how to get to this Albany Street."

Entering the hotel lobby, they saw a crowd of people in catering uniforms waiting at the elevator bank in the upper lobby, full of excitement like school kids on a tour, and not at all shy about showing it. They were babbling loudly in Russian.

"What the hey!" Perly said. "What gives? An invasion?"

"Wait," Galina said. She went up the staircase to the elevator bank and engaged one of the caterers in conversation.

While Galina bonded with her fellow Russians and Perly tried to soothe Lauren's still-ruffled feelings, Achilles asked the concierge for directions to Albany Street.

"Across West Street, in Battery Park City, near the riverside promenade," the concierge said. "Look for the dead end and the colonnade. You can't miss it. The cab driver will know where to take you."

"Thanks," Achilles said.

The elevators swallowed the Russian caterers, and Galina came back down the stairs.

"Well, this is interesting. Perhaps we need to rethink plans." She motioned for the others to follow her out of the lobby, onto the sidewalk.

"What is it?" Achilles said when they were outside. "What's the deal?"

"Entire penthouse floor has been rented for the night," she said. "One of our New Russian oligarchs is throwing party. Vladimir Grigorieff is his name."

"Which one is he?" Perly said.

"He's very aggressive, helped push first generation of oligarchs into disfavor. Owns autos, steel, timber, maybe some gold mines, I'm not sure. Anyway, plenty rich. He is here to monitor the summit, and tonight is his big party. *Big* party, do you get my meaning?"

"You mean we should crash it," Lauren said.

"Crash?" Galina said.

"Show up uninvited."

"What's the point?" Achilles said. "Don't we have work to do on the cipher?"

"Achilles," Galina said, with some impatience. "Bring your gaze up from sheet with numbers, and think of the larger picture. Didn't we just find out Sam Rains is really from Russia? Don't we suspect Mikhail of trying to spoil our investigation? Why would he do that? Is he dyed-in-wool Communist, seeking to bring old times back? Or is it possible someone has bought him? These are questions we need to answer. My instincts say we 'crash' the party." She smiled broadly, proud of herself at her quick pickup of a new slang word.

"They'll all be speaking Russian!" Achilles objected.

"Not so. Maybe some. Party has specific purpose. Grigorieff is trying to raise money for new project of his. Plenty of Americans there with money, people eager to part with their extra cash, give it to slick-tongued Russian entrepreneur." She laughed gleefully.

"What's the project?" Perly said.

"Racing cars. He is developing new Formula One from scratch, as you say."

"I'm not tracking your plan," Achilles said. "What does Formula One have to do with what we're investigating?"

"He is entrepreneur. Like your old robber barons. He enjoys fast cars, excitement. I think we might find something useful if we go there. Besides, I *must* go. Whether you come with me or not, I must." Her eyes glowed with a steely intensity that would brook no disagreement.

Achilles exchanged glances with Perly. He should have realized immediately that she would be under orders to check out any Russians who showed up for the summit. Perly's return glance said *yes*.

"You've convinced us," Achilles said. "Makes perfect sense. We're with you."

Galina sighed in relief. "Thank you."

They agreed to stick to their plan of reconvening in Achilles' room, with the ladies decked out in their party best, so they could think up some business personas to use as cover. Galina would be their "official" translator.

Galina took a cab home to change clothes, and Lauren took one downtown to the Tribeca Grand. Achilles didn't have time to get the worksheet from his room, but he still had his computer with him; he could refer to it if Malcolm needed details of the cipher. He and Perly hailed a taxi and gave the concierge's directions to the driver.

In ten minutes the cab had deposited them at the foot of Albany Street. Battery Park City had a fresh-scrubbed appearance, like a theme park; Achilles found it unsettling to be in a part of New York where everything, including the sidewalks, looked brand new. Couples strolled on the walkway by the river. The sun had already set, and the sparkling lights of the Jersey shore, far across the Hudson, reflected in the water. The pleasantly cool spring air was being pushed out by hotter, muggier air—not quite summer, but a preview. There might be another squall coming, a warm front moving through.

Once they located the colonnade they walked through it, looking for the derelict. A couple of Parks Department workers—*collecting handsome overtime, no doubt,* Achilles thought—industriously planted new shrubbery along the walkway. Before long the derelict came into view, sitting on a bench. Their very own derelict, so polluted with alcohol they could smell him from yards away.

"Malcolm?" Perly said as they approached cautiously.

The man looked up at them with a snarl in his eyes, if there could be such a thing.

"Sit," he said. "One on each side."

"Malcolm, what the hell is going on?" Perly said.

"I wish I knew," Malcolm said. "You've heard about Karl by now, I suppose."

"Yeah, of course. What triggered that?"

"He bitterly resented being cherry-picked by the Pentagon. We used to call him the Ringmaster because of his brilliant strategy for keeping active agents moving around and uncatchable. When I started running black ops, he was my mentor. He never forgave the fact that I got the nod for the Pentagon job."

"But you'd think he'd have been proud," Achilles said.

"So I would have thought. But he became obsessed with the idea that he, and the CIA, were being pushed aside."

"Pisser," Perly said. "But how did the storyboard play out? I mean, what made the DNI put the ban on him?"

"My recommendation," Malcolm said. "There's an impalpable menace surrounding this summit that I can't put my finger on. I could feel Karl spinning out of control, acting so irrational I couldn't afford to wait and find out after the fact that he was up to no good. I decided to launch a preemptive strike. And when he started making threats on my own life—threats I know he has the capacity to carry out, and the goblins who'll do the job for him—I concluded the best thing to do was make myself scarce, come up here, and keep an eye on the summit from a different perch."

"Do you have any idea where he is now?" Achilles said.

"No. None. That's what worries me."

"Which brings up an issue," Perly said. "I hate to say somethin' that may seem critical of you"—he was sticking his figurative neck way out, which made him nervous enough to start jiggling his knees—"but now that you've gone into hiding, the FBI is tryin' to take us off the investigation. They're sayin' we don't have a proper reporting structure, and their agent, Ramirez, is tryin' to put the ban on us."

"Don't worry about it. I spoke to both the president and the DNI before I came up here. They know what's going on. And you have Lauren on your side."

"I'm not so sure, anymore," Perly said. "She didn't cotton to the idea of us meetin' you alone, when she didn't even know you were in town."

"Tell her I'm sorry. I couldn't trust the chain of communication—there might have been leaks. I'll give you a phone number later where she can reach me. And don't worry about Ramirez, either. He doesn't know it, but he's already a piece of driftwood floating in the water."

Achilles allowed himself a few seconds of feeling he had won a great victory. Even though Ramirez supposedly belonged to the same team, he had put himself in the enemy camp by acting so disdainfully toward them. Achilles looked across at Perly and saw him beaming the same way. Malcolm noticed, and instantly deflated them.

"That doesn't mean you can go off half-cocked as if you have the fourth infantry division on your side. You're still on your own out there. You'll have to live by your wits. The FBI hates agents like you. Since they were tamed by the civil rights lobby, they have an institutional bias against anyone thinking creatively, or doing anything that hasn't been put on paper and gone through a hundred rubber stamps. So be on your guard."

Achilles and Perly, having been gently but thoroughly brought back to earth, murmured in assent.

"Now," Malcolm said to Achilles, "how's it going with the cipher?"

"Making progress, but it's slow. It would sure help if I could send what I have down to Arlington and put the trolls to work on it."

"Out of the question. Can't trust anybody—some of them might even be working for Karl. Just tell me where you are." Achilles began to open the case of his laptop. "No, don't bother with the computer. Just tell me."

Achilles quickly brought him up to date, including Galina's list of names.

"Not bad so far," Malcolm said. "Now you know who belongs to the society. Are you sure you have them all?"

"No. For one thing, there's the double zero. No name beside that number. We don't know if it's a vacant slot, or a person unknown."

"My guess would be person unknown," Malcolm said. "Any others?"

"Well, Galina thinks there might be another entire list, based on reversing the dominoes. There's the potential for forty-nine names, not just twenty-eight."

"Good thinking on her part. How's she going to find out?"

"She has her home team searching for the list. They found the first list, so if there's a second, they should be able to find it, too."

"Which reminds me," Perly said. "Malcolm—again, not to sound critical—but I'm curious about something. Why did we have to find out about the list from the SVR? If you knew about it, why weren't you able to tell us? I mean, we have to trust a Russian agent for our intel, and her loyalties are going to be with the SVR, after all."

"I think you can trust her," Malcolm said after some thought. "In respect to the source of your intel, that's not for you to worry about at this point."

"But why did she tell us to keep the Russian murders to ourselves?" Achilles said. "How are we going to get the locals really pumped up over this if they don't realize there've been other murders?"

"She's following the orders of her adjutant general. He and I agreed to this approach. If they can't trust their own PSB, we can't take any chances here either. Not the police, not even the FBI. You'll have to figure out how to deal with them. You are not, under any circumstances, to tell anyone about the Russian murders. As far as the locals are concerned, she's here to help coordinate security for the summit."

A tugboat struggled to push a huge cement barge upriver against tide and current. The Parks Department gardeners had worked their way closer to the bench, still busily planting new bushes. Achilles could feel their presence to such an extent that he became uncomfortable. Considering the tricks the SVR had up its sleeve, they could very well be Russian agents.

"Let's move to another bench," he said. "It's getting too crowded around here."

He and Perly made a show of helping Malcolm up, pretending he was a drunk stumblebum, and half-walked, half-dragged him south along the walk. Achilles noted with satisfaction that the gardeners made no move to follow.

"To answer the other part of your question," Malcolm said as they hunted for a new bench, "I didn't tell you because I had orders not to."

"Someone could give you that kind of an order, and you'd follow it?" Perly said. Achilles noted that Perly seemed to get bolder by the minute. On Tuesday, or even Wednesday, Perly would never have dared to ask such impertinent questions of their boss. In a sense, Malcolm had done this to himself. By allowing his unit to fall into a leadership crisis, and by going on the run incognito, he had inadvertently reduced his own rank to that of field agent, whether he had intended to or not. So the two field agents with him felt freer than they normally would to treat him as an equal.

"If the person giving the order is your president, then yes, you follow the order," Malcolm said. "You serve at his pleasure. Right or wrong, when it's a direct order and he's not asking for your input, either you follow the order or you resign."

Achilles and Perly both knew this was the first rule of serving in government, one which anyone who had been on board for any length of time knew by heart. Yet hearing it stated so baldly, by a member in the upper echelons of that government, came as a bit of a shock. The lower-echelon troops who hoped to get to the top someday would be surprised to learn there was no such thing as getting to the top. Not unless you ran for president and won the election. And even then, was that the top? Who gave orders to the president? Who, for instance, was the double zero, the unknown one, in the Society of the Domino Mask? Could that be the real leader, the person who ran the world economy? Did the president take orders from him? Achilles felt emboldened to ask yet another question.

"If you knew about the membership list in the society, but couldn't tell us, would that also apply to a second list? If you were aware of a second list, would you still be prohibited from telling us?"

They came to an empty bench, and Malcolm sat down with a sigh.

"You think you have power," he mused, almost to himself. "You think you can control events. But eventually you find out that even if you're a four-star general, there's always a five-star general."

He turned to Achilles. "As for a second list, the answer is yes and no. You already know about one list, and I'm not going to deny it exists, since you found out from a different source."

The gardeners noisily threw their tools into a wheelbarrow and moved farther away, to the next set of plantings.

"Those gardeners," Perly said to Malcolm. "City employees never work this late, do they? Do you think those men are our goblins, or Russian?"

"These days, who knows?" Malcolm sounded uncharacteristically dispirited. "Maybe they work for Karl. Or they could be Saudi, French, Brit, maybe even from Iceland. Today every country feels the need to have black ops, and goblins to run them. You're not a serious country unless you spend a big chunk of your GDP on intelligence gathering.

"Anyway, getting back to the second list," he said to Achilles. "I'll take the risk of telling you that yes, there is one, but I can't tell you who's on it. That would contravene my orders. I hope your Russian friend can come up with it."

"And you can't tell us anything about the structure of the society?"

"Achilles, this is one thing, even if I knew, I absolutely could not tell you, not even under pain of death. But the fact is, I simply don't know. I've seen the membership lists, but I know nothing of the power structure or the organizing principles. I don't even know when, or if, they hold meetings."

Achilles could see a squall line approaching across the water, raindrops beginning to hit the surface of the river.

"We'd better find some shelter," he said.

"You should go back," Malcolm said. "I just wanted to touch base with you." He handed each of them a slip of paper. "This is a cell phone number. You can give it to Lauren, too. I went to Radio Shack and bought a phone with prepaid minutes. Ironic, isn't it?" he said as they pocketed the slips of paper. "I can't trust my own secure lines, because I have to assume that Karl's men are monitoring them. Now I know how the drug runners do business. Anyway, go catch your cab, before the rain hits." He turned to go, then turned back. "One more thing—be careful."

"We are," Perly said.

"No, I mean, extra careful. I have this feeling that there's a torpedo in the water headed our way. I don't know who launched it, and I don't know what its bearing is, but I know it's out there, headed for us. Be on your guard." Malcolm turned to go, this time with finality.

"Malcolm, wait," Achilles said, "I have one more question. I want to try again with the second list."

"You're wasting your time."

"Maybe yes, maybe no. We just learned that one of the New Russians, an oligarch named Vladimir Grigorieff, is throwing a big party in the penthouse of the Soho Grand tonight."

"So far, that's not a question."

"The question is this: Grigorieff's name is not on the membership list of the society we already have. If I were to ask you if his name is on the second list, could you tell me?"

"The second list is for people on probation. It's not really a list of full members."

"But is Grigorieff on that list?"

"Yes. He's the newest addition."

CHAPTER THIRTY

The squall had passed when they entered Achilles' room; through his still-wet windows he could see a barrage of fierce-looking clouds, lit from below by the city's lights, scudding from west to east. The red, white, and blue spotlights at the top of the Empire State Building threw off columns of vapor, like a multicolored candle in a steam bath. A subtropic sogginess permeated the air, as if Virginia had sent its weather north, which indeed it had. They were in for a late-April hot spell.

"I meant to ask Malcolm how he does the derelict disguise so well," Achilles said to Perly as he booted up his laptop. He thought he might as well do some work on the cipher while they waited for the women to return.

"So did I." Perly kept pacing nervously and scratching his stubble, gazing out the windows at the cityscape. "I can't believe he actually has to drink that much alcohol to true up his cover."

The computer had just booted, and Achilles was opening files so he could transfer Galina's handwritten table to the format he preferred, when they heard a series of quick knocks on the door. Perly went to the door and opened it. Lauren stepped in.

Achilles, lost already in his computer, heard Perly make a whistle of appreciation.

"Achilles, pull your head out of the trough and look at this."

Lauren laughed when Achilles swung around, took in her beautiful new made-up-for-the-party persona, and let out a wolf whistle of his own. She was wearing a low-cut party dress, a pearl necklace, and matching pearl earrings. Her hair had been swept off her neck in an attractive chignon.

"We should arrange more of these social outings," he said. "It's been a long since I've seen the phenomenon of a woman made up to go to a ball."

"You travel in the wrong circles," she said, obviously in a much better mood than when they had left her.

"Right. Arlington goblins aren't allowed to mix with the Georgetown and McLean bunch. We've been contaminated by too many barbecues, too much frolicking in plastic swimming pools."

"No need to feel left out. I go because I have to. It's part of my job. Actually, if you want to take that part over, you can have it. Ninety-five percent of the parties are dull beyond belief."

"And the other five percent?"

"No comment." Her eyes twinkled with mischief.

"Speakin' of location," Perly said, "does anyone know where Galina takes off her shoes? Where do the Russians put up their U.N. staff?"

"Have no idea," Achilles said. "She didn't volunteer, and I didn't think to ask. Why does it matter?"

"Just curious. Wonder if someone at her level gets to live in a real apartment, or she's forced to bed down in a youth hostel."

"Never mind the talk about living arrangements," Lauren said. "Before she gets here, we have a few minutes to talk about Malcolm. How did your meeting go? What did he say?"

"He gave us a phone number where you can reach him," Perly replied. "Said he was sorry he hadn't been in touch with you, but he couldn't trust the communications chain."

"That's history. What else?"

"He filled us in on what went down between him and Karl."

"He seems to fear for his own life," Achilles said. "He's concerned that Karl, with control of so many goblins, could persuade some of them to do just about anything, including taking Malcolm out. When Karl threatened him, he took it seriously."

"Nothing new about the situation we're dealing with?"

"One thing. He confirmed there's a second membership list for the Society of the Domino Mask. It's a list of probationary members, and this Grigorieff, the guy whose party we're crashing, is on that second list. He's the latest addition."

"Nothing about anyone else on the list?"

"No, he wouldn't tell us. Said he couldn't. Evidently your boss of bosses has prohibited anyone from talking about it."

Lauren sat in the chair by the window, her brow furrowed.

"What's up?" Perly said.

"I don't like this, not one bit. I thought that sort of information passed through me exclusively, and now I see it doesn't. And all this dirty laundry coming out with an SVR agent planted right in the middle of us. Why don't we open up the doors to the Pentagon, the CIA, the NSA, the White House, let the SVR come have a peek at our files, interview all our agents?"

"They probably have already," Achilles said.

"In fact, there were a couple of gardeners hangin' out when we were talkin' to Malcolm just now," Perly said. "I'd swear they were SVR agents."

"Wouldn't surprise me a bit," Lauren said. "Which brings up an issue I've been meaning to discuss. No one has explained to me why we should be so eager to trust the SVR."

"Lauren, I've already had these thoughts," Achilles said. "But I don't see what choice we have at this point. And Galina's been incredibly helpful. She gave me a breakthrough on the cipher."

"Fine, if it was really a breakthrough. But what if she's fed you a nice piece of cotton candy? What if the Russian government itself, or some part of it, is really behind this, and they're using her to throw us off the track?"

"But Malcolm just confirmed…"

"He confirmed there's a second list, but if he's not allowed to talk about either list, he can't confirm if the lists are accurate, can he? Maybe someone planted wrong names on the lists to send us through the woods when we should be following the path through the meadow. Maybe there's a plot by some unreconstructed Communists to bring back the good old days."

"Yeah, that's really a possibility," Perly said. "Remember, at the meeting this mornin', Galina slipped and said 'Leningrad,' then corrected herself and said 'St. Petersburg.'"

Achilles groaned. "That was just this morning? It feels like last week." He didn't want to let his suspicious mind get hold of the scenario they were proposing. He had already struggled enough to trust Galina. "Lauren, what are you trying to say? Think carefully before you answer—if Malcolm isn't allowed to talk about the lists because of orders from the president, doesn't that raise the possibility of the president himself being involved? Is there a chance we have an updated version of Nixon and Watergate unfolding here, only much worse?"

Now it was Perly and Lauren's turn to groan. Perly slumped in the other chair.

"It's times like this when I wish I smoked," Lauren said. "We're just running in circles."

"And," Achilles continued, "if you're that convinced we shouldn't trust Galina, even though we've been ordered to cooperate with her, are you suggesting we disobey our explicit instructions? Should we break it off with her?

Tell her to go make her reports, do her work by herself from now on? And accept the consequences if things backfire, which they will?"

"You're being a sophist, Achilles," Lauren said. "You're turning everything I say around and throwing it back at me because you're becoming attracted to her. You can't let that cloud your judgment."

"You're absolutely wrong. I'm not becoming attracted. I'm already hopelessly in love. But I promise I won't let it cloud my judgment."

Perly and Lauren both laughed.

"Fat chance," Perly said.

There was a soft knock at the door. Perly opened it, and Galina entered. Achilles wanted to fall prostrate on the floor and kowtow. She had transformed herself from a mere mortal, a beautiful Russian woman, into an empress, a czarina, a walking plate of fresh beluga caviar, a Slavic Audrey Hepburn. Her tiny feet were encapsulated in nearly invisible sandals with transparent heels; she was wearing a plain black shift, which cut diagonally across her torso, her left shoulder covered, her right shoulder bare. Her neck and head were adorned with a diamond necklace and matching tiara, although, thought Achilles, the diamonds had to be rhinestones. He was not an expert on jewelry, a fact his ex-wife never tired of throwing in his face when he had brought home a present that failed to please her. Galina's upswept russet hair, held in place by the tiara, had gained new sparkle, like a maple leaf in autumn preparing itself for the hordes of photographers headed its way. She smiled expectantly, waiting for a compliment.

"Very nice," Achilles said.

"Not bad," Perly said.

"Oh, pouf!" she said, coming fully into the room and pulling out a fresh cigarette. "Would you face the firing squad if you actually paid a woman a compliment? Lauren, did they behave this way with you?" She lit her cigarette and blew smoke in Achilles' face.

"Of course," Lauren lied. "They don't know any better. They're men, after all."

"Okay, okay, enough gender-bashing," Achilles said. He went to the wet bar. "While we lay our plans for this black operation, I suggest we warm up with some beer, vodka, scotch, or whatever suits you. Any orders?"

"I need to think," Galina said. "I can drink plenty once we get upstairs." She sat on the bed, stubbed out her cigarette, and pulled a stash of business cards out of her bag. They were held together by rubber bands, which she busily stripped off, and then started rifling through the cards, hunting for some she could use.

"Anyone else want a drink?" Achilles said.

Lauren and Perly, staring at Galina with fascination, shook their heads *no.*

Finally she found what she wanted, and handed each one of them a card.

"You, Perly, are Lionel Packard, no relation to the computer Packards, you are from a different branch of the family, you are wholesaler of lumber products. Note your card says you are from Oakland, California. Your company, Bay Area Lumber, wants to expand its line of products for home building market. Lauren, you are Lionel's wife Judy, but your card shows you have your own business, you run chain of boutiques for fashionable women in the California suburbs, it's called Dame Judith, and you are here with your husband, you are on buying trip, you are both able to combine your business trips in this fashion. So, you two, you can stay arm in arm and prowl the room, no problem.

"Achilles—here is your card—you are Mitchell Hartman, a scout for group of auto dealers in New Jersey, you're curious if it might be time to add Russian entry to your lineup, now there are hardly any American brands."

"But there's only one card apiece," Achilles said. "People will be asking to exchange cards."

"Don't offer. If they bring it up, explain you have only one card left, so many people have asked, so sorry, you're cleaned out, but you'll write your information on back of one of theirs. I can't carry around a carton of these things."

"And what's your legend?" Perly said.

"Legend?"

"Your ID, your name, your fake persona."

"I am Marina Milanov. Translator you have hired from Berlitz school. This is your first Russian party, you only heard about it at some other business meeting earlier today, you didn't know of any translation services, you called Berlitz. Here's my card." She waved a card at them and deposited it in a beaded evening purse, an item Achilles hadn't seen since the last time he took a co-ed to a prom. "So," she said, getting up from the bed. "Are we ready?"

"Give us a minute," Perly said. "We got to practice." He looked at his card, then puffed himself up and bellowed at Lauren.

"Hey, Judy, find any new stock today?"

"Some great dresses…" She couldn't remember his name, panicked, looked at his card, then continued: "Some great dresses, Lionel, great stuff from the Philippines, how about you, find any new home products?"

"Come on, cut it!" Achilles said. "You have to act serious, here. These are going to be real business people."

"Thank you, Mitchell," Galina said.

Achilles was nonplussed for a moment, until he realized she was talking to him. "And Galina…," he began.

"Marina. I am now Marina."

"…Marina, I have an interesting piece of news for you about this man, Grigorieff, who's throwing the party."

"Oh?"

"Malcolm told us that he's a new member of the society."

"I know."

"You know? How?"

"You remember the quarter? The one in your pocket?"

"Yes, of course."

"You forgot to learn lesson from before." She strode to the desk, yanked open the drawer, and pulled a small object out of it. She plunked the object down on the desk.

"Meet me at elevator bank," she said tersely over her shoulder on her way out the door.

Achilles went to the desk and picked the object up.

"What is it?" Perly said.

"A quarter," Achilles said. "One of her bugs. She heard everything we said, including the stuff about her."

CHAPTER THIRTY-ONE

Galina was waiting for them at the elevator bank, pacing impatiently.

"Galina—Marina, I'm sorry…," Lauren said.

"No time to discuss it now. We have party to attend."

"We're sorry," Perly said, "but we have to be able to talk freely among ourselves. Surely you understand."

"Of course. You are three, I am one. Three Americans and one Russian. Once we reach party, you will find this ratio is reversed."

The elevator arrived; as the doors opened, revealing a cab full of Russian partygoers, Galina sailed into the group, merrily exchanging greetings with them in Russian. She introduced her companions all around; Achilles heard an outpouring of Russian, the names "Lionel," "Judy," and "Mitchell." The quick introductions were followed by heartfelt and bone-crushing handshakes from the men, pecks on the cheeks from the women. The air in the elevator reeked of Parisian perfume and Russian tobacco.

When the group stepped off the elevator, they were greeted by catering staff with trays of drinks and hors d'oeuvres. The penthouse, perfect for a party, had several large rooms and a wraparound terrace that afforded views of the East River bridges, lower Manhattan, midtown, the Hudson River, and New Jersey. The clouds had moved through, and there was a warm ambience in both the atmosphere and the party crowd.

"Excuse me for a minute," Galina said. "I will find Grigorieff and bring him to you." She melted away into the crowd, leaving the three Americans by themselves. They stood rooted awkwardly to the spot for a few minutes, until the elevator disgorged another group of partygoers, forcing the trio further into the room.

"This is nuts," Perly said. "We shouldn't have come. She's left us stranded here."

"I'm going to float," Achilles said. "Maybe I can find her."

He left Perly and Lauren on their own and wandered from room to room, striking up a conversation here (whenever he found someone who spoke English) or a quick nod of acknowledgement there (when the choice was Russian only). He tried to avoid getting into any serious discussions, but did his utmost to maintain his auto-dealer cover. In the central penthouse he saw a woman singing a Russian song, accompanied by a pianist. The singer had a beautiful, dusky voice that seemed capable of penetrating the din of the Holland Tunnel. The accompanist, a man with a familiar face and a modish five o'clock shadow, was someone Achilles had seen in magazines and on CD covers. Perhaps the famous conductor of the Kirov Opera, whose name he couldn't remember.

A couple of times he hooked up with Perly and Lauren again, and they floated around as a trio; but Galina/Marina, who was supposed to be their interpreter, had deserted them, and since so much of the conversation surrounding them was in Russian, they felt lost at sea. If Galina had meant to make a point that they couldn't do without her, she was certainly succeeding. Achilles began to think that with her missing from the team the whole thing was a charade, and simply a waste of everyone's time. He split away from Perly and Lauren to search in earnest for Galina.

He found her in the northern penthouse suite, where the host had installed a setup for audio-visual presentations. A crowd of people—including Galina and a tall, muscular man who enveloped her tiny body in a one-armed embrace—had gathered in front of a flat-panel HDTV hung on an interior wall. A promotional DVD was playing, extolling the accomplishments and virtues of one Vladimir Grigorieff, entrepreneur, industrialist, oligarch. It showed scenes of autos running off the assembly line, timber being felled, gold being smelted and poured into bars, steel being rolled. The film had a sound track narrated in Russian, with English subtitles. Every couple of minutes a scene played featuring Grigorieff himself, a handsome man with blond hair and a narrow face, who wore gold-rimmed glasses. The same man who was now clutching Galina.

Achilles watched closely, comparing the man in the room with his avatar on the screen. He had a prominent scar on his upper left lip, which from across the room looked like a harelip; but when Achilles saw a close-up image of his face on the screen, he noted that it was not a harelip but some other kind of scar. Some scenes of the hero at sport appeared, including one in which he was fencing with sabers, unprotected. Achilles realized with a jolt that Grigorieff was a fencer of the old school, who no doubt traveled in circles where a facial scar was considered a badge of honor. When the film ended, Galina saw Achilles, and brought Grigorieff over to him.

"Vladimir, this is Mitchell Hartman," Marina/Galina said. "He is one of my clients. He represents a group of car dealers in New Jersey."

Achilles took Grigorieff's outstretched hand. He knew enough to jam his hand firmly in the web between Grigorieff's thumb and fingers, to prevent the Russian from crushing his own hand—a move that Grigorieff attempted immediately. Even with the preparation, Achilles could feel the bones in his hand crunching.

"Mitchell, may I call you Mitchell?" Grigorieff said. "You see, in the new Russia, we know how to be informal," he laughed. "And you also see I'm not needing a translator, but she is very good, maybe I'll buy her for my own someday soon." He removed his arm from around Galina/Marina and patted her on the rump; she scowled and tried to move away, but he trapped her again and pulled her closer to him. She looked like a goldfinch caught in a lion's paws.

"Yes," Achilles said, steeling himself against the virtual assault taking place before him, "my auto group in New Jersey is interested in adding some exotic new cars to our lineup. I heard you were here, and wanted to see what you have."

"Next track on DVD, we show a new small car called the Koza; new limousine, the Grigorieff; and new Formula One we are developing, the Orlan. We are designing two courses—one in Moscow, one in Volgograd. Today, Moscow! Tomorrow, Monte Carlo!" he trumpeted to the room, and downed his glass of champagne. He plucked another glass from a passing tray, and chucked it down too.

"You don't think it would be better to start with Formula Three and move up?" Achilles said, exhausting in one question his entire pool of knowledge about car racing.

"No, no, absolutely not. You want to be at the top, you start at the top, that's the way you jump over the competition. Let them fool with puttputts—I go for the big stuff." He laughed and snatched yet another glass of champagne, downing it in two quick gulps. "Tell your associates, do business with me. I make you all rich in five years."

"I see from the film that you do your fencing the old way."

"Yes, saber, none of that protective crap. It's the center of the whirlwind for me. Why do you ask? Do you fence?"

"Mostly in college. Saber was my weapon also, but we had to wear the padding. Rules."

"Rules. Of course, rules. We had those too, God knows. In fencing, also in business. But no more. What is that saying one of your great entrepreneurs makes? Some guy from Silicon Valley. He says, 'To ask permission is to seek denial.' Someday, if you and I do business together, we should have a match. You with your padding, me without. Will be most interesting, to see who gets hurt the most."

He patted Galina/Marina appreciatively on the rump again, and began to move on. "Must tend to other guests. There are brochures on table by the door. Whatever appeals to you, help yourself. Brochures for timber, gold mines, racing cars—all the brochures you could want, English, Russian, French, German, name your language." He made a grab for Galina with his huge paw, but she eluded him and managed to hook herself onto Perly and Lauren, who had just joined them.

"Another of my clients," she said to Grigorieff. "Lionel Packard, and his wife Judy. They own…"

"Glad to meet you," Grigorieff interrupted, obviously not in the least interested in Lionel and Judy, or what they might own; he was in the middle of snorting some powder he had extracted from a small tin. He put the tin in his pocket, gave Lionel a peremptory shake of the hand, pecked Judy on the cheek with an equally peremptory kiss, and continued on his way. "Today, Berlitz!" he called to Marina over his shoulder. "Tomorrow, Grigorieff!" To the others he said, "Be sure to be sticking around! Ballerinas from Bolshoi come here after the curtain! Then I trade you, three ballerinas for one translator!" And he was gone, swallowed up in a crowd he seemed to love.

"What's happening?" Perly said.

"Grigorieff was putting the make on Ga—Marina," Achilles said. "Let's go. I think we've seen enough."

They left through the inner door, which led directly to the elevator bank. On the way out, Achilles rummaged through the pile of brochures on the table, but could only find German versions. He grabbed a few and stuffed them in his inner jacket pocket.

"Bastard," Galina hissed as they waited for the elevator. "No different from stories I heard about the Communists. Worse. The Communists used Marxism-Leninism, they patted women's behinds while they talked ideology, but at least they felt the need to talk ideology. The oligarchs think they can stuff bills in our brassieres and carry us off over their shoulders, no questions asked, no permission required."

"I'd swear you were enjoying yourself," Achilles said.

"In Russia, female guest is not rude to male host."

An elevator came, disgorging yet another load of chattering Russian partygoers. In the very back of the elevator cab was a lone man so lost in thought that he almost forgot to get out. As Achilles and his group entered the cab, the man came to his senses and looked up. With a flash of recognition, he stopped in his tracks and stared at them. They stared back, equally dumbfounded.

"Why, Mikhail," Achilles said, trying to break the spell. "What a surprise, to see you here. We heard about the party and thought we should check it out."

As the elevator doors closed, Mikhail stood on the other side, looking balefully at the four of them. He did not say a word.

CHAPTER THIRTY-TWO

"I am so sorry," Galina said during the short trip down to the fourteenth floor. "It never occurred to me that Mikhail might show up. I didn't prepare myself properly."

"It's all right," Achilles said. "We're not going to keep score on who makes what mistakes. I obviously made a mistake by going after Mikhail at the meeting."

"Not so," Perly said. "If he's tryin' to hide somethin', you might've smoked him out, just like we wanted."

The elevator reached Achilles' floor. They got off and went into his room. Everything remained as they had left it, even the quarter on the desk. Achilles picked it up and talked into it.

"Galina, can you hear me? Thank God I can call you Galina again."

She laughed and snatched the quarter away from him.

"I kind of liked that Lionel and Judy act," Perly said. "Gave me a nice buzz. Have to use it again."

"You'll need to think up your own names and print your own cards," Galina said. "Those are mine."

"Whoa, not to worry," Perly said. "We got plenty of our own legends."

Achilles took off his jacket and hung it in the closet. He noticed a bulge in the breast pocket and remembered the brochures from the penthouse.

"These might be interesting. Some of Grigorieff's brochures." He pulled them out of the pocket and tossed them on the bed. "Unfortunately, they were so picked over all I could find was German. Anybody here *sprechen sie Deutsch?*"

"We can't go back to the penthouse and search for more, not with Mikhail there," Galina said, pawing through the brochures in the vain hope she might find one they could read. "We have to get these translated."

"The weekend desk at Arlington," Perly said. "We can send 'em by messenger."

"Out of the question," Achilles said. "Malcolm said so. Karl's spies might see it."

"Galina," Lauren said. "What about your U.N. mission? Don't they have a German desk?"

"No, we can't do that. They will want to know why. And for all we know, someone there is on Grigorieff's payroll."

"Galina's right," Perly said. "We don't trust Ramirez and the FBI on our side, either. We got to keep this to ourselves."

"Then what are we supposed to do?" Lauren said, her voice rising in exasperation. "Stroll up to Berlitz tomorrow morning to see if they have any translators free on a Saturday? And if they do, how do we arrange payment? I mean, come on! No one here speaks or reads German, and time is of the essence."

"Wait," Perly said, waving a hand to put out Lauren's fire. "I got it." He pulled his cell phone out. "The party has to end sometime. When it does, the trash goes into the dumpsters behind the hotel. Chances are there'll be extra brochures, and they're gonna wind up in the trash. We'll get some that way." He rummaged through his pockets, found a slip of paper, studied it, and dialed a number. "Hello, Malcolm?"

"Brilliant," Achilles said.

"What is he doing?" Galina said.

"Malcolm is a derelict," Achilles said, while Perly was on the phone with the governor. "He can paw through the trash when it's put out, without anyone being suspicious. They may chase him off, but they won't think there's anything unusual about a derelict pawing through trash."

Perly completed his conversation with Malcolm and snapped his phone shut. "Done. He'll be out in the little park on Canal and Thompson, watching. When the party's over and the trash is put out, he'll start cuttin' bags open."

"Perly, you're a genius," Achilles said.

"Malcolm thinks so, too. If I may be so modest."

"Modest," Lauren said. "I'd hate to see you when you're boasting."

"He also said we should get some rest," Perly added, ignoring Lauren's jibe. "It'll be a few hours before the garbage is put out, and we have to be ready for action when he calls."

"Well, you and Lauren can go catch a snooze," Achilles said. "Galina and I are going to work some more on the cipher, right, Galina?"

Galina sighed. "For a little while. Then I go home and get my own rest. Can't think without rest."

Perly and Lauren left, Lauren still jibing at him for his false modesty.

"That's a natural pair," Achilles said to Galina as he closed the door.

"And us? Are you thinking we might be a natural pair?"

"I have to admit, I was furious upstairs. Wild with jealousy. I didn't know if I should try to take some drastic action to pry you loose, or if you were enjoying yourself, or what. Not a pleasant experience."

"Nor for me. I can tell you, I was not enjoying it. Unfortunately that's the way it is with these oligarchs. They imitate your old cowboys, but instead of riding ponies they're wearing Italian suits, use satellite phones, drive fancy cars. Someday your Hollywood will get a hold of some of these stories, and a new myth will be born about the Second Russian Revolution." She flopped on the bed and stretched out. "I am so exhausted."

"We have to keep going. Tired as we both are, we can't afford to lose momentum. Come on. Get out your pad, let's go to work."

He turned on the laptop and poured a couple of glasses of seltzer while he waited for it to boot up.

"Here," he said, handing her a glass. "This will flush out the booze, help us think."

Galina sat up, took the glass, and put it on the nightstand. Then she pulled a tablet out of her large shoulder bag, which she had left in the room during the party, and reacquainted herself with her notes.

"So before the meeting," she said, "we had string of meaningless letters."

"Right. And too many numbers. So let's put the digits at the end of the code instead of the beginning, see where that takes us." He created a new table on the computer, plugging the cipher values into new cells, and turned around to show it to her when he finished. She had fallen sound asleep on the bed. "Galina," he said. "Galina!"

"Hmm?" she said drowsily, propping herself up.

"Come check this out."

"Can't you do it on paper?" she said as she staggered over to the desk. "So much easier if you just hand me piece of paper."

"This way I don't have to keep drawing new grids. Take a look."

With the changes he had made to the code, the new version of the cipher read:

T-H-E-U-S-A-N-D-R-J-G-5-I-K-B-P-F-1-S-5-0-H-1-I-G-
W-K-L-8-G-I-E-D-6-V-4-1-N-H-X-I-G-I-5-W-M-9-I-6.

"What do you think?" he said.

"Might be promising," she said, beginning to wake up. "Starts with 'the US and,' or 'the USA.' Did you try full set of numbers on the pony cipher?"

"No." He pulled that file up on the computer and plugged in the new code: 33-02-50-16 gave him the letters S-C-G-M. "This is better. Scuggim may not be Sodm, but we picked up two letters."

"I think we should keep following this path. Somehow, these lists will open the cipher for us. We have simply not found right construction yet."

He looked at her through bleary eyes. Why did Perly get to have all the fun? Why had Achilles ever taken up code-breaking in the first place? Here he was with a gorgeous Russian woman in his room, unable to take advantage of her proximity because a group of letters and numbers held him chained to his computer.

"No," she said.

"No what?"

"No sex. Be careful, or I put you in same category as Grigorieff upstairs."

"What makes you think…"

"Your eyes tell all. With him, it's the hands and his loud mouth. With you, there is more politeness, and the eyes do the work, but the thoughts are the same."

There was no point in arguing. He returned to the cipher, as did she. For the next couple of hours they tried different formulas, different arrangements of letters and numbers, but nothing clicked. Eventually, Galina fell asleep, fully clothed, on the bed. Achilles went to rouse her, but she looked so peaceful that he couldn't bring himself to bother her. He decided to lie on the floor and rest for a minute. Within seconds he too had fallen asleep.

CHAPTER THIRTY-THREE

They were awakened by alarm bells clanging somewhere in the hotel, and loud sirens outside.

"What the hell…," Achilles said, getting off the floor.

"Achilles, what is it?" Galina said. "What's going on?"

"Don't know." He stumbled to the door and opened it. The deafening alarms resounded throughout the hallways, accompanied by an automated announcement coming over loudspeakers:

All guests are to vacate the building immediately! Do not take the elevator! Use the fire stairs! This is not a drill! Repeat, All guests…

Achilles slammed the door shut. "Quick, pack your stuff. We have to get out of here. There's a fire."

He stuffed his laptop into its case, Galina packed her shoulder bag, and they rushed out into the corridor, crouching low to avoid any smoke. They found the red *Exit* sign and hurried down the stairs, along with a stream of other guests and a few stayovers from Grigorieff's party, who were so drunk they kept stumbling and slowing the others down. On the lower floors the stairwell became even more crowded as firemen, oxygen tanks strapped to their backs and fire axes at the ready, shouldered their way against the crowd in the opposite direction.

The fire stairs led directly to the street. Frightened people, still in their night clothes, some covered only by blankets or sheets, were being directed up to Broome Street, two short blocks north.

"Over here, over here, over here!" policemen shouted, herding the guests like cattle to the other side of the barricades. The streets were clogged with fire engines, police cars, firemen laying hoses. Canal Street, Grand Street, Sixth Avenue, West Broadway, and Thompson Street had all been blocked off.

Achilles tried to take a minute to locate the fire, but a cop shoved him rudely.

"Keep moving!" yelled the cop. "Keep moving, no looking! No time to be tourists, folks! Keep it moving!"

At last they were a safe distance away, on the corner of West Broadway and Broome. There were no flames or smoke that Achilles could see.

"Must be Grigorieff's party," he said to Galina. "I'll bet one of his drunken guests set fire to the place."

"Always has to be fault of Russians, is that what you think?"

"Please, Galina. This is no time to be oversensitive. It's just a logical conclusion."

"Sorry, I can't think right anymore. I should go home. Would you put me in a cab, please?"

"We'll have to go over to Broadway—the cabs there will be going downtown, but you can have him turn around."

"Fine."

"By the way," he said as they walked east on Broome Street, "where do you live?"

"Why do you ask? Do you plan to sing under my window some night?"

He laughed. "You really are the prickly pear. I'm just curious. Natural curiosity."

"I live in the east 60s. Town house the mission owns. There are four of us in one room. We sleep on bunk beds. Does that satisfy your curiosity?"

"I'm sorry."

"It's all right. No need to be. I accept the conditions. They're better than I had at home."

An empty cab came by just as they reached Broadway; Achilles hailed it and put her in.

"See you in a few," he said.

She waved at him through the window as the cab pulled away.

When Achilles returned to the area around the hotel, more fire trucks were arriving, their sirens wailing, but there was still no sign of a fire. He decided to circle the building, see what might be visible from the back. Passing by one of the police barricades, he overheard a fire chief talking to a police captain.

"Accelerant…," the chief was saying. "Could have been bad, but the room was empty…"

Achilles reached Sixth Avenue and crossed to the other side, then walked south for two blocks until he reached Canal. He had a good view of the back of the hotel from this vantage point, and could see fire ladders extending upward, smoke pouring out of the broken windows of one room, the glow of flames.

Out of curiosity, he counted floors, allowing for the lobby on the other side of the building, and came to the conclusion that the fire was on the sixth floor. With that realization, he began to pay real attention. Sixth floor? What room? He noticed the karaoke club on Thompson Street, the one that had bedeviled him the previous night, directly below the flames.

The more he scanned the scene, the more he became convinced that the fire was in room 621. The fire chief had been talking about an accelerant. Someone must have firebombed his old room, thinking he was still there.

CHAPTER THIRTY-FOUR

"Got any marshmallows?" The question came from a man standing next to Achilles in the crowd of onlookers. His voice sounded familiar; Achilles turned and saw a homeless man with a crutch, hobbling on one leg—Malcolm, in a new disguise.

"The deli didn't have any," Achilles said, following protocol by avoiding eye contact. "Up until a few hours ago, that was my room."

"Good thing you're not in it now." The homeless man hobbled away. Achilles, sensing he should follow at some distance, split his attention between the fire and Malcolm's receding back. After several minutes he broke loose from the crowd and walked in the same direction, east on the south side of Canal Street. By then he had lost sight of Malcolm, but continued walking, knowing that his boss would show up when it suited him; and sure enough, after a few blocks the homeless man rematerialized behind Achilles.

"Keep walking," he said. "I'm trying to beg some money from you. Wave me off, but I'm persistent."

Malcolm made begging motions and Achilles made *get away* motions as they continued east on Canal.

"I forgot to mention to everyone that I'd moved," Achilles said, "so someone obviously thought I was still there."

"Yes, apparently."

"Or else they were after Galina. Are you really sure I can trust her? She knows everything we say to each other. She has bugs all over the place. Quarters as transmitters, earrings as receivers."

"I told you, I think you can trust her. Bugs are standard SVR procedure."

A Chinese man and his nervous-looking wife approached them from the opposite direction. Malcolm came closer, pretending to collide with Achilles.

"You're not reacting—push me away," he whispered. "C'mon, mister!" he shouted when the couple reached them. "Just a quarter, what's a quarter to you?" When Achilles pushed him away, he pursued the Chinese couple.

"How about it, how about you, can you spare some change?" he said, jabbing his hand under the man's nose. The man let loose a stream of invective in Chinese, put his arms around his wife, and picked up his pace. Malcolm hobbled back to Achilles, who had continued to head doggedly eastward.

"Obviously, I can't get near the trash to hunt for your brochures," Malcolm said when he caught up.

"Right. What do we do now? We need those translations."

"Go up to the Goethe House, across from the Metropolitan Museum. It's the German version of Alliance Français. They have bulletin boards. Find a translator there."

"Malcolm…," Achilles began, but stopped himself when he noticed a group of tourists approaching. He maintained his cover by waving Malcolm off like a pestilent fly.

"I was about to say," Achilles said when the tourists had passed, "that I think the Assistant DA is involved. He's a Brighton Beach Russian, and he showed up at Grigorieff's party as we were leaving. We think he doctored the Maguire photos."

"Exactly why I put you in goblin mode."

"But at some point we have to trust somebody. We have to get the police department to help us track down farriers, for instance."

"Only the minimum necessary. No more. That's an order."

"And there's Ramirez…"

"I told you, Ramirez is driftwood. Avoid him if possible."

"But he can still make trouble. Malcolm, we need some guidance. It's lonely out here."

"You and Perly are big boys, Achilles. That's why I sent you on this mission. Give me a buck, then yell at me to get lost."

Achilles fished a dollar out of his pocket and gave it to Malcolm. "Get the hell out of here, will you?" he shouted as he waved the bum away.

Malcolm pivoted on his crutch, retreating up an alley. "Sorry to bother you, mister," he yelled over his shoulder. "Thanks for the buck. My kids will bless you."

Achilles headed back to the hotel. Even at this late hour there was still plenty of traffic, including fire engines, ambulances, and NYPD/NYFD SUVs pulling away from the scene of the fire, honking their claxons and testing their sirens, just to let the neighborhood know the night's excitement had finished.

When he reached the Soho Grand the police were dismantling the barricades, and guests were being allowed back in. The fire and police departments had set up checkpoints to inspect IDs; because many of the guests had evacuated without their wallets, the lobby was packed with people in nightclothes creating a hubbub of loud disputation.

The elevators were so overloaded that Achilles could see he had no choice but to wait; his room was on a high floor, he was too worn out to walk, and in any case access to the stairs had been blocked so the firemen could bring their equipment down. He flopped in an easy chair in the lobby and drifted off to sleep, clutching his laptop.

CHAPTER THIRTY-FIVE

Achilles was roused by a hand gently pushing against his shoulder.

"Sir?" said a voice. "Sir? Could I see your ID, please?"

Slowly opening one eye, he saw a man standing over him. The man had a shaved head, and wore a black suit with a bow tie; a wilted carnation winked from the buttonhole of his lapel. Next to him stood a man in uniform.

"Hunh?" Although Achilles was still half asleep, his antennae were already sweeping the area for danger.

"Sir, I'm the night manager, my name is Freddy. The fire marshal, here, is checking IDs of guests before they return to their rooms."

Achilles fished for his wallet and showed them his Virginia driver's license.

"Smith, Achilles," he mumbled. "Room 1485."

The night manager and the fire marshal exchanged glances.

"Sir, we'd like to talk to you," Freddy said. "Could you please come to my office?"

"What for? What's up?"

"Could you please come to my office? We have a couple of questions."

Achilles forced himself to get up, and followed the two men to an office behind the main desk. Freddy was short and wiry, very dancer-looking, like most of the staff. The marshal could have passed for a relative of Frank Bernardo's, stocky and beefy, but Achilles guessed he would be Irish rather than Italian.

"Here we are," Freddy said as they entered the office. He arranged chairs for the other two men, then sat himself behind his desk.

"I'm Harry Malvern," the fire marshal said.

Achilles couldn't place the name. Irish? English? Didn't matter. "Couldn't this wait until the morning? I'm very sleepy."

"Sorry to bother you, but this is important. We understand that you were the guest in room 621 up until a few hours before the fire."

Oh, Christ, Achilles thought. *They think I had something to do with the fire.* "More than a few hours," he said. "I mean, I changed rooms in midafternoon. I hadn't been in that room for maybe twelve hours. And right now I'm completely worn out. Can't we have this discussion later, after I've had some rest?"

"This will just take a few minutes," Freddy said. "The day manager, when I called him, said you moved because of a smoking request. He told me that the woman with you insisted on smoking. Isn't it possible she might have left a cigarette smoldering on the mattress?"

"Are you telling me you didn't check the room out for twelve hours after we vacated? Seems a bit odd for an upscale hotel."

"Well, no," Freddy said, squirming in his chair. "But the staff might have missed…"

"So you're saying there's a possibility that a cigarette is burning in the mattress, the hotel staff comes in, changes the sheets, vacuums the rugs, cleans the bathroom, gets the room nice and spiffy for the next guests, and no one notices the smoldering mattress, in a no-smoking room, no less." Achilles turned to the marshal for some help, didn't get any, and turned back to Freddy. "Do you hire staff who've had their noses amputated?"

"Please—there's no need to be aggressive. We're only trying to ascertain a timeline here, determine the sequence of events leading up to the fire."

"Sorry. I just told you I'm exhausted. And I'm not being aggressive. I'm merely pointing out the logic of the situation." He turned back to Harry. "Besides, I think Mr. Malvern, here, will verify that the fire was started with an accelerant. A smoldering cigarette is not considered an accelerant, is it, Harry?"

"What makes you think there was an accelerant?"

"Heard one of your chiefs talking, out on the street."

Now it was Harry's turn to squirm. "Chiefs on the street, they're not up where the fire is, they hear rumors…"

"And they hear the walkie-talkies. So maybe they have pretty accurate information."

"Look, really, Mr. Smith," Freddy said. "Honestly, we're not trying to pin anything on you."

"I know you're not. You want to know if I can think of any reason someone would want to set fire to my room while I was asleep in my bed. Someone who might not have known that I'd moved. And since you hadn't rented the room to anyone else, I'm the only potential target."

"You, or your cigarette-smoking friend."

"Right. She could be a target also, but that requires the assumption that she was spending the night with me."

"Never mind that," Harry said. "Since you want to get right to the point, let's get to it. Are you involved in some activity that might cause someone to hold a grudge? I don't mean for you to reveal any of your business secrets, understand, but if we're going to get to the bottom of this, we need your cooperation."

Damn, Achilles thought. What was he going to do? The last thing he needed was to get hauled off to a New York City jail as a material witness to arson. He had to think fast. How was he going to get out of this?

As Achilles tried to devise an escape plan, Harry made a motion for Freddy to hand him the phone.

"I think we have a person of interest, here. Sorry, Mr. Smith, but I have to…"

Issue decided. "Wait a minute," Achilles fumbled in his pockets, looking for Justino Ramirez's card, found it, gave to Harry. "I think if you call this number, you'll get all the information you need."

Harry looked at the card. His eyes widened a bit, then narrowed. Apparently deciding to test for a bluff, he took the phone from Freddy and dialed the number. They waited while the phone rang on the other end. Achilles could tell that Harry had reached Ramirez's voice mail. No one manning the FBI phones this time of night. Harry hung the phone up without leaving a message.

"Until I'm able to confirm…," he began.

"Look, Harry—" Achilles was finally being forced to reveal his identity. *Sorry, Malcolm,* he thought, *but this is an emergency.* Malcolm! He should call Malcolm! Then he nearly broke out laughing. He could imagine the scene: he tells them the head of the Pentagon's clandestine service will straighten the whole thing out, and a homeless man shows up. Hopeless. No, he had to reveal who he was.

Achilles pulled out his Pentagon badge and showed it to Harry. "—I'm Achilles Smith, special agent for the Pentagon. I'm here working on a case that may have an impact on the G8 summit, which launches in a little over twenty-four hours. If you make the wrong move here, you'll be interfering with a federal investigation. There could be consequences." He had to find a way to make Harry back down. Because, come to think of it, he'd get no help from the FBI. Good thing Harry hadn't gotten through. Ramirez would be only too glad to leave a Pentagon man sitting in the local pokey for a few days.

But Harry would not back down. "All well and good, and I'd love to believe you. I mean, I do believe you. My difficulty is that we have had a serious fire, a major hotel had to be evacuated. The New York City Fire Department has to consider the public safety first. We can explore the issue of this investigation of yours on Monday."

"I'd like to make a call, please. And I'd like you to show me the courtesy of not making your call until after I've made mine."

"Go ahead."

Achilles pulled out his cell phone and dialed Perly. *Pick up, Perly, pick up,* he thought as he counted off the rings: one, two, three..."

"Hullo," came the sleepy voice at the other end. "Lyman here. That you, Malcolm?"

"Uh, Perly, no, it's Achilles. I have a bit of a problem here. I need you right away."

"Achilles, it's almost dawn, can't it wait?"

"Perly, I need you right now. I'm about to be detained as a material witness to arson. Someone firebombed my old room."

"Be right there," Perly said, suddenly wide awake.

"I'm in the hotel manager's office with the fire marshal." Achilles had an inspired thought: "Bring Lauren with you. Have her bring the photographs."

"The photographs? What for?"

"Perly, just do it, will you? Manager's office, behind the front desk." He snapped the phone shut. "That's my colleague from the Pentagon, and his friend, who is our liaison with the White House," he said to Harry. "Maybe they'll be able to convince you this is not a joke."

"Believe me, I don't think it's a joke," Harry said, still trying to maintain his *my-business-is-the-most-important-business* brusqueness; but Achilles could tell he was beginning to get a little nervous. In order to keep his balloon of self-importance afloat, Harry picked up his walkie-talkie and made the rounds of his chiefs to see how the cleanup was progressing. Achilles and Freddy sat and fidgeted, saying nothing, while Harry's walkie-talkie squawked and bleeped in the heavy predawn air.

Finally there was a rap at the door. "Yes?" said Freddy.

One of the desk clerks poked her head in the office. "People to see Mr. Achilles Smith? They tell me he's in the manager's office."

"Yes, let them in."

Disheveled and panting, Perly and Lauren stormed into the office, flashing their badges.

"What the hell's goin' on here?" Perly demanded.

"Where's Galina?" Lauren said.

"She's okay, I sent her home in a cab earlier," Achilles said.

"Your friend, Mr. Smith, recently vacated a room that has just been fire-bombed," Harry said to Perly. "We think he might have a few things to tell us. I intend to give him lodging in other quarters as a material witness."

"I tried to reach Ramirez, but the FBI wasn't home," Achilles said.

Perly sized up the situation immediately. "Lauren, you handle this. You know who you got to call."

Lauren pulled out her phone and punched in some numbers. "Hello," she said when she got a response. "Who is this? Sandy? Lauren Vogel here. Sandy, listen…"

Now Perly joined Achilles, Harry, and Freddy in a state of agonized suspense while Lauren explained things to Sandy, whoever that was. She pulled out a pen and pad and wrote some quick squiggles.

"Okay, thanks," she said to Sandy. "I think it would be a good idea for you to speak to him."

She handed the phone to Harry.

"Me?" he said.

"Yes, you."

Harry listened politely at first, interjecting "uh-huh, uh-huh," every so often. Then, finally, he ran out of patience.

"Look, I've got a job to do here. I don't answer to you people. You can't order me around, you got that?" He snapped the phone shut angrily and handed it back to Lauren. "Anyway, there's no verification. Anyone can get ahold of fake ID badges, call someone named Sandy who says he's at the White House. How the hell do I know you're not a bunch of slick drug runners, and one of your competitors tried to take one of you out? If you walk out of here, what's my guarantee you don't skip town?"

"Sandy anticipated that line of thought," Lauren said. "He's making some other calls that should enable you to put your fears to rest. Here. Call this number." She tore a piece of paper from her pad and handed it to Harry. When Harry saw the number on the slip, his eyes widened in disbelief.

"No—I can't call him. He'll be asleep."

"Dial it. By now he's expecting your call."

Harry dialed the number, using Freddy's phone. Freddy was sitting wide-eyed, like a kid in a corner watching his parents have their final pre-divorce battle.

The party at the other end picked up. "Sir," Harry said, his voice quavering, "I'm so sorry to bother you at this hour, sir, but you know, we've had this fire in the Soho Grand hotel, and I have a person of interest here..." His voice trailed off as he listened to the other party talk. "Yes sir, yes sir...yes sir, Mr. Commissioner, will do." Harry hung up the phone and shoved it back across the desk toward Freddy.

"You people sure have a hell of a lot of explaining to do. And someday I'll make you explain it. You can't run around endangering other people's lives with your cowboy games, acting like you're untouchable. I hope to God the mayor speaks to the president about this during the summit. I'll see to it he does." Harry stormed angrily out of the room.

"Well," Freddy said. "That was certainly an education." He stood up, prepared to escort them out.

"Not so fast," Perly said, his voice in official mode. "I haven't met you. What's your name?"

"Freddy. Freddy Simon."

"Freddy, we're just as interested in this fire as the fire department. We'd like to ask you some questions."

Freddy, now deprived of his partner-in-authority, showed outward signs of panic. "Can't it wait?" he said, his eyes trolling the phone and the door in search of an exit. "I have a hotel to care for, guests milling around in shock..."

"This will only take a minute." Perly turned to Achilles. "What do you think, Achilles? You had Lauren bring the pictures. Should I ask?"

"Absolutely." Achilles was so depleted he could barely think, much less talk.

"Freddy," Perly said, "do you know what time, exactly, the fire started?"

"About two, two thirty."

"And was there any traffic in or out of the hotel during that time?"

"Some. A few tourists out late on the town."

"What about the party in the penthouse? Was it still going on?"

"Winding down, but there were still some people up there. No one arriving, though. Only leaving."

"So you, or your staff, didn't see anyone come into the hotel who might seem suspicious?"

"No, nobody."

"Not even any uniformed services, policemen, anything like that?"

"No, no. They don't go upstairs. Sometimes a cop comes in to get out of the wet, if it's raining, or the cold, if it's freezing, but on a night like this, no cops would come in here…" Freddy paused, thinking hard. "Well, come to mention it, there was one. Wearing a helmet, leather jacket, and breeches. I figured he was a motorcycle cop. I did think it a bit strange that he came into the hotel and took the elevator. I assumed that someone had complained about the party, and he had been sent to quiet things down, but normally when that happens, they come to see me first…. Yes, that was unusual."

"Would you remember any salient physical characteristics?"

"Not sure I would. With those breeches, and the leather jacket, and the helmet…"

It was time to strike. Lauren, who had pulled out the envelope with photos, handed one to Perly.

"Did he look like this?" Perly said, showing the photo to Freddy.

"Yes, that's him, definitely. Square cheeks, a swarthy complexion. Sunglasses at night. That's the man."

Achilles and Perly flashed victory smiles at each other.

"Bull's-eye," Achilles said. "Sam Rains has been here."

CHAPTER THIRTY-SIX

"Freddy, there's one other thing." Achilles realized they might be able to glean some useful facts from the chaos surrounding the fire. "When your staff cleans up the penthouse, would you have them look for any brochures, or DVDs, or CDs, that might have been left behind in the confusion, and bring them to your office? We need to go through any of those materials that might be intact."

"I don't know. There's no apparent connection between the party in the penthouse and the fire in 621, and without a warrant..."

"Freddy, I'm not talking about an illegal search of someone else's belongings. This is your own property. That is, you represent the owner of this property, the hotel. If someone abandons their personal belongings on your property, you don't need a warrant to look at them, now do you? Do you need a warrant when someone leaves a bag behind in their room?"

"Well, no, we have to identify it, of course, ascertain the owner so we can return it..."

"Exactly. I'm not asking you to steal or keep anyone's personal belongings. Simply give us a chance to check it out before you return it to the owner. We have reason to think that some items from that party may, in fact, have some bearing on the fire, but we can't prove anything at this point. Can I count on you?"

"I'll leave instructions for the day staff. I'm going off duty in half an hour. Anything they find of that nature will be brought here."

"Great, Freddy, many thanks." Achilles and Perly shook Freddy's hand on their way out of the office.

And then, having managed to keep himself going this long, Achilles crashed. He had been deprived of a real sleep for four days running.

"Perly," he said as they got in the elevator, "could you and Lauren cover for me at the 8 a.m. meeting? I need to get some rest."

"Sure."

"And see if you can get Frank Bernardo to call off this fire marshal. I don't think he's through with us. Maybe one city agency will listen to another."

"Good idea."

"Oh, and Perly, someone has to go up to the Goethe house, across from the Metropolitan Museum, to look for a translator."

"Why there?"

Achilles explained to Perly about running into Malcolm on the street, and what Malcolm had told him to do regarding a translator for the German brochures.

"I'll put the precinct on it," Perly said. When the doors opened at his floor, the reek of burned upholstery and bedding hit them in the face. The hotel had obtained huge fans and placed them in the hallways to move the air and clear out the smoke.

"Perly, no," Achilles said, holding the elevator doors open. Despite his exhaustion, he had managed to keep Malcolm's orders in contact with the rest of his brain. "Malcolm doesn't want us going outside for this. At least make a couple of calls, see if they have anyone available."

"I'll do it after the meeting," Perly said. Then, grumbling, he walked down the hall with Lauren in tow, dodging a hotel crew setting up another fan. Achilles took the elevator the rest of the way to his floor, entered his room, and flopped on the bed with his clothes on. Finally he had a chance to get some sleep—the first he had had in months, or so it seemed, even though it had been only days.

As he slipped into unconsciousness, he entered a dream world devoid of sound or light; gradually, low buildings and narrow cobblestone streets formed around him. Horses passed by, their hooves clip-clopping on the stones, the metal of their shoes glinting in the sun. Then the clip-clopping became pounding and banging, as if the horses had traded shoes for hammers; the time frame shifted to winter and the horses became sleigh horses with bells jingling on their harnesses.

Achilles' brain slowly rose into a state of semiconsciousness, and he realized that the hammering sound came from someone knocking on his door, and the sleigh bells were the sound of his bedside phone ringing. He sprawled across the bed and fumbled for the receiver.

"Uh," he said into the phone.

"Achilles! It's me, Perly! We're outside, poundin' on your door! Wake up, let us in!"

"Uh," Achilles said again, and put the receiver down. He forced himself to get off the bed and staggered to the door. When he opened it, Perly, Lauren, and Galina burst in, a small weather system of sunshine breaking through the clouds of his night.

Lauren closed the door, while Perly tried to shake Achilles awake.

"You got to wake up, man," Perly said breathlessly. "Frank Bernardo's waitin' for us downstairs with a police van. We're takin' a trip upstate. He found our farrier, a guy in Millbrook."

"Millbrook," Achilles mumbled. "Sounds nice. Do they have beds?"

"Achilles," Galina said. "I heard what happened to you. I'm so sorry. But you must wake up. We have to go to Millbrook, Achilles, we have to talk to this horseshoe man."

"Mikhail didn't show for the meeting," Perly said as Achilles tried to wake himself up by taking a quick shave. "We told Bernardo what happened to your old room."

"What about Sam Rains? Did you tell him about Sam Rains?" Achilles swished some Listerine around in his mouth to clear his breath.

"Yeah, Bernardo's tryin' to put a search through on him and Mikhail, even though headquarters wants all troops to concentrate on the summit. I told you Frank is good, he's with us. He'll do the horseshoes with us while his troops beat the bushes. We scanned the photo of Sam and cropped it down, just him and the horse, so they can put it out to the troops, but we'll be lucky if anyone sees anything. They're on the lookout for some Islamic terrorists at the same time, and they're a lot more worried about them than our lone Indian."

"That's ridiculous. I know that getting ready for the summit is a big deal, but doesn't anyone understand that this investigation is part of that? Didn't Malcolm say he thinks there's a torpedo in the water, headed our way?"

"Malcolm's not in the loop right now, and nobody can see the torpedo. Their attention is on what they can see, which is that both presidents are flyin' up from Camp David together at dawn tomorrow, landin' at Newark, and takin' a Marine helicopter from Newark to the 30th Street heliport. There's a complete lockdown of the airspace over the river and Manhattan. Barricades for blocks around to keep protestors away from the heliport and the Javits Center."

Achilles, not yet completely awake, put on a clean shirt and fumbled to button it.

"Hey, man, let's hustle," Perly said. "We gotta hit the road."

"Wait a minute—why do I have to go? You and Lauren should go, and Galina and I can stay here to work on the cipher."

"Because you're the horse expert. You know what questions to ask."

"Achilles has a point," Lauren said. "Someone should stay here in the city in case something turns up. Millbrook is a long trip. We shouldn't all be out of range."

"He's gotta go!" Perly insisted. "I wouldn't even know where to begin!"

"Then maybe Achilles and I should go," Galina said. "We can work on cipher on the way. You two should be here to take care of emergencies."

"We might even uncover some background on Mikhail in the next couple of hours," Lauren said. "Maybe he'll lead us to his handler—I suspect, Grigorieff. I'd like to know why an assistant DA was going to that party."

Perly scratched his stubble for a few seconds, then gave in. "I gotta admit y'all have a point. Let's go. We'll walk you down to Frank and wave you off."

"Lauren," Achilles said on the way to the elevator. "Do you have a copy of the horse cop picture? I want to show it to the farrier."

"Sure." She pulled the envelope of photos out of her bag, found the right one, and gave it to Achilles, who put it in the side pocket of his computer case.

CHAPTER THIRTY-SEVEN

The firebombing had not helped the hotel's business any. The lobby was still full of guests milling around, most of them checking out, their voices raised in anger and frustration as harried members of the staff tried to make sense out of the confusion.

The smiling face of Frank Bernardo greeted them outside. He stood next to a nine-passenger NYPD van, jingling the change in his pocket.

"Hi, folks, get in," Frank said, holding the back door open for them.

"Frank, we have a change of plan," Perly said. "Achilles and Galina are goin' with you. Achilles is the horse expert, so he's the one who should talk to the farrier. Lauren and I will stay here and cover the Russian front. We'll set up camp in the precinct."

"Sounds good. Get in, Achilles, let's get going."

Achilles and Galina slid into the middle row of seats. Frank closed the door, jumped into the front seat beside the driver, and they were off, siren blaring. Perly and Lauren stood on the sidewalk, waving goodbye. Perly looked a bit forlorn, Achilles thought.

"Hell of a job, finding this farrier guy," Frank shouted over the siren as the driver threaded through the local traffic toward the highway entrance. "We kept striking out here in the city, even at the race tracks, so we widened the search. Had to bring the county sheriffs in: Westchester, Putnam, Dutchess, Nassau, Rockland, Bergen over in Jersey. Didn't want to, but we had no choice. It was Dutchess that found him. He's working at a major horse farm today, shoeing their entire stable."

"Did anything else come up at the meeting?" Achilles asked.

"Not much. Joshua Lin is still at the Chinese mission, holding their hands. There's a small team at City Hall working on the opening of the summit, but this job is off their radar until the summit is over. And the Stock Exchange, now that everyone's over the trauma of Maguire's murder, is back to business as usual. Markets are closed on weekends, period."

"How long do we have before we reach Millbrook?" Achilles said.

"Couple hours. It's parkway most of the way, but we have to do some back roads at the other end."

They lapsed into silence as the van made its way north toward Dutchess County and Millbrook. Frank switched off the siren once they were clear of traffic, bringing some relative quiet, so Achilles could think. He pulled out his laptop and turned it on. Galina extracted pad and pencil from her bag and set to work.

They wrestled with the cipher for the rest of the trip, but Achilles' state of weariness and the motion of the van did not help him any. The numbers swam in front of him, transposing digits of their own accord.

Galina kept at it, like a gardener weeding and turning the earth with a hoe. Achilles, through the firewall thrown up by his own laborious effort, could feel the energy of her mind working, the motion of her pencil and eraser as she wrote, crossed out, erased, wrote, crossed out, erased.

"Look at this," she said after an hour. "I moved digits, so they are between two sets of letters, instead of beginning or end, and here's how it translates into our ciphertext." She handed him a new page, with the ciphertext written out at the bottom:

T-H-E-U-S-A-N-D-R-J-G-I-I-A-B-P-F-E-S-I-D-7-E-I-G-
W-A-L-L-G-I-E-D-J-T-H-E-N-7-X-I-G-8-I-W-M-M-I-J.

Achilles studied her new text carefully. "This is getting somewhere. 'The USA,' or 'The US and,' we had those already. Now we have 'wall,' and 'then.' And here's a G8."

"And look at what comes after G8," Galina said. "I-W-M-M-I-J."

"'Summit,' is that what you're after?"

"Exactly. We can go back and reassign cipher numbers, then see how that changes rest of the text."

They turned off the parkway onto a side road, and were soon in horse country. The driver picked his way through the unfamiliar route toward the farm, while Frank studied a map and called out instructions.

"We'll get back to this after we've talked to the farrier," Achilles said to Galina.

She nodded assent and began packing her notes while Achilles shut down his computer.

———

They passed through a narrow valley lined with homes so buried in the woods they were nearly invisible, even though the trees were just budding; then the valley opened onto a long rolling plateau with well-kept houses, flowerbeds full of blossoms, white fences surrounding well-tended pastures, and large white barns with accompanying paddocks. The plateau fell off in the distance toward a low mountain range, and the whole scene made Achilles feel as if he had stepped into a Currier and Ives print.

"Here," Frank said to the driver. "Turn left at this sign."

The sign identified the farm as the "Clove Mountain Horse Farm, Breeders of Fine Morgan Horses." They drove up a long gravel driveway bordered by decorative fruit trees, coming to a halt before a large white stable. In front of the stable they saw a pickup truck emblazoned with signs that read "Mark Carroll, Farrier," followed by a Millbrook address. The farrier had set up a charcoal brazier for heating shoes, and a bench and anvil for shaping them. When the city team approached, he was busily filing away the excess wall from the right rear hoof of a horse he had tethered to the tailgate of the pickup.

"Are you Mark?" Frank Bernardo said.

Mark, who had already dropped the hoof by the time they reached him, sized them up out of the corner of his eye, then picked up the left rear hoof and attacked it vigorously with his file.

"Yep." He was a young man, probably in his thirties, with wide shoulders, an open but grizzled face, and thick thighs that looked strong enough to support the weight of an entire horse. "Mark, that's me. You Frank?"

"Yes. Did my lieutenant explain why we need to talk to you?"

"He said you wanted to know if anyone might've come to me lately to shoe any horses I don't usually do, especially any what needed horseshoes with extra borium dots."

"That's right."

"And I told him what I know. Don't see why you hadda drive all the way out here."

"Our normal procedure is to verify what we're told on the phone. And I have some colleagues here who weren't present for the phone conversation. They may have questions that my lieutenant didn't think of."

"So, okay, shoot," Mark said, dropping the left rear hoof and moving on to the left front. He tapped with his fingers just under the horse's fetlock, and the horse obediently lifted its foot for him.

Achilles stepped in. "Could you tell us anything about the man who brought the horse out to you?"

The farrier placed the foot between his knees, holding it firmly in his leather apron, and filed the hoof wall like a madman. A cloud of powdered hoof material flew into the air.

"Said his name was Ray," Mark said through the cloud of hoof dust. "Can't remember the last name, if he told me it. Said he worked for you."

"What?" Frank said. "Worked for me, Frank Bernardo?"

"No, no. Worked for the NYPD. You, the poh-lice."

"Didn't you think that was a bit odd? We have our own farriers."

"'Deed I did, but who am I to argue? Said he was on his way upstate, taking this horse up to the jolly farm where you send your nags for R&R, and the horse threw a shoe."

"And he didn't say why he felt it necessary to shoe the horse halfway through the trip?" Achilles said.

Mark finished filing the left front hoof and set it down, then went to the brazier, pulled out a red-hot shoe with a set of tongs, placed the shoe on the anvil, and pounded it with his hammer.

"Sure, I thought that was strange," he said, dodging sparks from the shoe. "Mosta the time, I don't care about weird things people tell me. This one, it was weirder than usual, so I asked. He said the farrier up at the jolly farm was on vacation, and his orders was to get the horse shod before he left it off. I 'specially thought it was strange when he paid me six hundred bucks, cash, for one horseshoe. 'Course, I woulda charged extra for the twelve dots. But I thought there'd be a big hassle with poh-lice paperwork, and all that."

"Are you aware that the police department doesn't use twelve dots?" Achilles said. "They only use four."

"Nope, didn't know. Did think twelve was a bit much, but he said it hadda be twelve."

"And what color was the horse?"

"Dark bay, blaze on the middle of its forehead." He dunked the shoe in a bucket of water, letting off a cloud of steam. "Nothin' unusual about its coloring."

Achilles pulled out the photo of the horse cop. "You sure it wasn't a chestnut? Did it look like this?"

Mark glanced briefly at the picture, then carried the shoe, still held in tongs, over to the horse.

"Nope. I reckon I do know my horse colors, and that's the wrong color. And the blaze on the face was a different shape." Sticking relentlessly to his own business, he took several nails from a pocket in his apron, put them between his lips, and tapped the horse's right front fetlock. The horse obeyed and lifted its foot.

Damn, Achilles thought. *How could we get this close, then come up empty-handed?*

Frank, sensing Achilles' mounting frustration, held out a calming hand and tried a different tack.

"Mark, what kind of conveyance did this Ray bring the horse to you in? Did you ask him why he didn't have an NYPD trailer?"

"Oh, but he did," Mark mumbled around his mouthful of nails. He deftly positioned the hoof on his apron, set the shoe in place, and hammered some nails through the holes in the shoe into the hoof wall. "Had the whole rig. Trailer, the SUV with the whirly lights, complete kit. No doubt it was one of your animals. That's why I couldn't figure why you was callin' up here."

"Was it a two-horse trailer? All our trailers are two horse, or larger."

"Yep, two horse. And it had two horses in it."

"Why didn't you tell us that before?"

"You didn't ask. You only been askin' about the one I put the shoe on."

"Didn't he want you to do anything with the other horse?" Achilles said.

"Nope. Just asked me to have a look, make sure the shoes was on tight."

"Did the other horse have the same kind of shoes?"

"Yep, six dots on each side of the arch, twelve per shoe."

"And Mark," Achilles said, "what color was the second horse?"

"Oh, that was a chestnut, not a bay. It was the horse in your picture."

CHAPTER THIRTY-EIGHT

When they had squeezed all the information they could from Mark, they returned to their van and began the drive back to the city, stopping briefly at a deli to get some food.

"So there were two horses on the scene the night of Maguire's murder," Achilles said, taking a bite of his turkey sandwich.

"Why so?" Frank said between bites of his corned beef on rye.

"Should be obvious. The horse in the picture didn't throw a shoe. The shoe came off the other horse. That means there was another rider, someone besides Sam Rains."

"Not necessarily. Maybe the same rider visited the scene twice, on two different horses."

"There is only one way to find out," Galina said. She, at least, had waited to swallow her food before talking. "Someone has to go back to your medical examiner's office and go through every picture, to see if there is any shot of other horse."

"Good idea," Frank said.

"I'll call Perly and tell him to go over there now," Achilles said. But his cell phone couldn't find a signal. "Damn. We're in a dead spot."

"Not a problem," Frank said. "I'll patch through Poughkeepsie to the precinct, have the sergeant on duty call the Office of Chief Medical Examiner."

Frank spent a few minutes putting the radio patch in place, and then, after reaching his sergeant at the precinct, gave him instructions on what to tell Perly and Lauren.

"And there's another thing," he said to the radio sergeant as he wrapped up the conversation. "We need a citywide inventory of all the SUVs and trailers used by NYPD mounted units. I want to know if any are missing, and if they are, which unit lost them, and when."

Achilles could hear squawking and scratching on the speaker, which somehow made sense to Frank, who signed off.

"He said that would be difficult on a normal weekend, and is probably impossible on this one, but he'll see what he can do," Frank reported.

"May I ask how you understood anything through that radio noise?" Galina said.

Frank shrugged. "You get used to it. You learn how to filter out the static. Every bit of static has a piece of information hidden somewhere inside."

Once they had reached the parkway, Achilles and Galina resumed their work. As they reviewed what they had accomplished on the way up, Achilles felt truly excited. At last they seemed to be making real progress with the cipher, which appeared more than ever to have a bearing on the summit. By assuming that the end of the message read "G8 summit," they made changes to the letters of the text, plugged the changes into the table, and then went through the ciphertext once more. Now it read:

T-H-E-U-S-A-N-D-R-J-G-S-I-A-B-P-F-E-S-S-I-D-7-E-I-
U-A-L-L-G-I-E-D-T-T-H-E-N-7-X-I-G-8-S-U-M-M-I-T.

"Damn," Achilles muttered. "We've gained 'summit,' but now the rest of the sequence is out of whack."

"This has to be right," Galina said firmly. "Look, after 'The US and,' we have RJGSIA. Must stand for 'Russia.'"

Russia, Achilles thought. *Bolshoi. Bolshoi Ballet from Russia.* He remembered with a jolt that he had made a dinner date for 5:30 with Jennifer, and 5:30 was only a couple of hours away.

"Oh, no," he groaned.

"What is it?" Galina said.

"I made a dinner date at 5:30 with my daughter. She's calling a show at Lincoln Center—she's stage manager for the Bolshoi. I set up dinner with her days ago. I have to cancel."

"I didn't know you had a daughter. How wonderful. A man should keep a date with his daughter."

"This is too important. We're really getting somewhere. We have to keep at the cipher."

"Achilles, think for a minute. Didn't Grigorieff say dancers from Bolshoi were coming to his party? If your daughter works backstage, maybe we can get in, I find opportunity to question dancers. I have instinct we might find out some more about him."

"So you could come to dinner with me. We'll sit in the park and work until it's time to meet my daughter. Sound okay to you?"

"Yes."

They returned to the cipher, scribbling, scratching, crossing out, erasing.

Just after the van reached the city, Achilles' cell phone rang. "Smith," he said.

"Perly here, ole buddy. We got your message. We're on our way over to the OCME right now. What is it you need exactly? The message was garbled."

"Ray Muller is carting two horses around. You need to go through all the pictures taken around the dumpster, see if there are any of a second horse and rider."

"Will do."

"And here's another goodie. The gun is starting to smoke, buddy of mine. Galina and I are pretty sure the cipher begins with something about the U.S. and Russia, and ends with something about the G8 summit."

Perly whistled. "How sure are you?"

"Sure enough that I'm telling you."

"I'd better call Malcolm. He needs to know about a big ticket item like this."

"Yes, do that. But wait a minute—before you hang up, have Frank's troops found anything on Mikhail?"

"Only that he didn't go home last night. Other than that, nothin'."

"Well, I'm supposed to have dinner with my daughter, and I was going to cancel, but it turns out she's working backstage for the Bolshoi, and Galina thinks she might be able to grill some dancers, maybe scope out some facts on Grigorieff. We'll keep working on the cipher while we wait for Jennifer."

"That's great," Perly said. "We'll meet you here at the hotel after dinner. We gotta eat too."

"Okay. Be sure to call the minute you know anything."

"Likewise." Perly hung up.

"Frank," Achilles said, "could you drop us off at Lincoln Center? It's just a few blocks from here."

"No problem. You have my cell number?"

"Yes."

"I'll be on call," Frank said a few minutes later as they clambered out of the van. "Keep in touch. I want to know when you crack the rest of that thing."

"Well," Achilles said as he and Galina watched the van push its way into the heavy post-matinee traffic, its siren wailing once again. "This will be interesting. It's the first time I've brought a strange woman to dinner with my daughter."

"She and I will get along fine. She'll think I'm only another Russian in her busy day. And please, just introduce me as your associate."

They found a bench in Damrosch Park, between the Koch Theater and the Metropolitan Opera, and sat down to work, ignoring the beautiful day around them.

The next step in deciphering the message was to try plugging "Russia" into the matrix. Unfortunately, this created even more problems with the sequence, because four different numbers would have to stand for S.

"This is a no-go," Achilles said after several frustrating minutes. "We can't have four numbers representing one letter, unless it plays out through the entire cipher. We have no system for that."

"But it may lead us somewhere. Let's keep working on it."

He tried to maintain focus, but his thoughts insisted on drifting to his daughter, and his failed marriage. He thought about those school plays unattended, the special events she lived through without a father there to cheer for her. He wondered if she would ever be able to think of him as a normal father, or, for that matter, if he himself would ever be able to contemplate having a normal life again—if, indeed, he had ever had one.

CHAPTER THIRTY-NINE

Five-thirty came. Time to meet Jennifer. Achilles stashed his laptop in its case and walked with Galina to the back end of the Koch Theater, not far from where they had been sitting in the park. Jennifer was already waiting outside, perched on the wall by the stage entrance. She was surrounded by a large group of excited dancers and balletomanes, all babbling in Russian, and yet she remained apart from them.

"Daddy!" she said, hopping off the wall and plowing through the group to give Achilles a big hug. He felt a little embarrassed, being called "Daddy" by a grown woman, but Galina seemed to take delight in it. She smiled warmly as Achilles and Jennifer luxuriated in their huggy greeting.

"Jennifer, this is Galina," Achilles said, when they had finished hugging. "One more Russian for you. She and I are collaborating on a project. I've invited her along."

"Wonderful," Jennifer said. She was tall and slim, with shoulder-length brown hair, and was dressed in jeans, running shoes, and a comfortable work shirt. She wore no makeup. "Where do you want to eat? There's a good Mexican restaurant right across the street—they know me there, and I have a quick turnaround."

"Okay," Achilles said. "Mexican it is." He turned to Galina. "That all right with you?"

"Of course. Whatever is working best for Jennifer."

After they had found a table and ordered their food, they were able to talk about their lives.

"Have you talked to Mom?" Jennifer asked from across the table.

"No."

"She asks about you from time to time." Jennifer glanced at Galina, to see if talk of Achilles' ex-wife raised any hackles. It didn't, so she continued. "She wonders how you're dealing with the change of venue."

"It's all right, although I miss the old campus. Things are more industrial at the Pentagon." He never revealed the details of his true work to his family, but they did know the basics. His changeover from CIA to the Pentagon had been too big to ignore.

Their guacamole was served, and they dug in with the chips.

"So," Achilles said, "how did you come by this job? Don't Russian ballet companies bring their own stage management?"

"They do, but local union rules say they have to use local people for actually running the show. So I lucked out."

"Must have been a lot of competition. I'm proud of you, being that high up on the list."

"Partly luck. The company has a secret angel who's paying the expenses, and he's somebody I know from the theater program at NYU."

"An American is paying for the Bolshoi to come to New York?"

"No, he's a Russian. When I met him he was a graduate student, ten years older than me. He had a patron high up in Yeltsin's circles who sent him over here to study economics, but he loved the theater, he was always hanging around backstage. Then he went back to Russia, became rich and famous after Yeltsin left office, and when he decided to sponsor this tour, he remembered me. So here I am."

"Extraordinary. You never know when your past will crop up and smack you in the face."

"This 'secret angel,' what you call him," Galina said. "May we know his name?"

"Grigorieff," Jennifer said. "Vladimir Grigorieff."

Achilles and Galina sat in stunned silence for what seemed like minutes. Jennifer must have wondered if they'd both had strokes, Achilles thought; but he was unable to pull up out of the dive.

"Daddy? Galina? Are you all right?"

"We're fine," Achilles said. "It's just peculiar…"

"We were at party last night," Galina said. "Party given by this very man. In fact, when we left, he mentioned that dancers from Bolshoi might be coming by after the show. Now it makes sense."

"Oh, yes," Jennifer said. "I heard some of them talking. They were really excited."

"Do you ever run into him?" Achilles said. "I mean, does he come by the theater?"

"He has a couple of times. He shows up on opening nights of new programs."

"Is tonight an opening night?"

"No, all the programs have opened by now."

The rest of their meal arrived, and they talked about more mundane things, mainly listening to Jennifer tell them excitedly of the backstage chaos involved with loading in and running a major Russian ballet company.

"Do you want to come backstage, take a quick tour?" Jennifer said to Achilles and Galina as they finished.

"We'd love to," Galina said. "I used to know some of the ballerinas. I might see an old friend."

————

After Jennifer had checked the two visitors past the guards, she took them up an elevator to the stage level and showed them around. Burly stagehands were doing a choreography of their own, hauling large pieces of scenery into place, nailing them down, sweeping the floor, adjusting the spotlights for the next ballet. Achilles noticed an overpowering odor, one he couldn't quite place, that reminded him of old woodworking shops.

"Amazing," he said to Jennifer. "And you're in charge of all this?"

"Actually, no. Each crew has its own boss. I just run the cues for the show."

"What's that strange odor?"

"Horsehide glue. They still use horsehide glue on their flats."

"What for? Haven't they heard of epoxy?"

"Actually, it's quite smart. It's water soluble. They just have to apply steam to the joints of the flats to take them apart for shipping. With epoxy, you couldn't. Saves a tremendous amount of storage space and shipping costs."

Galina, smiling broadly, spoke up. "Your intelligence services had same reaction when they captured one of our late-model MIGs," she said to Achilles. "They found out we were using miniaturized vacuum tubes instead of transistors. They thought it was great joke, sign of Russian backwardness, until they discovered purpose of the tubes."

"Which was?" This was a story Achilles hadn't heard before.

"In case of nuclear exchange, electromagnetic discharge in atmosphere destroys transistors. Tubes are not harmed. Your planes fall to earth, ours keep flying."

"Wow," Jennifer said. "I never thought of that."

"Same with horsehide glue," Galina said. "It still has many uses, as you can see."

"Yes," said a booming voice behind them. "We have many tricks in Russia that you in the West underestimate. Horsehide glue, miniature vacuum tubes, miniature rockets, for that matter."

They turned to see Vladimir Grigorieff, standing not two feet away. Grigorieff himself, saber scar and all.

"Vladimir!" Jennifer said. "I'm so glad to see you!" He enveloped her in a hug. "Let me introduce you to my father," she said, once Grigorieff had released her. Achilles desperately tried to signal her not to make the introduction, but too late.

"Vladimir, this is my father, Achilles Smith. And this is his companion, Galina."

Sunk. Achilles knew they were sunk. Grigorieff glowered at the two of them with intense, blazing eyes. The saber scar on his lip began to pulsate.

"Oh, indeed," he said finally. "Mitchell and Marina. So good to see you again."

Jennifer sensed that something had gone wrong, but she couldn't comprehend what it might be. She jumped in, trying to salvage the introduction.

"Daddy works for the government. Really hush-hush stuff, I'm not even allowed to know about it, isn't that right, Daddy?"

CHAPTER FORTY

"Well," Achilles said lamely, "we really need to be leaving. I'm sure you have work to do, Jennifer."

"Yes, it's almost half hour." She looked anxiously from person to person, wondering what could possibly have gone wrong, but not daring to ask.

"I'm so glad to run into you," Grigorieff said through a stiff smile, shaking Achilles' hand. "We must talk more about your business, now I know the government is involved." His voice was heavy with barely concealed sarcasm. Then he moved on to Galina and kissed her hand. "I will come by your school sometime, see how you do with teaching people our difficult language," he said to her in the same tone. "English speakers have such difficulty understanding the most simple Russian ideas, don't you think?"

"Yes," Galina said, trying her best to act normal. "Absolutely. You're right. Do come by, and I'll show you how I manage it."

Achilles and Galina gave the bewildered Jennifer a quick hug, then beat a general retreat to the elevator. His last view of his daughter was of her standing by the stage manager's desk waving goodbye, with Grigorieff's arm around her shoulders.

"Well, that was unfortunate," Achilles said to Galina as they hailed a cab.

"Worse than unfortunate. Now our identities are exposed. I'll never trust my instincts again."

"Don't be hard on yourself. How could you know? And in any case, seems to me that your instincts were right. If he's really the one we're after, this might help smoke him out."

"Or it will help us be dead."

They got in a cab and gave the driver directions to the Soho Grand. After they'd gone a couple of blocks, Achilles' cell phone rang.

"Smith."

"Achilles, this is Perly. How'd it go with your daughter?"

"Interesting. Turns out she knows Grigorieff from college."

"What? What the hell are you talking about?"

"I'll explain when we get to the hotel. Where are you now?"

"In my room. We just got back from dinner."

"Find anything?"

"You bet we did. Found a couple of pictures the geeks at the OCME didn't think were worth printing, because they didn't have any immediate forensic value. Wait till you see 'em."

"Did you get enlargements?"

"Better than that. We had a geek create a couple of digital files, so we can enlarge 'em on a computer screen."

"Good thinking. We'll come straight to your room."

"And, Achilles," Perly said. "We don't need a translator. We got some stuff from the party."

When the cab let them off, Achilles and Galina went straight to the elevator bank and up to the tenth floor. Galina, still upset and worried over the gaffe with Grigorieff, chewed on her lower lip, and seemed generally distracted.

"Galina, forget it," Achilles said as he knocked on Perly's door. "It's done. There's nothing we can do."

"You don't understand. This is more serious than you think. I must call home for instructions. If you don't mind, I'll stay out here."

"Okay."

"So," Perly launched right in as he opened the door, "what happened at dinner? Galina, aren't you comin' in?"

"I have to make phone call. I will be with you in a few minutes."

Perly looked quizzically at Achilles as he entered the room.

"She has to call home for instructions," Achilles said. "She wants privacy."

"Privacy? In the hallway?"

"She needs to be away from us. You see, my daughter has inadvertently blown our cover."

Perly sank into his easy chair, stunned. Lauren, who had been lying on the bed, sat bolt upright, all ears.

Achilles explained to them what had happened after dinner at the theater. As he finished talking, a piece of paper was slipped under the door.

"What is it?" Achilles said as Perly picked it up.

"It says 'Sam Rains, Yupik, Uma Tagi-tut-kak.'" He had to stumble through the pronunciation.

"That's Sam Rains's Yupik name. Why isn't she coming in?"

Achilles went to the door, opened it, and saw Galina pacing at the far end of the hall, talking on her cell phone. He motioned for her to come into the room. She held up fingers, indicating that she'd be another two or three minutes.

"She'll be here in a couple of minutes," he said when he went back in. "She's still on the phone. I guess she wanted to give us this right away."

"We got to show you some goodies," Perly said. "The hotel staff checked the penthouse. They couldn't find any brochures, but they found a copy of Grigorieff's DVD. It was still in the player."

"We should wait for Galina."

"Don't worry, you'll want to see it more than once," Lauren said.

Perly's laptop had been set up on his desk, with the DVD playback software already loaded, the screen flashing on the control menu. Achilles hit the "play" button. The video started with a sequence Achilles had already seen at the party: autos coming off assembly lines.

"Never mind that one," Perly said. "Skip ahead to chapter four."

Chapter four opened with a bucolic scene of horses at pasture, snow-capped mountains in the distance. A title scrolled by in Russian with English subtitles underneath, identifying the mountains as the Urals. Steeplechase jumps had been set up in one part of the pasture; in another, a line of poles created a makeshift grass-bound slalom course; and dummies on stakes had been positioned at intervals around the perimeter.

An announcer intoned a voiceover in Russian as the English subtitles continued to roll by: *Grigorieff Enterprises presents an entirely new sporting event, combining the elements of English steeplechase, American pole-bending, Russian Cossack maneuvers, and American bulldogging. We call it the equine tetrathlon. Our goal is to make it event in next Olympics.*

Grigorieff himself flashed onscreen, grinning broadly from atop a handsome bay horse.

This is our new breed, the Beloretski Quarter Horse, read the titles. *Cross between American Quarter Horse and Russian Kabardin. Aggressive, smart, highly maneuverable.*

Grigorieff spurred the horse into motion and began circling the pasture, gathering speed.

First, the steeplechase portion of the event. Maximum of one knockdown, one touch with hind foot allowed; otherwise contestant is disqualified. Grigorieff took the Beloretski through the obstacle course, horse and rider working together flawlessly as they cleared one jump after another.

Now comes the American sport, pole bending, a great favorite in western rodeos. One touch of pole allowed, no knockdowns. Grigorieff seemed to be one with his mount, cutting the corners so close that both horse and rider appeared to be more horizontal than vertical.

Next, Cossack maneuvers. In production version of event, the dummies pop up in random order. For this demonstration, stationary straw dummies are used. All dummies must be successfully "killed" before the contestant is allowed to proceed to final portion of event. Grigorieff, waving his saber, circled the pasture, lopping off the heads of most dummies, driving the saber into the "hearts" of others.

And finally, read the subtitles, *bulldogging. Contestant who has succeeded in killing all dummies now has 15 seconds to bring down the bull.* Grigorieff and his horse chased a bull that had been released from a chute. Cowboy style, he catapulted from the pursuing horse, grabbed the bull by the horns, and wrestled it to the ground, all in less than fifteen seconds.

"Incredible," Achilles said. "Just incredible."

"Wait," Perly said. "It's about to give contact info. Freeze the frame when you get to the address."

Titles rolled by over a video of Grigorieff taking a victory turn for the camera, smiling his crooked smile and waving his saber triumphantly. *If you are interested in being an investor, owning a part of the new Beloretski Quarter Horse breed, which is being developed especially for this event, then please write the following address:*

Achilles froze the frame the instant the address rolled onscreen:

Grigorieff Equine Enterprises
Double Six Ranch
Beloretsk, Bashkortostan
Russia
E-mail: BQH@grigequent.ru

"Good God," Achilles said. "There it is, the Double Six."

"This oughta be enough to get people like Stonewall and Maguire interested in investing, don't you think?" Perly said.

"Come see a man about a horse, have your head cut off," Lauren said.

"Galina has to see this," Achilles said excitedly as he ran for the door. "What is she *doing* out there? Galina!" he screamed in the hallway.

"*Da, da, harasho,*" Galina said into her cell phone as she scribbled notes on a pad. She looked at Achilles and pointed to the pad, making gestures to indicate she was taking down some important dictation.

Achilles returned to the room. "She's still getting instructions from her handlers."

"Okay," Perly said. "While we're waitin', pop this CD in and open the pictures. This is what we found at the OCME."

Achilles loaded the new pictures and opened one in the picture viewer. It showed the block on West Broadway where Maguire's body had been found, with two policemen on horses moving north, their backs to the camera.

"So there were two horses," Achilles said. "Just what I thought."

"Now zoom in on it. Look at the hardware hangin' from their saddles."

Achilles zoomed in on the area behind the riders' legs. On one horse, he saw a scabbard holding a cavalry saber; on the other horse, a similar scabbard with a saber, and also a second scabbard with the butt of what seemed to be a shotgun sticking out of it.

"Sabers and shotguns," Achilles said.

"You got it. And Frank Bernardo tells me that NYPD mounted units do not use sabers and shotguns. Now look at the other picture."

Achilles opened the second file: another version of the first shot Lauren had shown them, with the swarthy horse cop by the dumpster, but taken from a different angle, so the area behind the cop came into better view. Several yards away, there was another cop on a horse.

"So both horses were definitely there at the same time," Achilles said. "And the other horse threw the shoe that night."

"You got that, too. Now zoom in on the face of the second cop."

This cop, also wearing a blue helmet and shades, had a thinner, more Caucasian face than his partner. As Achilles zoomed in even closer, one thing in particular stood out: the man had a split upper lip. A saber scar. The second cop was Grigorieff himself.

"Galeee-na!" Achilles howled. "You've got to see this stuff, dammit!" He tore the door open and ran into the hallway.

Achilles stopped in his tracks.

She wasn't there. He ran to the end of the hall to see if she had gone around the corner to the main hallway. Not there either. He poked his head in the stairwells flanking the elevator bank. In one of them, he saw her shoulder bag lying on the landing.

"Achilles!" he heard Perly calling. "What's happening?"

Achilles ran back to the room with the bag, out of breath.

"We've got to call Malcolm and Frank Bernardo. Galina's missing. I think she's been abducted."

CHAPTER FORTY-ONE

They couldn't get through to Malcolm, but they reached Frank, and he had a van there in ten minutes.

"Tell me what you know," Frank said, after they had piled in. "Take us back to the precinct," he told the driver.

"She was out in the hallway, checking in with her handlers by cell phone," Achilles said. "But we don't know if they were here in the city, down in D.C., or maybe even in Russia." He quickly explained everything that had happened—the encounter with Grigorieff at the theater, the damning evidence on the DVD—everything he could remember. "The hotel staff didn't see anything unusual," Achilles said as he finished, "so Grigorieff's men must have taken her out the fire exit. We have to find that horse trailer. Wherever it is, that's where we'll find Sam Rains and Ray Muller, and I'll guarantee you that's where we'll find Galina."

"We hope, alive," Lauren said. "That trailer must be the killing lab."

Bernardo whistled. "Maybe it's time to call in Ramirez, get some SWAT teams together."

"We can't," Perly said. "Grigorieff's gang probably monitors the police band. They'll kill her the second we put out a bulletin."

"We should have thought of that earlier," Frank said as they reached the precinct. "Why did he take her, do you suppose? Why not you, Achilles?"

"Because Grigorieff probably figured she's closer to his track. The SVR knows more than we do, and I'm sure there's a lot she can't share with us. So he wants to take out the bigger threat."

"We have to go inside, make some arrangements," Frank said. "And I'm issuing sidearms to you people."

Frank told the desk sergeant to phone the other precincts, have them intensify the hunt for Mikhail, Sam, and Ray, and put Vladimir Grigorieff at the top of the list.

"Make sure they understand not to use radio," Frank told the sergeant. "We're dealing with people who monitor the police band. And I need one more man besides the driver. I need a partner. Get Joey, on the double. Have him meet us at the van."

Then Frank took Perly, Achilles, and Lauren to the supply sergeant and had Glock handguns issued to Perly and Achilles.

"What about me?" Lauren said. "Aren't I people? Where's my gun?"

"Are you trained?"

"If you get in trouble, what do you want with you, a useless female screaming for help, or one more person with a gun?"

Bernardo caved quickly. "One more," he said to the supply sergeant.

Lauren beamed with victory, and deposited the gun in her handbag.

They regrouped outside the precinct to plan their strategy. There were now six of them: Bernardo, the driver, Joey, and the three federal agents.

"Job one, find the horse trailer, is that right?" Bernardo said.

"Yes," Achilles said.

"Job two, see if she's in the trailer, or is being held somewhere near it."

"You got it," Perly said.

"Job three, we hope she's under light guard, find a way to free her without getting her or any of us killed. If she's under heavy guard and we can't do it, then to hell with radio silence, we have to call the SWATs, you get me?"

"Only as a last resort," Achilles said. "Once we do that, we may not catch Grigorieff."

"We'll have to take that chance."

"But we're gonna need help lookin' for the trailer," Perly said. "We can't scope the whole city by ourselves."

"You're the one who flagged a problem with the police band," Frank said, allowing himself to display a rare sign of exasperation. "In fact, now that I think of it, with the Russian and U.S. presidents arriving at dawn, and this being almost 9 p.m., every SWAT team and special ops man in the city is going to be on assignment. We wouldn't get help anyway."

"This is about the summit too, dammit," Achilles argued.

"We don't know that for sure. I can't call in SWATs based on partial information. Now everyone hop in the van. I'll join you in a minute."

Frank went back into the station house. As the others got into the van, Achilles tried reaching Malcolm again.

"Yes," came the familiar voice at the end of the line.

"Malcolm, we have an emergency. Galina's been abducted. We think Grigorieff's men have her. Grigorieff is the one. He uses his horse trailer as a killing lab."

Malcolm said nothing for a moment, then: "Go on."

"We're setting out with a team from the NYPD to hunt for the trailer. Do you have any ideas?"

"Are there any trailers missing?"

"They were supposed to do an inventory, but I don't know if they finished it."

"Probably his own equipment with a paint job anyway. You need to check every mounted unit rig that's on the street tonight. Don't put any of this out on the radio. Don't even use cell phones for police communications. You have to do the search yourselves. You should start up by Javits Center. I'll see what I can do on this end."

"Anything else?"

"I'll call you if I find anything out." Malcolm clicked off.

"Anything?" Perly said.

"That was Malcolm," Achilles said to Frank, who had come out of the precinct house and also been listening. "Our boss. He said to search up by Javits Center, check every MU rig that's deployed. And he emphasized not to put anything out on the radio, also said not to use our cell phones for police talk."

"Jesus, is there anything we can use? Does he want us to search on foot?"

"He must have his reasons. He doesn't go underground for the fun of it."

Frank chewed on this new information for a moment, then breathed a sigh of resignation. "Nothing to do but give it our best shot. Let's go," he said to the driver. "Stick to the river, they might be parked along 12th Ave. When we get up by the Center we'll work the grid, check the side streets."

"Frank," Perly said. "Are we really gonna work a grid all night? We got time for that?"

"It's the only way to find someone who is serious about hiding in a crowd. Gridwork is tedious, but it pays off."

As the van moved north, they encountered several roadblocks and police barricades; small knots of demonstrators had already formed, and the police were preparing for the landing of Marine One in the morning. Frank asked the men at each checkpoint if they'd seen an NYPD mounted unit being trailered into the area. There had been many, and several of them had come from lower Manhattan.

"We have our work cut out for us," Frank said to the others in the van. "The mounted units are being trailered in from all over. If Grigorieff has Galina in a trailer, she could be anywhere in the restricted zone."

They spotted a rig parked by the side of 12ᵗʰ Avenue near the Javits Center, and pulled over to examine it. Frank got out and identified himself to the officers. He asked for their IDs, inspected the trailer, then got back into the van.

"They're legit. I know their unit. They're from Troop B, on pier 76."

They spent most of the night in the restricted zone identifying mounted units. The constant need to pass through checkpoints, the press of the growing crowd—everything conspired to slow them down.

Achilles and the others were becoming increasingly irritated with Frank's methodical approach.

"We've got to cover more ground, Frank," Achilles said. "This could take days."

"Do you want me to call in the SWATs? The helicopters with searchlights, the works? What do you think Galina's chances are of surviving that? Work the grid, work the grid—that's what we have to do. It's the first rule for divers searching for a drowning victim, and it's the rule we have to follow tonight. Be methodical. It's torture, but it's our only chance."

Malcolm, thought Achilles. *Please, Malcolm, find something.*

His phone rang. "Smith."

"She's in lower Manhattan," Malcolm said. "She's not in a trailer. She's in a garage, that's where they've parked their gear. I don't know the exact street, but I know they're in a garage somewhere between City Hall and Canal Street."

"Great, Malcolm, how did you…?"

Malcolm's phone clicked off.

"Downtown," Achilles shouted excitedly to the others. "She's in a garage between City Hall and Canal."

"Go," Frank said to the driver.

Dawn had begun to break as they headed south. Achilles could see human figures dotted along the rooftops, silhouetted against the sky: SWAT teams positioning themselves for the landing of Marine One.

CHAPTER FORTY-TWO

Sunday, May 1, 6:20 am (EDT)

D riving downtown proved to be especially difficult because of the great numbers of demonstrators streaming into the area. Achilles saw signs protesting globalization, genetically modified foods, farm subsidies, immigration, Russian policy in Chechnya, the G8 itself—more viewpoints than he could count. Some demonstrators stood quietly in small groups, holding up their signs or singing hymns with arms interlocked. Others danced around fires they had set in trash cans, or hung off lampposts posing for the eager hounds of the press, who nearly outnumbered the demonstrators themselves.

At one checkpoint, the crush of the mob prevented the van from getting through. A group of demonstrators, apparently thinking this would be a good time to overturn a police vehicle, closed in and rocked the van violently from side to side, their distorted, angry faces giving Achilles and his companions a moment of real fear. Frank put in a frantic call on the radio, and a mounted unit showed up to disperse the attackers. Achilles heard horses' hooves, then the dull thuds of batons cracking skulls.

"Bastards!" a female voice shrieked as the horse cops bore down on their grisly work.

"Pigs!" from another voice.

"Cossacks, bastards, you have no respect for life!"

Then the van broke clear, heading down West Street.

"We'll start on Chambers Street and work our way north," Frank said to the driver. "There are lots of old garages on the side streets."

The van moved uptown from Chambers Street a block at a time, swinging crosstown toward the river and then back again, slowly moving along the awakening streets. This area was the antithesis of crowded midtown—no demonstrators, no police barricades, no SWAT teams on rooftops, none of the frenzy taking place farther north.

They reached the corner of Hudson and Leonard.

"There!" Frank Bernardo said, pointing to a decrepit one-story building in the middle of the block. "That garage there, on Leonard! Just around the corner from the precinct, for chrissake!"

An NYPD SUV, with a horse trailer attached to it, was parked on the sidewalk in front of the building's rolled-up articulated steel door. No one was in sight.

"Keep moving, so they don't see us," Frank said to the driver, then turned to Perly. "I know that garage. It's been abandoned for years. We're always busting crackheads there. No way is it an NYPD facility.

"Go north one block, then over to Varick," he ordered the driver. "We'll go in the back alley. You park on Varick and Leonard, and stay out of sight. Keep an eye on the front. If you see anyone go in or come out, call for backup. In five minutes, if you don't hear from us, ditto."

"Okay," said the driver. He let them out by the entrance to the back alley, and took off for his assignment.

Led by Frank and Joey, the group moved cautiously up the alley toward the back of the garage. Middens of broken glass and discarded drug paraphernalia made it difficult to navigate quietly, forcing them to step carefully and slowly. At last they were close enough for Frank to get down on his haunches and creep up to a back window. He raised his head a few inches to peek in, then returned to the others.

"She's in there, all right," he whispered. "Tied to a chair. Two men are in the front, saddling horses. One looks to be Sam Rains. I'll bet the other one is the hostler."

"Can we bust in?" said Perly.

"There's a door next to the window. We've busted in here so many times, it's got to be loose."

"Let's go," Perly said. "Let's do it."

With a quick burst, the men piled themselves against the door and broke into the back of the garage, their guns drawn.

"Police!" Frank Bernardo yelled as they ran toward Sam and Ray. "Down on the floor, down on the floor!"

The two men, stupefied by the sudden incursion, raised their hands in surrender, then sank to their knees. Frank and Joey pulled out their handcuffs and cuffed the prisoners to each other.

Achilles ran back to help Lauren, who was tearing at the tape that bound Galina's wrists and ankles.

"Are you all right?" Achilles said to Galina. Her eyes were wild with frenzy, and she was trying to speak through the tape that covered her mouth even as they tried to remove it.

"Grigorieff is going to shoot down Marine One helicopter!" she blurted, spitting pieces of tape out with the words.

"How?"

She rushed over to one of the horses and tapped the butt of what Achilles had thought was a shotgun. "This is new Russian missile, called Kolibri. May be small, but it will kill tank, airplane, or helicopter within 300 meters. He has one in PSB helicopter, and one here."

"We got to call the FBI—Secret Service," Perly said.

"Yes," said a familiar voice from the back alley, "why don't you do that?" Their old boss Karl stepped in the alley door, aiming a pistol at them. He was accompanied by Mikhail Goldovsky, assistant district attorney of Manhattan, also armed with a pistol.

"Karl, you bastard!" Perly said.

"Guns on the floor," Karl said. "Gently, no quick moves. Do it now."

Frank's group had let down its guard. Karl and Mikhail had the drop on them. They had no choice but to comply.

"Now, raise your hands," Karl said.

Mikhail shouted in Russian to someone unseen, out in the alley.

Grigorieff stepped through the door, dressed like a horse cop. "Good morning." He was holding the small tin Achilles had seen at the party, from which he took a pinch of powder, inserting a little in each nostril. He drew the powder deeply into his sinuses. "Did everyone sleep well?"

"You've gone off," Perly said. "What do you think you're pullin' here? And Karl, why are you mixed up with this cokehead?"

"No questions!" Grigorieff snapped. He signaled for Mikhail and Karl to herd the others to one side of the garage, away from the horses.

"I will give you brief moment of enlightenment," he said, strutting back and forth, "which you can take to the grave with you. I am new member of the Society of the Domino Mask. This society runs the world economy. They gave me miserable number, the one blank, lowest number possible on probationary list, like little child waiting for slot in good school." He looked at Achilles. "Do you remember when you asked why I don't start with Formula Three? 'I start at the top,' I said. Same here."

"But there's the double blank," Achilles said. "The double blank is lower than the one blank."

"Not true. Double blank is the exception. That is the Unknown One—he picks the lucky ones who get to be in the society. Whoever is double blank runs it all, runs the whole world. I want to be double blank, and not when I am old patriarch, but now, while I am young oligarch. I did not become billionaire in Russia by waiting patiently for others to die."

"So you thought you'd speed things up a bit," Perly said.

"My thinking is this," Grigorieff said. "If a few prominent members meet unpleasant deaths, then the others are afraid they might be next. Even presidents not safe. So then I smoke out the double blank, he is forced to come out of hiding. When I know who he is, we make a deal, because he wants to keep his head, and I become double blank. You see, by my way of thinking, I am only a carpenter, but I want to be number one carpenter in the world, not just any carpenter. The public, society, they are the lumber. The press, they are the nails and screws. The politicians, they are the saws, the screwdrivers, the hammers. None of it works without the hand of the carpenter. Without the carpenter, there is no economy, no society."

He turned to Achilles and Galina. "Did you ever decipher the message? No? Too bad. Russian SVR, American Pentagon, with all their experts, cannot crack a simple domino cipher. Soon the world will find out what it said."

"And even sooner," came a voice from outside the front door, "you will stay where you are and drop your weapons." The owner of the voice, flanked by two other men, stepped over the threshold and entered the garage. It was Malcolm, still disguised as the homeless man, but instead of a crutch he held a pistol, and so did his two men, who Achilles now realized had been the gardeners by the river. They were Malcolm's pod.

"Don't move! I mean it!" Malcolm said. The others stood frozen as he and his pod advanced a step.

"Who the hell are you?" Karl said.

Malcolm came forward another step. "Don't recognize your old colleague, Karl? How quickly you forget. Just as you forgot which country you work for. So he bought you, did he? Bought access to the Secret Service, the pass codes for the joint maneuvers."

"You pushed me aside, Malcolm. Nobody pushes me aside." He fired three quick shots, winging Malcolm's left arm. Suddenly another shot rang out, and Karl fell, wounded. Everyone dove for cover. Mikhail dropped his gun and ran toward the back office. Sam and Ray, still shackled, ran awkwardly in the same direction, screaming, "Don't shoot! Don't shoot!" Achilles, taking in each piece of action in a kind of disembodied slow motion, could see a smoking hole in the side of Lauren's handbag, with the muzzle of her Glock peeking through it.

Grigorieff paused for a second, standing upright like General Patton in the middle of a battle. But he had been overconfident, left himself exposed without a gun, and seemed strangely indecisive.

The wailing of sirens approaching the garage made up his mind for him. Grigorieff jumped on one of the horses and spurred it through the garage door.

"Stop him!" Galina screamed. "He will shoot down presidents!"

Achilles snapped to, quickly mounted the second horse, and followed Grigorieff out the door at a gallop.

"Radio the SWATs!" Malcolm bellowed to Frank Bernardo, "tell them not to shoot Achilles!"

Achilles headed up Hudson Street to the first cross street that cut over to the river. Grigorieff already had a good two-block lead on him. He leaned forward and yelled into the horse's ear.

"Let's go, Persimmon! Catch your buddy! No decent horse lets his stablemate get ahead of him."

He could see the rump of Grigorieff's horse in the distance as it burned up asphalt. They were now galloping up the bicycle path next to the river at full speed toward 14th Street, where a mob of protesters surged against the police barricades, blocking the way. Grigorieff, without a moment's hesitation, spurred his horse through the crowd. With his police uniform, they must have thought he was a cop gone mad. They scattered in panic, screaming and crashing into fences and planters.

As Achilles approached the barricade, he saw cops standing at the ready with their guns drawn, but he could tell they weren't sure quite what to do.

"Over the jump," he said to Persimmon. "Over, boy, this is your steeplechase, you can do it."

He felt a weightless sensation as the horse launched himself effortlessly, soared over the barricade, and landed safely on the other side.

Grigorieff was nearing 20th Street, with Achilles only a few feet behind him. Both men had drawn their swords. Grigorieff turned in his saddle and began swiping at Achilles with his saber.

"So!" he shouted. "At last we have our saber match! And you have no protection!"

Achilles ducked one blow from Grigorieff's saber, parried another, made a slashing attack of his own. Up ahead, at the heliport, he could see a huge blue-

and-white helicopter suspended in the air. *What the hell,* he thought, *that's not Marine One.* Then he realized it was the Russian PSB helicopter, waiting for the arrival of Marine One and its cargo of two presidents.

Thrust, parry, slash, parry, counterthrust. Achilles knew he had no hope of physically stopping the other man. His only chance of derailing Grigorieff's mad plan was to disarm him. He maneuvered Persimmon to the right side of Grigorieff's horse, and in between dodging saber thrusts from the Russian, strained to get his saber under the thong that held the missile scabbard in place.

Finally, at 29th Street, he succeeded. The scabbard upended, dumping the Kolibri out. The missile launcher skittered across the pavement.

Achilles and Grigorieff reined in their horses, jumped to the ground, and raced each other to the Kolibri. Achilles reached the missile a split second before Grigorieff, and kicked it out of reach. Grigorieff snarled and started slashing at Achilles with fierce, wild strokes of his saber. Much as Achilles loved being on horseback, he felt more at home fencing on the ground; in fact, he seemed to have the advantage. No matter how hard Grigorieff tried to get past his defenses, Achilles was able to fend him off, answering with deft ripostes. Then, in a moment of luck, one of his strokes broke the Russian's saber. Grigorieff stood dumbfounded, staring at the stub of his sword in disbelief.

"What's the matter?" Achilles croaked between gasps. "Have you gone soft, whacking the heads off people who are tied up?"

But Grigorieff's attention abruptly turned skyward, in the direction of a loud chopping sound: Marine One, flying low over the river, had arrived.

"Doesn't matter now," Grigorieff said, breaking into a grin. "Sabers are no longer important."

Achilles also looked skyward, following the direction of Grigorieff's gaze, and saw the PSB helicopter maneuvering itself parallel to Marine One. Something metallic glinted from the open side door of the Russian helicopter.

The barrel of another Kolibri, aimed at the presidents' craft.

Achilles dropped his saber and leaped for the Kolibri on the ground. Grigorieff, too preoccupied by the unfolding drama in the sky to react quickly, gave him the extra fraction of a second he needed. He swung the Kolibri toward the Russian chopper and pulled the trigger. The trajectory of the missile was short and brutal. The Russian helicopter disintegrated in a ball of flame, ejecting fiery pieces of debris as it plunged into the river. Marine One immediately initiated evasive maneuvers and headed back west.

"Nooo!" bawled Grigorieff, launching himself at Achilles, swinging the butt of his saber. Achilles tried to defend himself with the missile launcher, but it was too heavy and cumbersome to be effective. Grigorieff was all over him, pounding him like a raging bear.

"Don't move! Don't move!" a voice cried nearby.

Achilles turned to see Perly and Frank Bernardo, guns drawn, racing toward him, followed by SWAT teams dressed in black. Then he felt a sharp pain in the back of his head and lost consciousness.

CHAPTER FORTY-THREE

When Achilles woke up, he was lying in bed in a hospital room, surrounded by concerned-looking faces: Malcolm, his left arm in a sling; Perly; and Lauren. His head ached fiercely, as if it had been lacerated by a wheat thresher. He could feel the constricting sensation of bandages wrapped tightly around his skull.

"What happened?" he managed to whisper.

"We were a few seconds too late," Perly said. "The Beloretski Madman tried to off your head with the butt of his sword."

"The presidents? Are they safe?"

Malcolm put a finger to his lips and closed the door.

"Absolutely," he said when he returned to the bedside. "Thanks to the work you and Galina did on the cipher, we thought it would be prudent to send in an unmanned Marine helicopter as a decoy. The presidents came in later, on a tourist helicopter. They want to meet you and thank you, but it'll have to wait until you get out of here, and then it will have to be a secret meeting. No medals in the Rose Garden. You did a great job, Achilles. Too bad it won't be in the history books."

Achilles fumbled on his nightstand for a cup of water and swallowed it greedily. "Don't need medals or footnotes in history books," he grumbled. "Just want to know what the hell the full cipher said."

"A true cryptanalyst," Malcolm said. "He comes out of a near-coma and asks for the solution to his latest puzzle."

"We almost had it. We almost had it. Has anyone figured out the code?"

"Galina was working on it with her handlers when Grigorieff's men kidnapped her. Now it's finished, and she's bringing it by on her way to the airport."

"Airport?"

"She has to rejoin her team. They need her at home."

"Where's Grigorieff?"

"On his way to a submarine that's leaving soon for the North Atlantic, where our people can interview him without being disturbed by the ACLU or cable TV talking heads. When we're through with him, the Russians can have him."

"What's the storyboard? What are we telling the public?"

"You and Grigorieff are Chechen rebels, name of Gada Arsanov and Murat Lakaev. You were planning to shoot down both helicopters, but you only succeeded in getting the Russian helicopter. Both of you have been handed over to the Russian authorities, who requested jurisdiction. You're already on your way to Moscow."

"No extradition hearings?"

"The extremely sensitive nature of the case, certain secret protocols... You can figure out the rest."

Achilles laughed, but regretted it immediately, because the motion made his wound throb. "Brilliant," he said, when he had recovered from the jolt of pain. "And I suppose there are a couple of rebels by those names in their jails already."

"Exactly. And as we speak, their pictures are being shown on television all over the world. In fact, the crew of that PSB helicopter was a group of Chechen rebels Grigorieff recruited for a suicide mission. The Russians are searching for the bodies of the real crew. They'll probably find them in a mineshaft somewhere in the Urals."

"What about the others? Ray, Sam, Karl, Mikhail?"

"When Karl gets out of the hospital, he'll be dealt with quietly. Mikhail is sitting in the U.S. Attorney's office, singing into a recorder. He'll get a plea bargain and be put in the witness protection program, to keep him from blowing the storyboard. No decision yet about Ray and Sam."

They heard a light knock. Malcolm opened the door, revealing Galina, dressed in a business suit that, despite her best efforts, failed to mask her femininity.

"Galina," Malcolm said. "Come in."

"I have only a minute," she said. "Car is waiting to take me to airport. I must return to Russia, work on finding rest of Grigorieff's gang. The other people on domino list are fearing for their lives." She went straight to Achilles and planted a kiss on his cheek. "A code-breaker playing part of hero. No one in SVR will believe it."

Achilles held her hand. "I'm glad you could get here."

"I came to show you the code." She removed a manila envelope from her bag, pulled a piece of paper from the envelope, and handed it to Achilles.

On the paper was a vertical grid with two columns of domino numbers and four columns of letters and digits arranged in order—A-Z, 0-9—in three sequences.

"See how clever," she said. "The cryptographer makes three passes through the domino numbers, so no letter has same code number twice in a row. Person on other end doesn't even need a written key. Once he knows the system, he has the key memorized. No need for computers or electronic transmissions."

"Never mind how it works," Lauren said, impatient to get her hands on the paper. "What did the message say?"

"Should come as no surprise—'The U.S. and Russian presidents will die at the next G8 summit.'"

Galina hugged Perly and Lauren in turn, then shook hands with Malcolm.

"It has been a great pleasure working with you," she said stiffly, in her best formal tone. "I hope we can do it again sometime."

"So do I," Malcolm said. Achilles thought he noted a hint of familiarity in Malcolm's voice.

Next Galina returned to Achilles' bedside and pulled a small note-sized envelope from her bag, placing it on his nightstand. "This is for you, later," she whispered. "When you are alone." She planted another kiss on his cheek. "Take care." And then she was gone.

"We should let Achilles rest," Lauren said once Galina had left. "After all, he just took a nasty knock on the head."

"Achilles," Malcolm said, "the rest of us are going back to Washington. Check in with me the moment the hospital releases you. We'll need to have a thorough debriefing, and then I'll arrange that secret handshake with the president."

He went to the door and waited for Perly and Lauren to make their farewells.

"Ole buddy," Perly said, "I'll never make fun of your fencin' again. No footballer could have pulled off what you did."

"The horse helped," Achilles said. "The horses!" he said to Malcolm. "What happens to them? I want that Persimmon."

"They're on their way to the NYPD horse farm. For now they're evidence. We'll see about getting Persimmon for you."

"What you goin' to do with him?" Perly said to Achilles. "Stow him in your bathroom in Arlington?"

"They have stables, jerk. You board the horse and ride it on weekends."

"I can just see you," Lauren said, laughing. "Tearing up and down the fields, practicing the equine tetrathlon."

"Not a bad idea," Achilles said. "It really should be an Olympic event. Grigorieff may be a madman, but even madmen can have their moments of genius. That's why people want to believe them."

Malcolm gestured to the others that it was time to leave. Perly and Lauren joined him at the door.

"Malcolm, wait," Achilles said. "One more thing."

"What's that?"

"My daughter, Jennifer. She went to college with Grigorieff. I'm afraid that with his connections he might be able to have her kidnapped or harmed to exact revenge for my part in his capture. She's calling the cues for the Bolshoi Ballet right now, and he's the one who paid for the tour."

"You want us to put her in the witness protection program?"

"She'd hate that. Isn't there some way to protect her without putting her in a cocoon?"

"It's a question of resources—I'll see what I can do. Obviously, if the Russians are concerned about Grigorieff's gang, we have to consider that also. I promise you, Achilles, no one in your family is going to get hurt."

Malcolm and the others left, closing the door behind them.

Achilles rubbed his throbbing wound for a moment, wondering how to put some backup protection in place for Jennifer. Not that he didn't trust Malcolm's word, but a little redundancy wouldn't hurt. Maybe he could get Frank Bernardo to help.

He remembered the envelope on the nightstand and retrieved it. Galina had been in such a hurry she had addressed it in Cyrillic: Ахиллес Смит. He opened it and extracted the contents—a short note, which she had mercifully written in English, and a shiny quarter inside a small Ziploc bag.

Don't forget, she had scrawled, *Russian lady is never without her earrings. Until our next meeting. Love, Galina.*

THE END